Precious Treasure

by

Terry Segan

Precious Treasure

Cover Art by *Jennifer Greeff*

The Wild Rose Press, Inc.
PO Box 708
Adams Basin, NY 14410-0708
Visit us at www.thewildrosepress.com

Publishing History
First Edition, 2022
Trade Paperback ISBN 978-1-5092-4023-4
Digital ISBN 978-1-5092-4024-1

Published in the United States of America

Janie dragged herself out of bed and into the bathroom. Turning on the tap to fill the sink, she bent over and splashed cold water on her face. The refreshing drops rolled down her forehead, cheeks, and chin, pulling her out of her funk. Sightless, Janie reached for the hand towel hanging nearby and dried her face as she stood upright. Opening her eyes, she leaned in to examine the damage of the late night on her complexion. Her reflection looked back, as well as that of a young man standing behind her. Janie's heart leapt to her throat as she whipped around and found no one there. When she looked back in the mirror, only her image remained.

This is too much, she thought. First nightmares and now hallucinations. Janie shook her head. With the assault of information thrown at her in the last twenty-four hours, her imagination cartwheeled out of control.

The visions had to be a result of the wine, newspaper articles, and journal. This knowledge didn't calm the raised hackles on the back of her neck. The foreboding in Brian's letter snaked its way up her spine threatening to encircle her throat and squeeze tight. His writing had a tone of uncertainty and fear— uncharacteristic of the man she had married.

Dedication

This book is dedicated to a man who is my best friend, husband, and hero.

Despite knowing everything about me, you're still here. Thank you for that, Paul, and for all the love and laughs we share.

PROLOGUE

July 14, 1813

"Your son is gone, sir." Captain Williams shuffled his feet and awaited a response from his passenger. Receiving none, he turned and walked away.

The bow of the *Renegade Red* dipped as it rode off the crest of one wave and began its journey up the next. Jacob Pelter bowed his head as he braced against the rail. Ocean spray danced across his face.

Fleeing the British occupation, the Pelter family had made their way to the South Shore of Long Island where Captain Williams and his crew waited with a long boat. They were ferried to the ship. In just a few days of sailing, they should have arrived in Virginia—if a British frigate hadn't broached the horizon, forcing the *Renegade Red* to go farther out to sea. This added days to the journey.

When Jacob's eldest son and namesake had taken ill, the ship's physician could do nothing but isolate him. Abigail insisted on attending to their son. She too succumbed to the fever earlier that day.

Jacob's hands balled into fists at the memory of his wife's excitement for this voyage. He recalled her cheerful depiction of how their temporary life in Virginia would unfold. They had escaped the British occupation and would face this challenge together, as a family. When the struggle for this country was done, they would return home.

As the ocean churned, Jacob's anger grew with every scathing drop the sea hurled at him. King George would regret the devastation his army had wreaked on the Pelter family. Someday Jacob, with his remaining son and daughter, would retake what was rightfully theirs. Those foreign bastards would pay!

CHAPTER 1

Present Day

Carol snipped away at Janie's hair, talking a mile a minute. "So, I told him he can just keep the DVD collection if he's that attached to it. It can help fill all those lonely nights he's got ahead of him."

"Oh, Carol, why not try working this one out instead of bolting? You've only been married three years. Besides, I like how he gives your friends a discount at his butcher shop. He is the best in town."

"Well, he may be the best butcher in town, but when it comes to the husband department, he's lacking. You know we've had this conversation before, and you're not talking me out of it. Besides, it's already final except for a bit of paperwork with the judge. Let's move on to something worth talking about. Like your love life," she said with a devious glint in her green eyes.

"Not that again. I'll agree to a subject change, as the current one is giving you a little too much zeal with the scissors." Janie watched in the mirror as her friend waved the sharp cutters. "You might forget it's me under this cape, and I'll end up with a buzz cut."

"I worry about you, Janie. And I just met this wonderful man, but he's a little tame for me." Carol stopped to admire her own reflection in the mirror and pat her blonde locks before resuming her work.

"By that you mean he's too close to your own age."

"I didn't say that. But John is a year or two older than us. He runs a lawn care service. You know the one with the cute talking lawnmower on the side of the trucks? I've told him all about you, and he said he'd really like to meet…" Carol rambled on.

At least this topic calmed her, and the cutting resumed at a normal speed. Janie had no desire to see piles of brunette tresses scattered on the floor instead of attached to her head. When her friend took a breath, Janie jumped in. "Why would you do that? I told you I'm not ready. Besides, what if—"

"Stop! Don't go there. It's been eight years." On Janie's shoulders, Carol rested her full hands. In one she held a pair of scissors, the other, a trimming comb. "It's time you face the facts, sweetie; he's not coming back. If Brian were alive, he'd have contacted you. There's no way he would have deserted his family. Honey, he's dead. There's no other explanation. Even the police came to that conclusion."

Janie stared at her friend in the mirror. "How can you say that? They never discovered a trace of foul play. There wasn't any blood in or around the car. They searched thoroughly and found no indication of violence or a break in," she said. "It still makes me angry the way the authorities tore apart our lives and tried to make it sound like he simply ran off, possibly with another woman." She clenched her hands into tight fists. "They didn't even consider how he'd been edgy and losing weight!" With a gasp, she halted the rant unfairly aimed at her best friend. After a few deep breaths, she splayed her fingers open and backed away from the precipice her nerves teetered upon.

"Sweetie, however his car got left in the ferry parking lot at Orient Point may have had nothing to do with where he ran into trouble. Your husband might not have been alive by then."

"You know I won't give up hope until they produce his body."

"You're only causing yourself harm by holding onto a past probably gone and buried." In a softer tone, she asked, "I guess that means you won't file the papers either?"

"My family thinks I should. Even his family thinks I should, for the insurance money. As if that would make things all better—get a settlement to replace my husband. The kids' college is assured; Brian took care of that long ago. I'm doing well with the real estate business, so we don't need the money. I see no reason to go through with having him declared dead." Her face warmed with a flush.

"Janie, it isn't about the money, and you know it. You need to get on with your life. The girls seem to have moved on better than you." Carol walked over to her purse, pulled out a business card, and offered it to her friend. "Here's John's number. Can I tell him you'll call? You've got to start rebuilding somewhere."

Janie stared at the card, then shook her head. "No. It's too soon. Last week I pulled out all of Brian's old files and am going to sift through them again. There must be something there—some clue of where he went that day and why he never told anybody. If he was cooking up some surprise for the kids and me, that could be why he told Jenny he was digging for treasure—at least that's what she claimed. Obviously, he didn't plan on being gone long or he would have told his assistant, Meg. He never forgot or missed an appointment, especially with a client."

"Jenny was only four years old at the time. Who knows what he really told her?"

Janie's eyes brimmed as she gazed at the floor. Her body heaved as she stifled a whimper.

"I'm not letting up on you, sweetie. If I don't give you a kick in the pants to get on with life, who will?" Carol held out the man's number.

As if in slow motion, Janie extended her arm, grasped the card, then tucked it into her purse. If nothing else, this would temporarily get her friend off her back.

"Carol, I know you mean well. So, keep kicking, and maybe I'll have the gumption to go along with one of your dating schemes—eventually. Goodness knows you've given me more than sympathy all these years. I know I need to move on with my life, but it's hard living in the same house and working in the same office Brian had been. Sometimes when I sit at his desk and lean back in the chair, I consider replacing it, but I can't bring myself to let go of another piece of him, no matter how small."

Her thoughts drifted to a meeting she'd had with her lawyer two weeks prior instructing him to prepare the paperwork declaring Brian dead. Janie didn't feel up to sharing the news with anyone yet. Closure needed to happen, but if she didn't talk about it, this final step would be virtually painless—maybe not as real. The court date was scheduled for Thursday.

"Honey…Janie? Have I gone and lost you? Hello?"

Janie shook her head, clearing the cloud of sadness.

"Sorry, I zoned out for a moment." She forced a smile. "I'm back."

"Good. What do you think?" Carol unsnapped the cape and handed her a mirror so she could view every angle of her hair.

Janie threw back her shoulders and puffed out her chest. "Too gorgeous for words."

Both giggled as Janie got out of the chair.

After settling the bill and striding outside, Janie's shoulders slumped, and her step slowed to a crawl. A nagging doubt made her question her actions—again. The court proceedings meant more than accepting her husband was gone. It forced her to admit he was never coming back.

CHAPTER 2

Later in the afternoon, Janie picked up Mom for a doctor's appointment. With soft brown eyes and an oval face like her mother, there was no doubt which side of the Barton family Janie resembled.

When she drove into the hospital parking lot where the physician had an office, her older brother Jeremy's dented blue sedan sat parked near the entrance. The women exchanged worried glances.

"I hope nothing's happened to one of the kids." Mom's eyes widened as her hands twitched in her lap. "You know how rough those three boys are. Always into one dangerous sport after another."

"Mom, they play soccer and tennis. You make it sound like they practice knife juggling." She forced a chuckle. "Let's cut through the ER on our way to Dr. Sherdla's office."

The automatic doors swished open with a blast of crisp, antiseptic-laced air. They rushed to the emergency room waiting area. Janie's brother, Tom, glanced up from where he sprawled in a chair reading a magazine. Both he and Jeremy inherited the height in the Barton family while sharing the same brown hair as their younger sister.

"What are you guys doing here? Don't tell me Jeremy called you too?" He sat up straight.

"Mom has her appointment today, and we saw

Jeremy's car outside. Is one of the kids hurt?" Janie gripped the top of the chair in front of her. "You weren't telling them they could fly off the roof like a pixie, were you?"

"Oh, please. Ruth threatened to rip my head off if she ever caught me doing that again." He bristled when mentioning the name of their headstrong sister-in-law. "Besides, our nephews aren't as gullible as your girls." Tom smirked, his turned-up nose accentuating the impish grin. "I was at their house helping with a project. Jeremy brought me along to the hospital for protection."

"Why does this sound like something involving Ruth?" Janie wrinkled her brow and placed her hands on her hips.

The tension in Mom's shoulders eased. She shifted the purse strap from where it had slipped down her arm.

"Jeremy and I were putting up that flagpole holder his wife's been nagging him about. From atop the ladder, he dropped one of the screws in the grass, so I went back to the garage to find another. Ruth came out to oversee the progress of the operation," Tom said in an official sounding voice.

"This is beginning to sound too dramatic," Mom said. "I'm going to my appointment. You can fill me in on the details later, Janie. I'll meet you over there." With her slightly hunched back and steady gait, she ambled past the nurses' station and through the double doors.

"The suspense is killing me. What happened?"

"As I returned, I heard Ruth trying to get her husband's attention—probably to say she wanted the driveway shifted over two feet or a swimming pool dug." Tom shrugged. "I don't know. Anyway, Jeremy didn't hear her over the noise of the electric screwdriver. Annoyed at being ignored, she shook the ladder. He lost his balance and dropped the screwdriver."

Janie asked, "Please tell me he didn't fall and break something?"

"No, he held on. Unfortunately, the screwdriver wasn't as lucky. It bounced off Ruth's head and hit the ground."

"You're kidding? It landed on her head?" Janie covered her mouth holding back a laugh.

"I believe I said bounced." He snickered. "It made a nasty gash. Hopefully it didn't damage my screwdriver. I was afraid to look while she held her bleeding head."

Janie nodded with a giggle. "No wonder Jeremy wanted you to come with him. I'm surprised she didn't castrate him on the spot. Is he in there with her now?"

"No, he's down the hall on the phone."

"Who's he calling, the Witness Protection Program?" Janie's laughter grew louder.

Tom cracked up. "No. They already turned him down. They were afraid of losing too many agents on the case. I think he's dialing a shelter up in the Yukon."

"Well, it was nice chatting with you. I do *not* want to be here when Ruth gets out with her head stitched up. If Jeremy is lucky, he'll be out of the doghouse by next summer." Janie started down the hallway her mother had taken. She wouldn't want to be in that house tonight when the drugs wore off. After hearing what had happened, the kids would probably be hiding in their bedrooms. "You might want to lie low yourself for a while. Just by you being there she'll find a way to blame you too. I'll call later for updates."

"Thanks, Sis. I knew I could count on you for support...and guidance," Tom yelled after her. He looked over at the room Ruth was in, then down the hall toward Jeremy and shook his head chuckling. "Hey, Janie," he called before she got too far down the hall, "is dinner still on for tomorrow night?"

"Of course. You think Jeremy will be alive to attend?"

"Oh, I'm sure of it. Ruth will only hurt him a little bit. Nothing obvious. See ya tomorrow." He waved.

****

The whole family met at Janie's the next night. After dinner the usual chaos ensued. While the women cleared the table, the men tried to stay out of their way. All five kids stampeded out the back door. Despite the age differences, the cousins got along well. Truth be told, the boys were quite protective of their younger cousins. Mom went outside to watch them play on the new tire swing Uncle Tom hung up the previous weekend.

Janie had purchased a new ceiling fan for Jenny's room, so Tom and Jeremy tackled the installation job. It was nice having brothers who knew things when it came to tools. Brian never excelled at home improvement projects and would hire somebody for anything they needed done. Janie didn't like to impose on her brothers' talents, but this wasn't a difficult task.

The savory aroma of roast beef hung in the air. With most everything cleaned up, Tom's girlfriend went outside to join Mom. Despite the unmarried status, Mom treated Cassie like a daughter.

Ruth lingered in the kitchen fussing with the napkin holder on the table. Janie braced herself to endure her sister-in-law's version of what happened yesterday. The two women had never become close but maintained a decent, if not strained, friendship. Despite her petite frame, Ruth projected a strong presence with her overbearing demeanor and cropped red hair.

"Janie, I don't quite know how to start this. We haven't been the closest of friends over the years, but I consider you my sister. Heck, I've known you longer than most of my friends." Ruth tucked a loose strand of hair behind her ear.

Janie stopped loading the dishwasher and turned toward the other woman. "Yes, of all the girls batting their eyes at my brother in high school, you were the only one he cared about."

"You know my friend, Phyllis, down at Judge Marlowe's office, don't you?" asked Ruth.

Damn this small town. Janie bristled at the direction of this conversation.

Before she could break in, Ruth continued. "Now, Janie, I know what you're thinking—small town, gossip flying. That's not the case. Phyllis called me out of concern for you and how hard this has been with Brian gone." With Janie on the verge of tears, Ruth pushed on anyway. "I'm the only one she's told, and if nothing else, Phyllis is honest. Since you didn't say anything at dinner tonight, I thought I'd talk to you privately."

"Ruth, look," stuttered Janie, her lips trembling. "I know I should have told the family. Actually, I'd planned tonight's dinner to announce it but chickened out in the end. Everyone has always been there for me. But I just can't yet—especially not Mom. I know she worries about me and still hasn't come to grips with my husband being gone. This would send her blood pressure off the charts. Please don't—"

Putting up a hand, Ruth said, "No, Janie, that's not what I'm getting at. I respect your decision to do this quietly. It's up to you when to tell the family. But since I already know…if you want…I could go with you tomorrow. If you don't want me there, I'll understand. It never hurts to have a little moral support."

Janie bit her upper lip as she leaned against the counter. The lingering scent of dinner, which had given her a sense of comfort only moments ago, now turned stale in her nose. She crossed her arms and rubbed her elbows. With a sigh, she said, "You know, it wouldn't hurt to have a friend. Thank you, Ruth. I'll meet you there, if you don't mind. Please don't tell Jeremy. He'd insist on Mom knowing."

"Insist on Mom knowing what?" Tom asked as he walked into the kitchen carrying a toolbox.

Janie forced a smug grin. "Insist on Mom knowing you really didn't touch her television set when you told her you'd fixed it."

"Oh, very funny. By the way, Jenny's fan is up and running. You'll get my bill in the mail," joked Tom as he carried the tools out the door to his truck.

With someone else knowing about the proceedings, the reality of Thursday threatened to choke her every breath. Janie faced the sink, pretending to wipe it down. A chill seeped through her body. How would she get through tomorrow without losing her mind?

CHAPTER 3

"With the authority vested in me by the State of New York, I declare Brian Holgram legally dead." Swinging the gavel to punctuate his declaration, Judge Marlowe ended the proceedings.

Janie flinched as the resounding bang echoed throughout the courtroom like cannon fire. Her heart pounded, trying to escape the confines of her chest. Determined not to break down, she almost lost the battle when her sister-in-law's hand lightly gripped her arm.

In one fell swoop, Brian was dead and Janie officially a widow. People had been calling her that for the past few years anyway. She knew the consensus around town—he wasn't coming back. At least her husband had been an upstanding guy. Outside of the authorities, nobody thought for a minute he'd abandoned his family. All these facts offered little comfort as her life's happiness drained from her body onto the floor for someone to mop up and toss away like dirty wash water.

Rising from the wooden bench, Janie followed Ruth toward the back of the courtroom while Sam, her lawyer, gathered his papers into a briefcase. The second they stepped into the hallway her legs turned to rubber. She grabbed for Ruth's arm. If her sister-in-law hadn't caught her, Janie would have collapsed.

A security guard supported her other arm and led Janie to a bench. "Here you go, ma'am. Rest here a moment." The wood creaked as she leaned against the backrest.

A clerk walking past opened a bottle of water and put it into Janie's hand. "Sip on this, Mrs. Holgram, nice and slow. You'll be okay."

After ten minutes, Ruth asked, "Feeling any better?"

Janie nodded. She took another sip. "Thank you for the water." She acknowledged the clerk who still hovered nearby. After a few more minutes, her pulse slowed to a normal cadence. She stood and walked out of the building on her own volition.

The women trudged down the stone steps of the Court House, their heels tapping on the white marble. Sam caught up with them and placed a hand on Janie's shoulder causing her to turn around. He offered her a large packet. "I'm sorry I couldn't deliver this to you sooner."

Why would he? Her copy of the official paperwork didn't mean anything until today. She slipped the envelope into her briefcase with a mumbled thanks.

Ruth suggested they stop at Calloway's Diner on the next block. Janie could collect herself before driving home.

Fifteen minutes later, Janie and her sister-in-law sat in a corner booth at the restaurant. An aroma of cinnamon and nutmeg filled the air. Each woman, with a hand wrapped around a mug, poked a fork at a huge slice of apple pie. It was the diner's house special, but it didn't feel special today.

"…for the best. You know that," Ruth said.

Janie's eyes refocused on the woman sitting across from her. "I'm sorry. My thoughts drifted. What did you say?"

"Oh, nothing but well-meaning gibberish." Ruth sighed. "Things I'm supposed to say at a time like this, but they sound pretty hollow to me. Small wonder you tuned me out."

"No. I'm glad you're here. More than you could know. It's all sinking in. Maybe coffee isn't the drink I need right now." Janie's chuckle sounded more like a whimper.

"When will you tell the rest of the family? I'd say you have until tomorrow at the latest before they run the story in the newspaper. Mom never reads the local rag, but somebody is bound to come across an article and mention it. Might be better if the news came from you." Ruth reached over and squeezed Janie's arm. "Brian's family should be told. I know his parents aren't alive, but you could call his sisters."

Janie met the other woman's steady gaze. "You're right. It's just…I mean…you know what I mean. Tomorrow will be soon enough. Tonight, I want to be alone with Jenny and Natalie. I'm struggling with how to break the news to them."

Ruth sipped her coffee. "Maybe it's time for a memorial service. You've gone this far. The healing won't be complete unless he's put to rest. You wouldn't have to erect a headstone if it doesn't feel right."

Janie dropped her fork, spilling crumbs over the edge of the plate. "Now you're pushing beyond my limits. Let me get through telling my kids and Mom. You can tell Jeremy tonight. Call Tom too, if you don't mind."

"I'll take care of it. The rest can wait."

Ruth paid the tab, and they left the diner. "I'm parked around the corner from the Court House. Would you like me to drive you home? We can get your car later."

"No. I'm okay to drive. I probably won't be later," joked Janie as she mustered her courage. Stepping closer, she said, "Ruth…"

"You're welcome," Ruth said with a compassion in her voice Janie had never heard before.

Her sister-in-law wasn't a warm person, but she leaned over and hugged her anyway. Sniffling, Janie spun on her heel and hurried across the street to the public parking lot. Unlocking her car, she clutched the handle, tears streaming down her face. Her body wracked as she took in jagged breaths. Finally, she opened the door, tossed her purse and briefcase on the passenger seat, and got in.

The drive home and rest of the afternoon were as much of a blur as the twenty minutes with the judge. Janie didn't remember arriving at the house but found herself sitting in her car on the driveway. The tears had dried, leaving her skin taut from the salty moisture. She had no idea how long she'd been there, but the school bus lumbered down the block. With deliberate effort, she forced herself to exit the car and scurry inside. After dropping her keys on the kitchen counter, she went to the bathroom and washed her face. Janie spent the rest of the afternoon sitting in Brian's home office—now her office. Would the numbness ever go away?

The girls came into the house, yelled a hello, then bounded upstairs to their bedrooms. They left her in peace until Natalie popped her head into the office asking about dinner.

Janie told her to call out for delivery. She couldn't remember if they'd decided on chicken or pizza. Whatever got ordered, she wouldn't eat much.

At the dinner table, Janie tried to garner her strength and begin a conversation. Her nerve failed, and an awkward silence descended over the fractured family. She picked at the Kung Pao chicken and rice Natalie had ordered, but none of the food made it past her lips.

Too drained for a conversation with her daughters on the day's events, Janie put the news off until tomorrow. Would she be considered a coward for withholding the day's proceedings? She didn't care. The delay gave them one more day of having a father who could be alive.

Later, she crawled into her pajamas and turned down the bed. Before getting in she went downstairs to retrieve her briefcase from the office and an open bottle of wine from the kitchen. A full glass of wine already sat on the nightstand, but she expected to need more than one pour tonight.

The judge had said the official copy of the paperwork would be available next week. *So, what did Sam give me?*

Once situated in bed, she pulled the envelope from her valise. Turning it over Janie froze at the neat, uniform script. Her name and address were handwritten—in Brian's hand. She stared at the envelope, afraid to blink and discover it was really an office clerk's scrawl.

A combination of fear and hope forced her to slow

down, resisting the impulse to rip open the envelope and dump its contents on the bed. There had to be an explanation for the past eight years. Maybe Brian stayed away for the family's safety and lived in a foreign country. She allowed herself a moment to savor this fantasy, her lips curving up at the corners. Hope dissipated and fear gained ground as she chided herself for believing such an idea. It couldn't be his Last Will and Testament. With his death finalized, Sam would arrange a meeting for it to be read. Did she really want to know what lay inside?

Her fingers shook as she carefully tore the flap, as if by prolonging the process it would change what the documents held. Janie removed the contents, finding a variety of items. There were two newspaper articles, neatly clipped, edges of the thin paper curling with age, and a real estate file, like hundreds she'd seen at work. This one had a blue label, which meant it came from Brian's home office. Bringing a hand to her mouth, Janie stifled a sob as his old, organized life spilled through to the present.

Among the paperwork was an odd-looking book. Her fingers brushed across the rough leather cover. It looked like an old journal. She flipped through the yellowed pages covered in a crude, faded handwriting. The words could still be read with some difficulty. She set the book aside and sorted through the other things.

Janie started with the most familiar item, picking up the real estate file labeled Brassel Field Property. Her husband had talked about this parcel, but she couldn't remember his ever selling it. Now, as his replacement at the office, Janie was familiar with all the current files in the cabinets at work, and this wasn't one of them. It could be in the archives if it hadn't shown any recent activity. Brassel Field lay in the middle of Suffolk County on the north shore. Brian told her this property had been an old farm since before the American Revolution. According to the file, all the original structures were long gone. One of the previous owners had rebuilt, probably using the plot for a summer home, like most of that area.

Next, she perused the newspaper articles. The first, titled "Turnerville Teens Find Skeletal Remains," included a picture of a young Brian with his best friend, Larry, standing next to a skeleton. The two eventually became real estate partners as adults—the same office Janie now shared with Larry. The article read:

August 24, 1992—Police were called out to investigate the discovery of a skeleton found in a small underground cave on the north shore of Long Island. Two boys from Turnerville, out for one more hurrah before leaving for college, made the find while exploring a wooded area near their campsite on Filmore Beach. Brian Holgram, 18, lost his footing and slipped into a small cave hidden by the overgrown brush on the side of the trail. The teen wasn't injured but got more than a little startled when he found himself face to face with a skull.

After being pulled out by his friend, Larry Carson, also 18, the two called the authorities, thinking they'd found the remains of an old smuggler in a loot cellar. This area, comprised mostly of farms since before the American Revolution, has escaped the rise of modern housing developments and tract homes so popular on Long Island over the last forty years.

After a thorough search of the cave and

surrounding area, all remains were taken in for examination. Amongst the items were bits of clothing, a pocket watch, and an empty musket located near the resting site. While too soon to speculate, the skeleton could possibly have been there since Colonial Times or the Civil War. Once local experts have established the era of the belongings, the identity of the corpse may be revealed.

Until then, the boys are off to college and life goes on—at least for the living.

The second article, dated three months later, was titled "Union Soldier or Confederate Spy?"

November 18, 1992—A skeleton found in a small cave near Filmore Beach by two Long Island teenagers on August 22 has been identified. The remains of the body, as well as uniform buttons and a musket, have been dated as being from the Civil War era.

Research conducted by local Civil War expert Rafferty Boggs determined the uniform remnants to be from a Sharpshooter brigade out of New York City. Thanks to a pocket watch found at the site, authorities believe the teens found the resting place of a Confederate soldier named William Carver.

After studying historical and church records, Boggs was able to trace the young soldier's Southern heritage. Two brothers, William and Benjamin Carver of Virginia, left for war in May of 1862. From the approximate age and height of the skeleton, it is believed to be that of the older brother, William.

His actual history gets confusing at this point since he died in a Union uniform. Was the young man a Confederate spy, or had he switched sides to fight for the North? Records of conspiracy were not always recorded accurately, so the truth may never be known. Damage to one of his ribs suggests a bullet to the chest led to the teen's demise.

After contacting surviving descendants of the Carver family outside of Richmond, the young soldier has been laid to rest in a family plot in Virginia. Whatever his circumstance, he is now at peace, surrounded by loved ones.

Janie leaned back against her pillow. *Why had Brian never told her about this discovery? And why did he find it necessary to leave her this information as if it were a legacy of some kind?* She'd been in high school herself at the time. Articles like these wouldn't have been front page news so would have gone unnoticed by her. People were always finding things from colonial and Civil War times throughout Long Island. She would have to ask Larry about their finding the remains.

Next Janie grabbed the leather-bound journal. As she opened the cover, a paper fell out with her name on it in Brian's handwriting. Unfolding it, she found a letter dated the month he disappeared. It read:

My Dearest Janie,

If you're reading this, I'm no longer with you and the girls. I'm truly, truly sorry. I never dreamed this whole thing could go so far. It started when Larry and I were carefree teenagers. You've probably read the articles included saying we found a skeleton thought to be a Union soldier. From a pocket watch he'd been holding experts discovered the boy came from a family in the South. There was more, however, that we kept to ourselves. Thinking we'd found an old pirate, Larry and I dug around the skeleton hoping for buried treasure.

Stuck in the wall next to the skeleton we found this journal wrapped in oilcloth. It must've protected the book for it to survive these 150 years in the ground. After reading it we agreed to place the journal aside for ten years. We decided by then we would have the means to follow through on this adventure and solve the mystery. It seemed like a good idea at the time. In hindsight, I see how naïve we were, but how could we possibly have known? I stuck the journal in a box with my old high school books and forgot about it. Six months ago, I came across it when helping my parents clean out their garage.

It was a secret between Larry and me. But then it turned into a nightmare shortly after we picked up the pursuit. We thought about burning the book and walking away. Unfortunately, it had a hold on us that couldn't be vanquished. The two of us decided if we solved the mystery it would end. We were wrong. The closer we got the worse things became. Then, someone else found out, but we still don't know who. I'm not even sure if it wasn't Larry's doing that brought this other party into the mix. I don't know who to trust anymore.

The whole situation has gotten worse on levels I can't begin to explain. If I tried, you'd think I'd lost my mind. I have a plan that might work. If it doesn't, I regret I might never see you again. The only reason I leave this for you now is maybe, if you are threatened, you can use it as a bargaining chip. I can no longer protect you. The final key has always been with you and the girls.

Be very careful who you trust. I wasn't and paid the ultimate price. I'm leaving this in Sam's care. He has no idea what it is, and I trust him enough to never ask.

Please know I'll always be with you and the girls. I pray things go well so you'll never read this.

Love always,
Brian

CHAPTER 4

Janie covered her eyes and shook her head. This was something out of a bad movie, not real life. Not her life. Instead of feeling closer to Brian, this pushed him farther away. Uncovering her eyes, she picked up the letter and read it twice more before turning her attention to the leather-bound journal.

May 14, 1862

Jumping off day. Mama always called new beginnings "jumping off." Kind of like when we were little and we would jump off things to start us on a walk. It really fit the beginning of our journey.

My name is William Carver. Me and my family abide in a tiny town in Virginia name of Rockville. About six miles outside of Richmond. I don't expect to lose this journal, but if it be found please return it to my mama. Forever would I be grateful.

Mama did give me this journal to record the tale of our adventure with the Confederacy to eliminate the Union threat to our country. Not being a slave-holding family, and not believing in the possession of people by others, we are not sure if this is the right side to be on. But Daddy always said it was our obligation to defend our country. Guess when he died five years ago, he never thought we would be fighting our own kin, so to speak.

Last night I bid farewell to my Becky. We are to

marry when I return from battle with the family fortune. Here is where my devotion goes beyond love of country. And I must set down our past to begin my story. Years ago I made a promise to Grandpa Peter. I would return to the land our family came from fifty years ago. Great-grandpa Jacob Pelter was a profitable landowner and businessman on Long Island in the state of New York. His family had been happy and thrived. Then the British tried one more time to take this country from us.

Great-grandpa Jacob was too old to fight. He feared for his family, especially Great-grandma Abigail and beautiful daughter, Mabel. Her being of marrying age Jacob could not risk her virtue at the hands of the British. Other families tried to abide in peace with the invading army but paid a price very dear.

Jacob took the family and set off for the home of his sister in Virginia. Distrustful of the captain and crew of the cargo ship Jacob secured passage on off the south shore of Long Island, he chose to bury the bulk of the family wealth on his land. He left behind sums of cash and all of Abigail's fine jewelry. He believed the day of their return would not be far off. The trip south lasted longer than ever they thought. Plagued by British ships, the captain of their vessel was forced to journey out to sea and to prolong the voyage to evade capture. A slight discomfort felt by his eldest son, also named Jacob, blossomed into fever. My great-grandpa held the rest of the family away, yet Abigail insisted on being at young Jacob's side. Before the journey was over, both son and mother perished.

Jacob landed in Virginia a broken man. By the time the British were beaten back, he had not the heart to return north. The shattered family made a home in Virginia. It did not compare to what he left, but here he chose to live out his days. The surviving children, Peter and Mabel, cared for their father deeply but would never replace the loss of their mother or Jacob's first born.

Mabel married Henry, a local boy and apprentice to a printer. She bore two girls. The first, Grace, died two days after birth. With the birth of Annie, both mother and child succumbed.

Peter, my grandpa, married Catherine. Life was simple and happy. From the day I could sit on Grandpa's knee, he told me about the treasure left behind. When I was a boy of only eleven, Grandpa made me swear upon his death bed I would restore the family to the standards that Great-grandpa Jacob had made for us. To make fast my oath, he gave me the pocket watch I always seen him carry. It was passed from Jacob to him and was very dear. Mama being his only living child, Peter thought it proper to pass the watch on to the eldest boy of the family. It is a honor I cherish. The inscription reads "Precious Treasure" and the date 10-12-12, with the family name Pelter below it. It is a date to remember in the history of my family. That is all I can set down on it right now.

The Army of the Confederacy put in place the conscription. Every man between the ages of 18 years and 35 years is to join. Mama thought this would be the time for me to make my way to the family land. Once our army defeats the Union soldiers, it would be in my reach to go there. Against both our desires, Benjamin insists he help. He is only 17 years of age and claims it is his duty as a man of our family. Benny means well, yet never was quite right in the head. He is simpler than most. Maybe that is why Mama says he is her most precious treasure. Benny is the most loving soul anybody could know. Maybe he is what this country needs more right now.

Mama did not want him to swear against our Lord under oath. My mama is a very clever woman. She wrote the number 18 on a piece of paper and had Benny put it in his shoe. When his turn came to swear he was over 18, he did not lie. Many others in our town have done the same out of respect for this country.

We hope to be home with our belongings no later than fall. No war against the north could last longer than a few months. We can then return to our lives. Only our lives will be better. And none too soon for Mama. She has been poorly with a bad cough. I fear she be worse before better.

Mama is preparing Benny for our trip to the training camp. He is excited to be going. Only hope our journey is swift so I will return to my life and new beginning with my Becky.

June 23, 1862

To my great dismay we are still in Virginia. Our whole regiment thought we surely would be on our way north by now. Our days are spent marching. We practice drills from the first bugle sounds of reveille at five in the morning 'til we fall into our bed rolls at nine-thirty after the bugle sounds taps.

Our sole existence is run by the bugle call. It tells us when to rise in the morning, when to march, when to eat, and when to sleep. Every night they take roll call to be sure none of us run off. To be named a deserter is a serious offense. Two boys from Belton took it in their heads to run off. The experienced soldiers tracked them down and drug them back. They stood guard duty three nights. No sleep for three days. They look like death walking.

Benny is in good spirits. No matter how much other men poke fun at him being simple, he takes it in proud stride. To him this is just a game. I fear the day we truly go to battle. He promises to stick at my side when that time comes. I pray he is able.

They gave us muskets on the third day here. Benny is one of the best shots in the regiment. All that hunting we done back home served him good. He can outshoot most men here. My aim is mostly true. I hope I can do my duty when it is time. I expect shooting another man, no matter what his offense, will be harder than hunting rabbit and deer.

August 14, 1862

With our days all the same, nothing was new to set down until today. Tonight is our last at training. All the men are anxious to be on the way and do some good. Rumor has it we are joining with the Confederate Army of Northern Virginia under command of the great General Lee.

It was a long time coming. I hope we complete our task quickly and be on our way. This war is gone on longer than any man thought it would.

September 1, 1862

We are camped near the land of our first victory. Still in Virginia, we are at Manassas. The old soldiers say this was the second battle the Confederates fought on this very ground. We defeated the Union troops.

There should be a bout of music and celebrating at our triumph. There are those that chose to make merry.

Those of us fresh from our first battle are still in mourning for the soldiers not returning from the fields. Tommy and Joseph, two boys I knew since toddling around on my first steps, now lay side by side. Both went down as we charged the field. All the drilling and marching did not prepare any of us for the tragedy of death. Victory does not taste as sweet as we thought it would.

Benny is fine. Mama would have my head if he was not. True to his word, he stuck at my side. Loading our muskets was routine in training. It took on new meaning with shots landing near us. The sound of cannons was enough to make you want to turn tail and run, but we held our ground. We did General Lee proud.

I hope this victory will help us continue our journey north. Now I am too weary to write more.

September 18, 1862

Today we took many casualties. Beside the creek of Antietam, in a town called Sharpsburg, more friends died. Finally we marched our way to the state of Maryland, only to be welcomed with cannon and musket fire.

The battle was fierce. Benny got a blow from a sabre, but with luck it glanced off the strap of his haversack. It should have been a fatal blow, had it not hit where it did. We retreated to cover with others from our company.

On the march here we lost many to sickness. Our company is only strong by half because of the effects of measles. It is a nasty disease when gotten as men instead of children.

Both sides took heavy losses, yet today we see this

is one more battle to be followed by many. Mama, I fear our hope of being home by autumn will not be seen. Thoughts of spending the whole winter away from you and the family sadden me, yet we dare not shirk our duty. The punishment would be harsh, and the family's honor sullied.

October 16, 18........(rain spattered pages)

...three months have we dug in to our winter camps. No troops can fight in such conditions. We spend our days scrounging what little rations the army can offer. Hard tack is much of our stores, and we are grateful for it. Before we complained of the poor rations we were forced to scavenge. Now we rejoice in every crumb handed out.

Supplies are low. Some men have taken to trading with northern soldiers. The camp is so close to ours that we hear them playing music at night, as I expect they hear ours. Benny went with a few others for some trading. It made me worry, but Frankie swore to watch out for him. They met up with some northern boys and traded tobacco for coffee. That drink has been in short supply. We are all grateful for the kindness, as are the Union boys for the tobacco. It seems if we can help each other in that way, why can't we do that in other ways instead of all this killing?

I never will understand the need for this aggression yet stick to my duty. My prayers still go to this getting over quickly. Until that tim....(more water damage)

June 30, 1863

My story stopped for a spell because of a long recovery in a field hospital I endured with many of our regiment. The fever would subside and then be back twofold. Many of my fellow soldiers will not make it back to duty. The graveyard behind the infirmary is become overly full.

The illness seemed to pass by Benny. I worried for him each day I could think clearly to do so. There are many days I do not remember. True to his word last winter, Frankie took Benny under his wing and kept him safe. He never did say it himself, but other men mentioned it a time or two.

The great army of Northern Virginia made it farther north this time. We are in Pennsylvania outside a place called Gettysburg. Most of the men never been farther north than Maryland in their whole lives. Benny and me never travelled out of Virginia. It is a beautiful place, yet the troops are amassing, and I fear we are set for another battle. I pray this will pass swiftly, and we will continue north to put an end to all battles.

July 1, 1863

Another grueling day brings much death to both armies. Benny and me have lasted the day. I am retiring after four hours of guard duty. Sleep will not come just yet.

We took few prisoners. Though it is not allowed, while guarding them, we talked of our homes. Two soldiers do not wear the Union blues. They are in green uniforms and carry a new kind of rifle. It is a breech-loading rifle.

Never have I been so fascinated with a weapon. Our own muskets load from the front. This forces us to stand and most times be seen. These rifles load from the back. The shooter can remain hidden from sight. The two soldiers tell me they are in a special regiment of sharpshooters for the Union. Most regiments are made of men and boys from the same town. This bunch was gathered from many states by a rich man in New York City. They are the best long-distance shooters around. Sadly these two boys got separated from the regiment during the fighting. That is how we took them.

They seem like plain folks just like me. Hard to think of them as the enemy. Maybe that is why we are not supposed to talk to the prisoners. If we start to feel for them, we may not do the right thing on the battlefield.

CHAPTER 5

Brian stood before Janie wearing a Confederate soldier's uniform. Saluting, he turned on his heel and marched away.

"No, Brian. Don't go! Wait! Wait…"

Janie awoke gasping for breath. Her sweat-drenched pajamas clung to her skin. The buzzing of the alarm clock shattered the veins in her temples. Hazy fragments of images flashed through her head. With incredible effort she reached over and turned off the offending noise. Focusing her sight on the digital screen, it read 6:03. Beyond the clock, the empty wine bottle mocked her. That explained the grogginess. The contents of Brian's envelope lay scattered across the bed. The leather-bound journal rested beside her pillow. She shoved it away as if it offended her because it didn't offer any helpful clues.

She had stayed up most of the night, struggling through William's diary as best she could. The first few pages proved difficult, but it began making sense once she figured out the rhythm of his entries. Beyond his family history, there were snippets of historical information written by the young Confederate soldier. He logged battles he and his brother, Benjamin, fought in, but nothing useful to her—or Brian. The crude writing took a long time to decipher, especially on pages where the ink had faded or smudged. She passed out before finishing.

Janie dragged herself out of bed and into the bathroom. Turning on the tap to fill the sink, she bent over and splashed cold water on her face. The refreshing drops rolled down her forehead, cheeks, and chin, pulling her out of her funk. Sightless, Janie reached for the hand towel hanging nearby and dried her face as she stood upright. Opening her eyes, she leaned in to examine the damage of the late night on her complexion. Her reflection looked back, as well as that of a young man standing behind her. Janie's heart leapt to her throat as she whipped around and found no one there. When she looked back in the mirror, only her image remained.

This is too much, she thought. First nightmares and now hallucinations. Janie shook her head. With the assault of information thrown at her in the last twenty-four hours, her imagination cartwheeled out of control.

The visions had to be a result of the wine, newspaper articles, and journal. This knowledge didn't calm the raised hackles on the back of her neck. The foreboding in Brian's letter snaked its way up her spine threatening to encircle her throat and squeeze tight. His writing had a tone of uncertainty and fear—uncharacteristic of the man she had married.

She dressed for work then woke the girls on her way downstairs. Both arose chipper. At least they got a good night's sleep. Janie hadn't set up the coffee the night before. With a deep sigh, she prepared the pot to brew then laid out the cereal bowls and milk for the girls.

Throughout the morning, Janie did her best to keep the routine normal. Her voice remained even and her movements deliberate. Despite her concerted efforts, the earlier appearance of a man in her mirror kept distracting her from her morning tasks.

"Everything okay, Mom?" Natalie asked, seated at the breakfast table.

Janie turned from the counter where she'd been putting together the girls' lunches. Struggling to keep the quiver out of her voice, she said, "Fine, honey. Why do you ask?"

"Well…"

Extending an arm out, Janie gripped the edge of the counter. Someone told them. Guilt raced through her at not being the one to explain this new development.

"As much as I love squash," Natalie said, "I'd rather have an apple in my lunch, if you don't mind."

With a tilt of her head and brows scrunched, she peeked inside the bag and grimaced. Beside a sandwich and bag of chips sat a yellow zucchini. She looked at her daughter, and they burst out laughing. "Are you sure? I thought I'd spice up the menu."

"Maybe you could throw in a pear or banana for variety, you know, something from the fruit family?"

Jenny giggled at her sister while holding in a mouthful of cereal.

Picking an apple from the refrigerator, she replaced the squash. Janie checked what she'd put into Jenny's bag but found it to be the usual fare. Not wanting to sully their cheerful morning, she once again put off telling the girls about the court proceedings.

When good-bye kisses and proper lunches were handed out, Jenny and Natalie left for the bus stop. Janie gathered her things for the day. A desk full of papers awaited her at work.

First, she needed to stop by Mom's. No sense putting it off. The news would be more upsetting if heard from someone else.

Her knuckles whitened as she gripped the wheel on the short ten-minute drive to her mother's. Parking behind Tom's truck, she let out a sigh of relief. Having the support of her brother this morning gave her strength.

Mom and Tom sat at the kitchen table, each holding a mug. The scent of bacon lingered from their breakfast. Dirty dishes sat on the counter.

"Hi, Janie." Tom gave an awkward smile. "Ruth called me last night, so I thought I'd drop by this morning."

Confusion shone in Mom's eyes, but Janie understood. She conveyed a silent thank you to her brother with a weak smile.

"What's going on?" Mom asked, setting her coffee down a little too hard and sending drops onto the tablecloth. "I should have suspected something when you showed up unannounced for breakfast, Tom. You haven't done that in ages."

Not wanting to prolong the scene any further, Janie blurted out her news. "Yesterday I went to court and had Brian officially declared dead." She flopped down in the chair next to Tom, drained of energy as if she'd run a marathon.

The only sounds heard for the next few moments were the clock ticking on the wall and the whir of the ceiling fan overhead.

In a quiet voice, Mom said, "It was time."

"How can you be so calm?" Janie's shoulders trembled.

"It was eight years last month. I expected you to declare this a year ago. As much as it hurts, you needed to lay Brian to rest."

Tears rolled down Janie's cheeks. How could something so difficult be taken with such grace? Sometimes she underestimated this woman. While age diminished her mother's memory, her heart always knew the right course.

Tom, unnaturally quiet, took his sister's hand in both of his. "Janie, Mom's right. It was time. We all knew, but you had to decide on your own."

Uncertain how to respond to their unified acceptance, Janie cast her eyes downward, wiping tears with the back of her free hand. Mom poured a cup of coffee and set it in front of her daughter. Tom released his hold, and Janie mechanically took a sip. Both the brew and her brother's presence gave her comfort.

After a few false starts, conversation progressed with talk of present events. Thankful at not having to relive the details of court, Janie thought about telling them of the packet Sam presented to her. In the end she chose not to—for now. Sharing the information would alleviate her stress of hiding possible clues, but she didn't want to offer false hope. She carried enough of that for the whole family.

Mom asked her brother, "Is Cassie excited about your trip this weekend?"

"Very. She's never been to the Catskill Mountains before."

"When are you going to marry that nice lady?" Mischief rang out in Mom's voice.

Tom tipped back in his chair. "When she can afford to keep me as a house-husband."

Mother and daughter rolled their eyes in unison at his long-standing joke.

He checked his watch. "I had better get to today's job site or the owner will have my hide. He's probably left several voicemails already." Pulling the phone out of the holder clipped to his waistband he turned on the ringer.

Janie followed him outside to the driveway and wrapped her arms around his neck in a warm hug. "Thanks for being here, big brother. You knew how hard this would be for me."

"Yeah, I know. Now you owe me big time, little sister." Tom smirked, returning the squeeze. "You don't think I provide these moral support services for free, do you?"

"Thank you for that touching sentiment. Just when I think you've decided to act like a normal person, you completely blow the notion out of the water." Janie pulled away.

"Normal? What do you mean normal? There's no one normal in our family." Climbing into his pickup, he gestured with his thumb. "By the way, think you could move that heap from behind my truck? Some of us have jobs to get to."

Janie grinned and hurried back inside for the keys. Rather than linger any longer, she grabbed her purse and kissed Mom on the cheek.

"Janie, it's okay to let go. You did the right thing."

"I know. It doesn't feel right yet, but it will." She hopped into her car and backed out of Tom's way. For the first time in twenty-four hours, some of the tension seeped from her body.

Driving around her and down the street, Tom

tooted the horn and waved out the window, his hand making a peace sign with two fingers.

Janie's momentary calm retreated as she shifted her car into gear. Tonight she needed to relate the court proceedings to two more important people—her children.

CHAPTER 6

"Good morning. Here are your messages." Meg, her reading glasses hanging from a chain around her neck, held out a pile of pink notes as Janie walked past the front desk. "Larry called and won't be in until noon."

Janie stopped and took the papers from her assistant. "Anything I need to cover?"

"No. He wasn't sure whether you would be taking another day off, so I rescheduled his morning appointments." Meg tilted her head, her silver hair curling beneath her ears.

Continuing down the hallway, Janie caught Meg's reflection in the window beside her office door. Instead of going back to work, the woman stared after her. Their eyes met in the glass, then Meg snapped back to her computer, replacing her spectacles on her nose. Janie shook it off. Her face must look a wreck from lack of sleep.

A few years ago, when Janie took Brian's place at the realty office, Meg patiently walked her through everything. Never once did the assistant show frustration or annoyance. Despite Janie having been in the real estate business years prior, many things had changed. After six months it got easier.

Had it not been for Meg's constant efforts at keeping the work moving when Brian disappeared, the business would have closed. The woman surprised Janie by remaining here in this small operation. With her skills, she could have gone to any large office and gotten a higher paying position with better benefits.

Before Janie knew it, the clock read five o'clock. Her stomach grumbled, reminding her she'd skipped lunch.

Meg poked her head into the office. "Unless you have anything else, I'll be heading home."

Janie looked up from her paperwork. "Nothing else, thanks. Have a nice weekend, Meg."

"Thank you, Janie. You too." It had taken Meg months before she started calling her Janie instead of Mrs. Holgram.

The same exchange took place between Meg and Larry before the outside door clicked shut. Shortly afterward, an eerie sensation rippled through her. She looked up and nearly fell out of her chair. Larry stood in the doorway. His stocky frame filled most of its width. Only being a couple inches taller than Janie, he still dwarfed her with his broad shoulders and barrel chest.

"How long have you been prowling around there?" Janie asked.

"Long enough to see you need a break. Go home."

She gestured to the papers in front of her. "I want to finish this last offer. Are you heading out now?"

Larry stepped inside and flopped down in one of the chairs opposite her desk. The legs jiggled and groaned. He looked disheveled with his shaggy blond hair and mustache in need of a trim. "Janie"—his hands fidgeted in his lap—"Meg showed me the newspaper— the article about Brian. You made it official only yesterday. Why are you here? You've been holed up in this office as if your life depended on it."

"I'm sorry. I should've told you." Janie hung her head before making eye contact again. "It's too raw right now. As far as coming into the office, where else should I be? Moping around my house won't make anything better. Here I can stay busy."

"That's not what I meant. I didn't expect you to come running into my office telling me you'd declared Brian dead."

Janie winced.

Softening his tone, he asked, "Why aren't you home with your kids? All this can wait."

"No, it can't. I haven't been pulling my weight in the last week. Clients won't wait forever." Janie straightened the papers on her desk, tamping them harder than necessary. "Besides, I haven't told them— the girls, I mean. I couldn't bear to yesterday, so I was waiting until tonight."

"Putting it off won't make it any easier. Besides, by tomorrow some of their friends may know." Larry rested a hand on the desk. "Go be with your children. You need them right now."

Her chair creaked as she leaned back and sighed. "You're right. I'll finish this offer and head out. How about you?"

"I'm going to burn the midnight oil a bit longer. See you Monday," Larry told her as he got up and walked toward the hallway. Stopping at the door, he added, "Lock the door on your way out, will you?"

"Sure, Larry." She stared after him, appreciating his concern.

Janie finished the proposal and left it on Meg's

desk. A sense of accomplishment flooded through her as she looked over the pile of work completed, despite it only being a distraction. Thoughts of what she would say to Natalie and Jenny kept getting in the way.

With her purse and briefcase in hand, Janie headed across the parking lot. Halfway to the car, she went back to lock the building's front door. As she turned the key in the slot, Larry walked toward her office. When the bolt clicked home, he turned with his brows arched and mouth agape. Flashing a grin, he waved as he walked past her office toward the file room.

How odd. She had no doubt Larry was going into her office. Nothing unusual about it, since they worked on clients together, and he probably needed paperwork. But why pretend to head for the file room instead? Must be her imagination playing tricks.

Removing her key from the door, Janie jumped. The reflection of a man in the window stared back at her. She turned and asked, "Can I help you...?" The parking lot remained empty save for her car and Larry's. Janie whirled back toward the door, but only her image reflected in the glass with a view of the office beyond. With nerves jangling, she hurried to her vehicle, got in, and locked the door.

Cars packed the roadways causing the drive home to take longer than usual. She gripped the wheel, inching through crowded intersections and being cut off twice by overzealous drivers.

Arriving home, Janie walked into a kitchen filled with the savory scents of macaroni and cheese bubbling in the oven. "Mmm, something smells good." She placed her keys and purse on the counter.

"Hi, Mom," Jenny said. "We decided to pull one of

your frozen casseroles out for dinner. I hope you didn't have other plans."

"Nope, that sounds great. I'll whip up a salad to go with it," offered Janie as she set her briefcase on the opposite counter.

"Already taken care of," Natalie said, entering the kitchen. "I put it back in the fridge until dinner time. The macaroni should be done in fifteen minutes."

Her children had gotten so independent. When did that happen? "Good. We have a few minutes." Her voiced cracked, and she cleared her throat. "Come sit down. I have something to tell you."

They took seats at the table. Natalie arched her brows and Jenny leaned on her elbows, nesting her chin on her hands. Both were miniature versions of their mother with long brunette tresses and athletic bodies.

Janie eased onto the chair next to Natalie. She cleared her throat. Both girls gazed at her, expectant looks on their faces. "Girls, I went to the courthouse yesterday. I know we've all prayed someday Daddy would return." With trembling fingers she tucked a stray hair behind her ear. "As the years have passed, hope's faded. There's no easy way to say this. Yesterday, I had your father legally declared dead."

Natalie and Jenny stared at their mother with wide eyes. Natalie fidgeted with the napkin and fork in front of her.

Jenny's lip quivered, and tears slipped down her cheeks. "What do you mean you had Daddy legally declared dead? You can't do that." Her voice escalated as she lifted her head from where it rested. "He's coming home to us. He's not dead. You can't just decide that!"

"Jenny, honey, I didn't just decide that." She reached over and placed a hand atop her twelve-year-old's. Jenny's cool skin did nothing to alleviate the heat building inside of Janie. "You know it's not that simple. I believed he would come back. But it's been—"

"No," screamed Jenny, ripping her arm away from her mother. "You can't do this."

"Jenny, listen to me." Moisture brimmed her eyes as her voice quaked. She retracted her hand and placed it over her heart. "It's been eight years. If Daddy were still alive, he would have come back to us. We need to move on with our lives."

"How can you forget him like that?" Jenny glared.

"I haven't forgotten him." Tears leaked down her face, and her chest felt about to explode from the rapid beating inside. The oven timer dinged but not as loud as the ringing in her ears. "I'll never forget Daddy, but he's gone, sweetie. I'll always love him and hold his memories dear to my heart. You must believe I'm looking after what's best for us. It's time for our family to heal."

Jenny bolted out of her chair, almost knocking it over. "Heal? How could our family ever heal with Daddy gone? Does it mean now you'll look for a new daddy?"

"Please, listen to me, Jenny. Nobody can ever replace Daddy, but we're still here and owe it to him to live our lives as best we can. Part of that is accepting he's gone. Try to understand."

Her daughter tore from the room. "I'll never forget Daddy," she shouted, pounding up the stairs.

Janie leaned her head back and stared up at the ceiling. She massaged the throbbing veins in her neck.

Her shoulders rose, echoing the tightness of her neck. The scent of the macaroni and cheese wafted through the air. Her stomach roiled, and the thought of dinner no longer sounded satisfying. She reached out and gave Natalie's shoulder a squeeze. "Do you hate me too?"

Natalie gasped. "Oh, Mom, I don't hate you. Neither does Jenny. I know you're doing what's best for us. She's upset. It's…well…it's like losing him all over again. Except this time there isn't hope he'll come back. Is there?" Natalie's cheeks also glistened with moisture as she searched her mother's face for an answer.

Janie cupped her daughter's wet cheek, using a thumb to wipe away the tears. "No, Natalie, he isn't coming back. I know Jenny's hurting. It's how I felt when I got home yesterday. I wanted to scream at somebody and say it isn't fair, just like Jenny is doing now. Even though she was only four when he lef…went away, she remembers him. Being the last one of us to see him, the scene is scorched into her memory."

"Mom, we'll be okay—all of us. Jenny will calm down. I think it's harder on her because she was his baby."

Janie's eyes shone at her fourteen-year-old. "When did you get to be so old and wise?"

"I think the same time you decided to quit feeling sorry for yourself and moved on with raising us alone."

"We aren't alone, you know. Grandma and your aunts and uncles have always been there for us." Janie slipped an arm around her older daughter and pulled her close.

Natalie rested her head against her mother's shoulder. "I know, Mom. Jenny does too. She needs time to get used to the idea."

Janie nodded and gave her daughter a squeeze before getting up. She turned off the oven and set the casserole on the stove to cool. Natalie set out the salad and dressings from the refrigerator.

Walking upstairs to her daughter's bedroom, Janie lightly rapped on the door. No answer. Instead of knocking again, she put a hand on the knob. It wouldn't turn.

"Jenny, open the door. Please."

"No! Go away!" Her daughter's tear-filled voice came from the other side.

"Jenny, open the door. I want to talk with you. Don't shut me out like this." Janie placed her palm flat against the door as if willing the bolt to release.

After an eternity of silence, the lock clicked. Footsteps stomped across the room, and the mattress springs creaked. Turning the knob, she walked in. Jenny lay sprawled across the bed with a pillow over her head. The scene brought a smile to Janie's lips. The girl had done this since the age of two whenever she got upset. If only hiding from the world could be that easy.

"Please talk to me. I want you to understand I'm not doing this to forget Daddy. It's time to put his soul to rest. Hoping for something we know will never happen isn't good for any of us."

Jenny's muffled voice came from under the pillow. "You want to forget him."

"There isn't a day that goes by I don't think about your father. We can't live our lives expecting him to walk back through the front door anymore. It's been eight years. Daddy isn't coming back. You don't have to accept this right now, but at least try to live with the idea. Turn around so I can see your face."

Reluctantly, Jenny rolled over and sat up next to her mother, still clutching her pillow. "Don't you love Daddy anymore?"

"Of course, I love him. And I love you and your sister. You're the two most important people in my life. Our lives need to go on with our family the way it is now. Do you understand, sweetie?"

"Yes…I…Mom…" The girl tried again. "It hurts."

Janie held her child close and rested her head atop Jenny's silky brown hair. The scent of honeysuckle shampoo tickled Janie's nose. "It hurts me too. We need to help each other through the pain."

Jenny nodded through streams of tears, her eyes rimmed in red. After a few moments, they went downstairs. Halfway down the steps, Jenny looked at her mother. "Mom, I don't really hate you."

"I know. I'll always know." Now if only she could stop hating herself for what she'd done. *Would she ever really move on?*

CHAPTER 7

Sitting around the dining table, none of the three could summon an appetite. They pushed macaroni noodles around their plates and picked at the cheese. The salad went untouched. Feeble attempts at conversation increased the tension engulfing the shattered family until an uncomfortable silence descended.

Janie had taken eight years to come to grips with Brian's disappearance, culminating with her court actions yesterday. The gavel slamming down seared through her mind as she watched her daughters process the news, delivered like a battering ram to their innocence. Forced to deal with the finality of losing their father only an hour ago, it would take time for the girls to accept. Lots of time.

Natalie and Jenny left the table and trudged up the steps to their rooms. Janie cleaned up the meal then tackled a load of laundry and ironing before heading upstairs.

She stopped at Jenny's room first and knocked on the partially closed door.

"Come in," Jenny mumbled.

Janie sat on the bed next to her daughter. "Did you want to talk?"

"Will we have a funeral for him?" Her eyes glistened.

Janie placed a hand on the stuffed dog her daughter clutched. She ran her fingers over the rough fur now matted from years of loving. "Do you want us to have one?"

"No. Is that wrong?" She bit her lip.

"No, it isn't wrong. Maybe after a while we may want to. We don't have to decide anything tonight."

Jenny let go of the toy and threw her arms around her mother. "I really don't hate you."

"I know, sweetie. You don't have to keep telling me; I believe you." Janie pulled away from her daughter. "Ya know, I don't hate you either."

Jenny smiled.

Janie kissed her daughter on the cheek and left the room, leaving the door ajar.

Moving on to Natalie's, she leaned against the door jamb. Her daughter lay in bed reading a book.

"It's okay, Mom." Natalie spoke first. "We don't have to talk about it now."

"We can if you want?"

"Maybe tomorrow. At least this explains the squash in my lunch." She giggled.

Kissing her oldest goodnight, Janie went to her room and flipped on the overhead light. Halfway hidden by the covers of her unmade bed the leather-bound journal beckoned. A chill trickled through her raising the hair on her arms.

She changed into pajamas and went into the bathroom to brush her teeth and remove her makeup. After drying her face in front of the mirror, Janie cracked open one eye. She let out the breath she held at seeing only her reflection. Back in the bedroom, she extinguished the overhead light and crawled under the blankets. As she turned on the bedside light while grabbing the journal, she heard a soft *pop*, and the room remained dark. The book slipped from her fingers and hit the floor with a thud.

Quietly cussing under her breath, she swung her feet over the edge of the bed to retrieve a new bulb. She needed to continue reading. The saga of the two brothers during the Civil War captivated her, as did the necessity of finding the connection between them and Brian. He'd always been a history fanatic, but that shouldn't be a reason to go missing.

As Janie approached the stairs, the light from Natalie's room spilled into the hallway. Jenny had gone to sleep. *It's a wonder the girl didn't pass out a couple of hours earlier.*

An empty box of bulbs sat on the kitchen counter. She tossed it at the trash and missed. Rather than picking it up, she left it where it landed. At the top of the basement stairs, she hit the light and descended the creaky flight. Despite their groans, the steps were by no means rickety. Brian saw to getting them reinforced before they moved in years ago, especially with her being pregnant at the time. No sense having any potential hazards.

The basement possessed the same damp, musty smell found in most homes close to the ocean. Crossing the floor to the workshop area brought a sad smile to her face. She had given Brian a set of tools for one of their anniversaries. He never made it a secret as to how un-handy he was around the house. Home improvements weren't one of his gifts, he liked to say. As a joke, she'd labeled each one with big bold letters and included a pegboard to hang them on. He took the gesture in stride and erected the pegboard over an old cabinet he dubbed his "work bench."

Lost in memories, Janie opened the right-hand compartment. The hinges creaked as she swung the door wide enough to find what she needed. Turning back toward the stairs, her body stiffened, and her mouth gaped in silent horror. The bulb slipped from her fingers. It took eons before shattering on the cement floor into a million pieces. A young man wearing a Confederate Civil War uniform stood before her.

A scream lodged in her throat, not gaining enough momentum to reach her lips. Panic-stricken eyes bulged from her head as her first thought went to the children's safety. *Were there others in the house?*

Standing three feet away, the man, more of a boy really, didn't move any closer. A pained expression writhed across his face with his brows wrinkled and jaw taut. Already scared out of her mind, the sheer torture in his eyes sent new tendrils of fear throughout every nerve-ending in her body. He opened his mouth as if to speak but uttered no sound. Instead, he mouthed the words, "Help me, Janie. Help me."

Janie picked out a clear path to the staircase. Forcing her feet to move, she bolted for the exit. Hitting the first step and throwing herself up the next, she glanced behind and stopped. Save for pieces of glass and filament scattered by the work bench, the floor stood empty.

She hesitated a moment longer, then tore up the stairs two at a time. Slamming the door, she threw home the bolt and leaned against the wood, panting, grateful they'd never removed the lock once the girls had grown.

Getting her breathing under control, Janie shivered as she ran through the scene in her head. No doubt it happened. The torture on the young man's face and in his eyes pierced her like a knife. His anguish echoed through her to the bottom of her soul.

No point in calling the police. What would she tell them? *Yes, officer, I saw a Confederate soldier in my basement, but he disappeared.* They'd be out the door and calling the psych ward in seconds.

The busted light forgotten, Janie ran upstairs to check on the girls. Jenny lay safely asleep in her bed. Natalie had drifted off with her book still in hand and the light on. Janie turned off the lamp before returning to the ground floor. She made a quick tour of the house, going into every room, turning on lights, checking each closet and nook. Nothing. Everything was as it should be.

Back in her room, she looked at the journal lying innocently on the floor where it had fallen. *Could it be normal for people to hallucinate under stress?*

Janie opened her nightstand drawer and tucked the book away, hands still quivering from her experience. She debated whether to put it downstairs, completely away from the bedroom. "Now you're being ridiculous," she said aloud. Slipping herself under the covers, she left the overhead light on all night.

Horrible nightmares tormented her dreams— visions of Civil War soldiers, Brian, and death. Lots of death. Several times she awoke on the verge of screaming only to find herself safe and alone. Falling back to sleep, she experienced the horror again. This loop repeated over and over with different variations. At one point she dreamed of Brian in a Confederate

Uniform mouthing the words, "Help me, Janie. Help me." Never uttering a sound, his voiceless lips formed the words repeatedly. Sometimes his face morphed into that of the young man she'd been seeing, who continued the silent tirade. "Help me, Janie. Help me."

CHAPTER 8

Groggy and sticky with sweat, Janie dragged herself out of bed. Her limbs weighed heavy with exhaustion, yet additional sleep eluded her this morning. She shivered as images of the basement scene flooded her memory. Standing under a hot shower, she scrubbed harder than needed, as if she could wash away the fright of her nocturnal visitor.

Like yesterday, the coffee had been forgotten the night before. As the brew dripped into the pot, the kitchen filled with the scent of French roast, helping to raise her spirits.

Conceding she could no longer handle the situation alone, she picked up the phone to call Tom. About to dial, she put the handset back in its cradle. He and Cassie were away on a trip and wouldn't get back until Monday night.

Natalie came bustling into the kitchen wearing her soccer uniform. "Morning, Mom. Aren't you going to pack the cooler? My first game starts in an hour." She helped herself to a bowl of cereal.

"I'll take care of it after my coffee. Julie's mom is picking you up, right?"

"Yeah. Coach wants us there a half an hour before the game. I'm sure there will be a pep talk involved. Rah, rah." She waved pretend pom-poms in the air.

"Don't be disrespectful. She's doing a great job

with your team." Janie opened the refrigerator. Nothing inside could be used for their lunches and snacks. With the stress of the last couple of days, she hadn't planned ahead for this weekend of tournament play. Natalie had games all day today, and Jenny's team participated tomorrow. She'd need to stop on her way to the field.

"I know. I'm only kidding." She shoveled her breakfast.

Janie turned to her daughter. "Are you okay? I mean, after what I told you last night. Did you want to talk about it?" She clasped her hands together.

Natalie leaned back in her chair. "No, Mom. I'm good. It still hurts, but like you said, it'll take time to get used to knowing Daddy really isn't coming back." She pushed her half-eaten breakfast away. "Guess I'm not as hungry as I thought. Want me to get the cooler from downstairs?"

Janie busied herself rinsing dishes. Over her shoulder, she said, "I'll take care of it. Thanks. Get your gear ready so you don't keep your ride waiting when they arrive."

"Okay." Natalie placed her bowl on the counter by her mother and hurried upstairs to her bedroom.

"Make sure your sister is awake, please," Janie called. She turned from the sink, and her shoulders tensed as she approached the basement door. The mess on the floor needed cleaning. If she didn't take care of the broken bulb, one of the girls might step on it. Janie grasped the deadbolt but didn't unlock it. Instead, she went to the utensil drawer and selected a wooden rolling pin. Holding it up in a ready position, she slid back the lock. Cracking the door a few inches, Janie peered down the stairs. The light shone from the ceiling, enabling her to see all the way to the bottom. Raising her weapon higher, she thought, this is ridiculous, and swung the door wide. Setting her back straight and chin up, she strode down the stairs.

In the light of day, she had doubts about the previous night's occurrence. Yet in her mind's eye she saw every detail of the young man's contorted face. Her moments of terror while staring at his agonized expression forced her to accept the reality.

Get a grip, she thought. The glass fragments remained where they'd landed. She set down the rolling pin, grabbed the broom leaning against the wall, and swept the pieces onto a dustpan. After pouring them into the trash, she opened the cabinet to get another bulb. This time she stood sideways while searching, so she wouldn't have her back to the only exit.

Securing her prize, she picked up the large, red cooler from the other side of the workbench and scurried up the stairs without a second glance. She once again bolted the door.

Before she and her younger daughter left for the soccer field, Janie removed the half-read journal from her nightstand and locked it in the office filing cabinet. So shaken from her experiences in the last day, she would wait until she could talk the situation over with Tom before proceeding further. As much as she needed to finish going through everything Brian had left, her nerves couldn't handle any more.

****

The soccer schedule monopolized the whole weekend allowing very little time for anything else. Nightmares haunted Janie's slumber robbing her of restful sleep. Over those days she found herself drawn

58

to the home office where she stood before the filing cabinet. The journal beckoned to her to be read, but fear of eliciting more sightings weighed heavier. She resisted until Tuesday morning arrived when she called her brother.

Tom answered on the second ring. "Hello?"

"Hi, it's Janie."

"Who?"

"Janie."

"Who?"

Grasping the handset, she admonished, "Cut that out. Will you ever grow up? Never mind. I don't need an answer."

"No, you don't," chuckled Tom. "What's up?"

"Are you free for lunch today?"

"Your treat?"

Snorting through her nose, she said, "Yes, if it will get you to come."

"You know I'm kidding. Of course. I'd love to have lunch with my favorite sister," Tom replied.

Ignoring another one of Tom's dumb jokes, she asked, "Where and when is good for you? I don't know where you're working today, but I prefer earlier, if that's okay."

Tom hesitated. "How about eleven at Fredrick's Deli. I've got a job down the street from there. Everything okay?"

"Yes, of course." She gripped the phone tighter. "Eleven o'clock at Fredrick's sounds good. See you then."

"Okay. Hey, Sis? You did the right thing—about Brian, I mean."

"I know." Her voice cracked. "It hurts, but like

everything else, I'll get through it."

"Darn straight. You're tough as nails. Why do you think I let you protect me from the bullies on the playground when we were kids?"

"Yeah, getting beat up by all those girls must've been pretty tough on you."

"Funny. I gotta run. See you later." Tom ended the call.

Janie had a lighter hitch to her step after talking to her brother. He may not be able to shed any light, but it would help to share this bizarre situation. Brian's note warned not to trust anybody, but surely that didn't include Tom. He would never do anything to hurt her or the girls.

After getting the kids off to school, Janie called her assistant at the office.

"Good morning, Charger Realty," Meg answered, her voice crisp and professional.

"Good morning, Meg, it's Janie. I won't be in until about noon today. Unless something's come up, I shouldn't have any pending appointments, do I?"

"Let me check your calendar." Janie heard Meg tapping computer keys. "No. Your morning is clear." She never wasted words, especially on the phone.

"Great. I'm meeting Tom at Fredrick's Deli at eleven; can I bring you something back?" Meg would decline the offer as usual, but Janie asked anyway.

"Thank you, no. Will that be all?"

"Yes. Thanks for holding down the fort," Janie said. "See you later."

"Goodbye."

"Humph," Meg sighed. She couldn't wait for the day Charger Realty would be a distant memory. She would bide her time. Meanwhile, she thought, this might be a perfect opportunity.

Back in the kitchen, Janie slipped the phone into its charger on the counter. Her assistant's demeanor unsettled her when she acted more dismissive toward Janie than professional.

When ten forty-five rolled around, Janie grabbed her purse and keys then left through the kitchen door.

She lucked out and found a close parking space less than a block away. As she walked down the sidewalk to the deli, the smell of corned beef with mustard lured her inside. The Reuben sandwich had been Fredrick's claim to fame since they opened thirty years ago and remained her favorite. Her mouth watered and her appetite returned.

Tom waited at a back table. He spoke with a sandy-haired guy with well-formed biceps standing across from him by the counter. Janie didn't recognize the man, but his denim jeans and T-shirt suggested he worked construction or some other outdoor occupation. When she got close enough to read his shirt, it had a cartoon of a lawnmower and touted Cooper's Landscaping—the company owned by the man Carol wanted to set her up with. Her hands fisted nervously as she prayed he wasn't the owner.

"Janie," Tom called as he waved her over to the table.

"You weren't planning on starting without me, were you, big brother?" She struggled to relax, but her fists remained balled.

"Wouldn't dream of it. Besides, I thought you said you were buying?"

Janie smirked.

Tom grinned at his sister. "Hey, have you met John? He owns all those trucks with the cutesy talking lawn mowers on them."

"No…no, I haven't," she said with a tremor in her voice. She had no intention of volunteering her connection to Carol.

"Well, Janie, this is John. John, Janie. You can shake hands and be polite now."

"Does this guy ever stop joking?" John gestured with his thumb. Breaking into a gleaming smile, he reached out. "It's a real pleasure to meet you. Don't worry. I won't hold it against you that you're related to this guy. Every family's got one."

Accepting the handshake, Janie replied, "It's nice to meet you. And no, he doesn't ever stop."

"I believe we have a mutual acquaintance. Carol Dell? She's a hairdresser."

She shifted her stance. Busted. "You mean stylist. Don't ever make that mistake in front of her, especially if she's armed with scissors. It could get ugly."

"Good advice. Well, I wouldn't want to get in the middle of important family business. My order's ready anyway. Tom, I'm sure I'll see you around. Janie, glad to meet you. Maybe we'll run into each other again." He winked as he scooped up his bag and sauntered toward the door.

"I do believe he likes you, Sis." Tom glanced at his sister sideways.

As John walked away, she admired the way his jeans clung in all the right places, especially his muscular thighs and calves.

"And I do believe you're enjoying his retreating backside."

Her face flushed with warmth. "What? Oh...don't be ridiculous. Besides, he's a friend of yours. How nice could he be?" Despite the denial, she remained caught up on his rugged looks. John stood about six feet. Maybe Carol's idea had some merit.

Janie surprised herself. She couldn't remember the last time she'd noticed a man in that way. Since Brian's disappearance, she hadn't even considered other men. Now betrayal coursed through her veins as if she were cheating on him.

Ignoring her discomfort, Tom led her to the front counter where they could place their lunch order. "So, what are we eating? I'm going for the Italian sub with an extra-large soda. How about you?"

Janie didn't hesitate to order the corned beef on rye she'd been obsessing over since Tom suggested Fredrick's. She'd given up fighting for the bill long ago and allowed him to pay.

When their order got called from the back counter, Tom picked it up. Janie dove hungrily into her Reuben savoring the tender corned beef and toasted marble rye bread. After talking about their mother's latest antics and life between big brother and his wife, the conversation lulled. Tom broke the ice. "Okay, Janie, give. What's bothering you?"

Putting down the remaining half of her sandwich, she stuttered, "I...I don't know where to begin. You see...well...things have been...happening. I'm not sure how to handle them."

"Like financial matters? Is the roof falling off? You want me to teach Jenny to drive? Give me a little more to go on," Tom said.

"Okay. Let's start with before Brian disappeared."

Tom would usually take this opportunity to interrupt again, but occasionally he knew when to sit back and listen. She looked from side to side, leaned in closer, and lowered her voice. "Did he ever mention finding a skeleton when he was a teenager?"

"A skeleton? You mean a real bag of bones, so to speak?"

Janie slouched back in her chair. "Yes. Right after high school graduation, while camping at Filmore Beach, he and Larry found remains in a hole in the woods."

"Did he tell you about the discovery right before he went missing?"

She shook her head. "On Thursday after court Sam gave me a large envelope addressed in Brian's handwriting. He had instructions from Brian to give it to me upon his death. Obviously, my husband hadn't planned on going missing and his lawyer waiting eight years for delivery. The packet contained an odd assortment of...things. Two of them were old newspaper articles. The first reported how Larry and Brian found a skeleton. He never said anything to you about it?"

"Nope. Never mentioned it. Why would he? It happened so long ago." He bit off a large bite and chewed. "Do you think it has something to do with his disappearance?"

The butcher paper crinkled as Janie pushed the remains of her lunch aside then propped her elbows on the table. "Honestly, I don't know what to think. If it doesn't, why would it be important for me to have the articles after his death?"

"I have no idea. You said there were two articles.

What did the second one say?"

"It revealed who Brian and Larry found—a soldier from the Civil War. The buttons and boots left from his uniform determined it was Union, but his engraved pocket watch had a surname belonging to a Confederate family in Virginia. Historians traced it back to the south and discovered there had been two sons who fought in the Civil War. DNA and forensics confirmed him to be one of the brothers, probably the older one because of the watch. After being hidden in an underground cave for 150 years, the bones were shipped back to Virginia and buried in the family plot."

Tom stopped eating. "This is fascinating. Being a history buff, Brian must've loved being part of the discovery. I remember him watching documentaries about Gettysburg and other battles. But, Sis, why do you think it has anything to do with his disappearance?"

"I know, I'm grasping at straws." Janie looked into her brother's eyes. "He also left me a real estate file in the packet for Brassel Field. I remember him speaking to someone on the phone about that property a week before he disappeared. Guess I hoped this information might jog your memory if he mentioned it. Did he ever talk about that property?"

Tom slurped his soda through the straw. "No. I honestly can't remember his mentioning that either. Have you followed up on the lead? Maybe see if the property ever sold or who owned it at the time? What about taking this stuff to the police? They're trained to research and ask questions. It might be better if you let them handle it."

"You mean it might be safer." She leaned back, crossing her arms and legs.

"Something out of the ordinary happened to Brian. Poking around in things he might have been involved with isn't one of your better ideas."

Janie ran a hand through her hair. "The thought crossed my mind, but I'm not sure who to go to. Brian enclosed a note telling me not to trust anybody. I wish he'd confided in me."

"He probably didn't want to endanger your life or that of the girls. You should turn this over to the police." Tom touched her hand. After a moment's silence he added, "You won't do that, will you?"

"Not yet. I'm afraid if I do the information will slip through the cracks. It's an eight-year-old case that's gone cold."

"Was there anything else in the envelope?"

Janie uncrossed then re-crossed her legs. "No, that's all." New doubts gnawed at her regarding the last few days and how the story would sound out loud. She didn't tell Tom about the journal. Also, being closer to noon, the deli had a steady stream of foot traffic, and any further discussion should be held in private.

"Tom, why don't you come over for dinner tonight? You can look over the stuff and tell me what you think. I've told you everything I can remember, but maybe you'll catch something I missed."

"A home cooked meal, not out of a can? How can I refuse?" Tom grinned. "What time do you want me?"

"How about six-thirty? That'll give me enough time at the office. I took the morning off, so I have some catching up to do. I don't want to hold you up from the job site any longer either."

"I do need to get going. I'm glad you told me about this. It sure is a mystery, but maybe it's got a simple explanation. Might have been important to Brian at the time but meaningless now. We'll look the stuff over together and see what we come up with."

Walking outside, Tom gave his sister a hug and strutted down the block. Janie got into her car, hesitating a moment with a hand on the ignition key. *What might I be dragging him into?*

CHAPTER 9

Janie wrestled with her decision to share William's journal with her brother. If he read it, the apparition may haunt him too. The idea of a ghost haunting either one of them unsettled her nerves, but she didn't know how else to explain the strange encounters.

Tom arrived at six-fifteen through the side door. The smells of cilantro and lime permeated the kitchen, and he made a show of inhaling deeply. His nieces pounced on him before he could set down the Chocolate Melt-away cake he brought for dessert. Natalie rescued the box as it teetered in his hand. The jacket he carried wasn't as lucky and slipped to the floor. He scooped it up and hung it on a hook by the door.

Pulling at his arm, Jenny shouted, "Uncle Tom, Uncle Tom. Come see my science project for school. It's a volcano."

"Does it explode and spew lava?" Tom jumped up and down like a two-year-old.

"Of course not. It's supposed to be a replica."

"Oh, too bad." He stopped hopping. "Maybe I could rig it, so it does." His face brightened.

Both girls' eyes lit up.

"Tom, as Jenny said, it's supposed to be a replica. The last thing I need is fake lava all over my den and the school."

"Aw, Mom, you're no fun," whined Natalie.

"Yeah, Mom, you're no fun," Tom mimicked his niece.

Shaking her spatula, voice stern, Janie said, "You may go look at the project. Then you'll need to wash up. Dinner's on the table in fifteen minutes."

Jenny dragged her uncle out of the room. "Okay, Mom, we'll go look at it."

"Your compliance is greatly appreciated," Janie yelled after them, giving the fajita mix in the pan a stir. Her two daughters' excitement and laughter filled her with joy.

Light-hearted banter continued throughout the meal. Tom's infectious playfulness gave a welcome break from the trauma of the last few days.

Afterward, Janie tasked the girls with cleaning up dinner so she and Tom could have an adult talk in her office. She didn't want the girls knowing anything about the documents received from her lawyer or the strange mystery involving their father.

Leaning back in the desk chair, Tom read the two articles. "I never knew about Brian finding the remains of a Confederate soldier. I'm almost a bit jealous he got to make such an incredible discovery." After looking through the property file, he added, "This doesn't tell me much, Sis. You're the expert here on real estate."

"There's nothing special about the place, except for its history. Do you know where Brassel Field is?"

"I'm sure I've worked in that part of Suffolk County. Most of those lots in the area date back to the first settlements of Long Island. Filmore Beach is nearby, which is the obvious connection to Brian's articles. Still doesn't tell us why he included them, if the authorities removed the skeleton and shipped it to Virginia. I bet historians combed the area for additional artifacts years ago. Not to sound harsh, but beyond that, who cares?"

Janie perched on the edge of the desk, studying her brother. He was right. Who cares about an old skeleton and ancient piece of land? Hopping off the desk, she picked up her briefcase, where she'd stashed the contents of the packet before dinner. Despite being a personal message to her, Janie retrieved Brian's letter and handed it to Tom. "This is why I care about what those articles and file might mean."

The chair creaked as Tom leaned forward and plucked the letter from his sister's trembling hand. When he finished, he read it again. After an interminably long time, Tom said, "I would call this a hoax, except Brian never joked like this. Why did he have to be so cryptic? There aren't many helpful details. What does he mean by the key has always been with you and the girls? I wish he'd left you the journal, then you might have had a shot at figuring this mystery out."

Janie balled her hands then opened them again. "All of these bits and pieces are connected. Brian said someone threatened him. I remember him being jumpy those last couple weeks but chalked it up to stress at work."

"And you don't have any idea who it could've been or why?"

She shook her head. "Not a clue."

"What could this journal have in it that made it so valuable? I guess the age of the book made it worth some money. People might pay big bucks for an authentic Civil War diary."

"Maybe when he wrote the letter, he didn't know the person's identity. He or she could have contacted Brian in any number of ways, other than in person." Janie looked down at the floor then back up. Securing her brother's gaze, she said, "There is something else. I haven't been completely truthful, Tom." She reached into her briefcase and withdrew the journal.

"You do have it. Let me see." Tom shot his arm toward her, but Janie pulled the book out of reach.

Sweat formed on the back of her neck. She hugged the diary to her chest. "There's more. Before you read this journal, you need to know everything. I wish I'd been given a warning before cracking open the cover."

"Janie, you're shaking." Tom jumped up and put his arm around her shoulders. "All this stuff is hard to swallow, but I'm sure whoever was after Brian gave up long ago. They would've contacted you by now if they thought you had anything worth getting."

"That isn't what scares me. I'm a little embarrassed to tell you this part, because when I say the words out loud…it doesn't seem possible."

Tom pulled away and leaned against the desk. "Hello, this is your brother you're talking to. Remember, no matter how crazy or weird, I always listen."

"You listen, then proceed to cut up and make fun. I can't take jokes right now."

"You're scaring me, Sis. Just let it fly, and I'll decide for myself how to react."

Her jaw taut, Janie said, "Promise you won't make fun of me. My sanity is on the verge of going over the edge."

Tom held his right hand up with three fingers showing. "Scout's honor."

Janie looked at him sideways but proceeded. She'd gone this far. He'd never let her stop now. "The first night, after the court date...well...I started reading the journal...William's journal. He's the soldier who wrote it. I fell asleep before finishing. The pages are yellowed and some of the handwriting faded, so it's hard to decipher."

"That's expected with a book this old and having spent 150 years in the ground." Tom kept his tone steady. He nodded for her to go on.

Stress clouded her face, and she squinted, as if seeing everything again. "I had horrific nightmares—images all jumbled together."

"Images of what?"

"Brian and William, both in Confederate uniform. Brian stood in front of me wordless, then turned and walked away. I yelled for him to come back, but he marched off. The next morning, I washed my face, and when I opened my eyes, there was a man standing behind me."

"In your bathroom?"

Janie trembled. "Looking back from the mirror. Maybe he was in the bathroom. I don't know."

"Slow down. You're not making sense."

After several calming breaths, Janie tried again. "I went into the bathroom and washed my face. When I opened my eyes, I saw my reflection in the mirror and a man wearing gray standing behind me. It only lasted a second. I turned around, and the room was empty. I looked back in the mirror and only saw myself."

"Janie, sit down. You're shaking so hard, I'm

afraid you'll collapse."

She eased onto the desk chair still clutching the book with both hands.

"Do you want some water? Wine? Sedative?"

Janie flashed her eyes. "Tom, you promised."

Holding up his hands in surrender, he said, "Sorry. Just trying to lighten the mood."

"You don't believe me."

"I didn't say that. It's just…well…okay. Did you see him again?"

"Yes. When I locked up the office Friday night, I saw his image in the glass door. Again, when I turned, he was gone."

"Did it look like the same guy?"

Nodding her head, she forced herself to finish. "Yes, I'm sure. Because I saw him one more time later that night. Only it wasn't a flash in a mirror or door. He showed up in the basement right in front of me."

Tom rubbed his arms. "Geez, you're giving me goose bumps. What happened? Did he say anything?"

"No, but the pain in his face seared through my soul. He appeared to be suffering. His mouth formed words, but no sound came out. He mouthed 'Help me, Janie. Help me.' "

"Help him do what?"

"How should I know?" she snapped.

Sitting on the desk in front of her, he said, "Okay, fair enough. This is so fantastic. Are you sure you really saw him?"

"Yes."

Tom tapped his foot, not speaking.

"Say something," she pleaded. "Do you think I'm crazy?"

"For once, I don't know what to say. My little sister, the sanest one in the bunch, just told me she's seeing ghosts."

"Not ghosts. Only one ghost. I'm sure it's been the same young man each time."

"Okay, one ghost. Glad we cleared that up. Did you already make an appointment for a CAT scan, or shall I do it for you?"

Slapping her brother's knee, she said, "Cut it out. I told you I can't handle your humor right now."

"Who's joking?" he asked. "Let's look at the logic. I'd say, let's be adults about this, but I don't think it'll help." He gave her a crooked grin.

The tension in her jaw eased.

"Hear me out."

Janie nodded.

"The reflection in the mirror and window could have been a trick of the light. You're stressed with your head full of images about this guy and his exploits in the Civil War."

Janie opened her mouth to protest, but Tom held up his hand. "I know, you said you really saw them. Let's think about this a second."

"Fine. Explain what happened in the basement. That was a full on, straight ahead apparition—no trick of the light or reflection. I stared into the man's tortured face. A good two or three minutes of terror shook my body. I saw it! The ghost was real! I did not imagine it!"

"Well, you've certainly made your point clear. Okay, let's say you did see…something."

Janie's anger at her brother's disbelief replaced her fear. "Fine. I saw something."

"Okay. You saw something. It was late, and you were tired. Maybe you'd finished that whole bottle of wine I saw in the trash."

"I wasn't drunk. I know what I saw."

"Let's move on. You believe you saw a ghost, possibly the spirit of the young soldier who wrote the diary, whose remains Brian and Larry found, so, you don't want me to read it?"

"Yes. No. Oh, I don't know. Forgive me for trying to protect your sorry ass from being as scared out of your wits as I felt the other night. Here. Go ahead and look." Janie dropped the diary onto the desk.

He stood. "I don't mean to be the devil's advocate here but think about what you're saying."

"Tom, on some level, you make sense. Never in my life have I believed in visitors from beyond until I read this journal and things started to appear. The occurrence in the basement didn't happen in my head. I'm too rational a person to randomly believe in spiritual beings. There's no other explanation for what's been going on."

Tom fingered the rough leather cover. "Humor me a minute. If this is all connected to Brian, why isn't Brian's spirit visiting you? Why some stranger?"

"Do I look like an expert on supernatural visitations? There doesn't seem to be an owner's manual available. Your guess is as good as mine. This whole conversation is ludicrous." Janie flailed her arms. "I'm telling you what happened, plain and simple."

"Okay. Let's not micro-analyze this. I can't offer any reasonable explanations. Can I take this home?" Tom asked.

"No," Janie spurted, louder than she'd meant to. "I

mean, no. The language is difficult, and it's faded in parts making it hard to read. I'm only part way done. After the scare in the basement, I locked the book up in here and haven't touched it since. I wanted to get your take on this bizarre situation first, but I do need to finish it. Only getting to the end can I begin to piece together what all of this means and how it connects to Brian. At least I hope I'll be able to find a connection. Why don't I leave you alone for a while, and you can look through it here?"

In a sarcastic voice he asked, "Gee, would you like me to leave my driver's license and promise my firstborn to make sure I don't slip out the back door with it?"

"Don't be silly. You'll never have children. My two have scared the notion of procreation right out of your head." The corners of her mouth lifted. "Your license will be fine."

Standing, Janie motioned for Tom to take a seat then left him alone in the office, closing the door behind her. As much as she wanted him to experience what she saw, if only to prove she wasn't crazy, she hoped he would be spared. Despite being visited three times already, she didn't know how she would react the next time. Maybe reading the journal would cause the spirit to transfer his attention to the new reader.

CHAPTER 10

Three hours later the girls were asleep, and Janie paced the kitchen. Stopping to fill the kettle for tea, a loud crash resounded down the hallway. She dropped the pot in the sink with the water still running. Bolting for the office with her heart in her throat, she slammed through the door and found Tom getting up, rubbing the back of his head.

"Sorry to startle you, Sis. I must've tipped over too far in the chair."

"You scared the daylights out of me."

"You thought I had a visitor, didn't you?" He winked.

Janie's mouth gaped open, closed, then opened again. "Are you sure you weren't pushed?"

"Okay, calm down. And yes, I'm fine, thanks for asking."

Fidgeting with her wedding ring, Janie asked, "Well? What do you make of the journal? How far did you get? Did you..." Water running from the kitchen faucet made her stop. She held up one finger and dashed out.

When she returned, Tom said, "Finished it. I skimmed over some middle parts of the brothers' training and battles. Did you know there's a page missing?"

Janie put a hand to her cheek. "No. I've been

carefully absorbing every word and haven't finished yet. What part is gone?"

He bent open the back cover, holding it out. "The end. The last page of the journal, as in the one that tells where the treasure is buried."

"Do you really think there's anything after all these years? It got buried almost two hundred years ago. Could Brian have gone treasure hunting, like he told Jenny, the morning he…when he…it happened?"

"Anything is possible. Have you talked to Larry about this? After all, he and Brian made the discovery together as teenagers."

"I thought about it, but Brian's letter said not to trust anyone. Since he didn't say one way or the other, I have no way of knowing if Larry threatened him. He's always been so good to me, but with Brian leaving this package, I guess nobody is ever who they seem. Besides, if he knew what Brian was up to, don't you think he would've said something to me by now?"

Tom tossed the diary onto the desktop, then stood the fallen chair upright. "You're not holding anything else back, are you, like the last page? If you want me to help figure this out, you need to level with me."

"No, that's everything. I didn't even know the ending was torn out until you mentioned it."

"Okay. Obviously, Brian thought the Brassel Field property belonged to the soldier's family. Why else would he have left the file? I think before we go any further, you need to finish reading William's account. This way, we both know everything your husband left behind."

"Seems logical, but I'm a bit hesitant to read it at…"

"Do you want me to spend the night?" Tom placed a hand on her arm. "I don't need to be at the job site until ten tomorrow, so I'll have time to swing by my place and change."

Janie covered his hand with her own. "Would you? I'd be more comfortable knowing you were nearby. The guest room is all made up; you can make yourself at home."

"Don't fuss. I know the way. Finish reading, and we'll talk in the morning about our next move."

"Then you'll help me?"

Feigning indignation, Tom responded, "Huh! Like you needed to ask me. The nerve." He pronounced the last word with a heavy, New York City accent.

"You have to admit it isn't every day you're asked to be involved in a paranormal mystery. I didn't want to assume."

"Look, it's late, and you have reading to do. Go upstairs, and I'll lock up and get settled into the guest room."

Gently picking up the tome, she turned to leave the office. Stopping, Janie said, "Thanks, big brother. I don't know if I could've gotten through this alone."

"You're welcome. Besides, how could I possibly give up a chance to see dead people? And if I didn't agree, you'd be stuck with that blonde bimbo friend of yours from the beauty parlor as an accomplice."

"Stop it. Carol has been a great friend over the years. She just has a problem hanging on to her husbands."

"Right. What's she working on now, number eleven or twelve?"

"You know you could have been number three or

four, had you played your cards right."

"Lucky me. Go read." Tom shooed her toward the stairs.

Janie went to the back of the house instead. "I need a cup of tea first; would you like one?"

"No, I'm good, thanks." Tom headed toward the living room. "I'm gonna watch some television before crashing. Good night."

CHAPTER 11

Janie slipped two fingers through the delicate handle of the cup, blew on the liquid, then took a sip. The chamomile soothed her nerves—somewhat. With the journal in her other hand, she went upstairs and got into bed. Her palms felt clammy, and she shifted several times against the pillows before settling. The chore couldn't be put off any longer. She had to find out what became of the two brothers. Obviously, William died on Long Island, thus the reason for her having his journal. But what happened to the treasure and younger brother Benjamin?

July 10, 1863

For the past week Benny and me have been in a Union field hospital. My journal stayed securely hidden in my uniform, or else we would be found out. This is the first chance I dare reveal it enough to set down events of the last battle.

After two days of fighting, General Lee was forced to retreat after suffering severe losses. Or that is what I am told. On the last day, I woke up to find the sun down and Benny lying beside me. We were among other soldiers, most dead or close to dead. When first I opened my eyes, I lay face to face with Benny. I thought he too was dead. He jumped when I shifted because he thought he had lost me, and all he could think to do was lie down and play possum.

My head hurt something awful, and I felt a stickiness down the side of my face. I later learned it was blood. My blood, from a blow to the head. I knew it was not a bullet because it would have killed me for sure.

Benny had his left hand wrapped in a rag so soaked with blood it looked black. When I unwrapped it, his thumb and finger were missing. His eyes were glassy.

As we got to a stand of trees, I spotted the two men in green I been guarding two days before. Both shot in the head. Most likely by our men when they knew the battle was going wrong. This was the chance we needed.

I stripped the uniforms off both and made Benny put one on while I the other. We did our best to put our uniforms on the bodies, so no one would notice. Benny's hand gave him pain, but he did as I told him. The clothes were big on us, but not enough to look unnatural.

That is how we joined the 1st United States Sharpshooters of New York. Since the regiment was a mix of men from different parts of the north and west, we had a good chance of not being discovered as Southerners. That also helped explain the way we speak.

We were found by Northern soldiers and taken to the field hospital. Now they are sending us back to New York to fully recover. Benny never will since his hand is damaged. I sometimes get dizzy if I stand too long. They say that is from the fierce blow to my head. No good to anyone on the battlefield.

We will travel north with other Union soldiers too sick to continue the fight. Benny is withdrawn and barely speaks, even to me. Maybe it is best so nobody finds us out. He does not understand why we cannot tell others about our true quest.

August 3, 1863

Our trek north has taken more days than we thought. Forced to stop at hospitals along the way and retrieve others heading north, the progress goes slow. Rations are few since most are sent to the boys in battle. All are weak from hunger, making progress even slower.

Benny has taken a turn for the worse. His injury is mostly healed over but still pusses and gives him pain. He has grown pale and thin. I fear he will get too sick to walk. We do not know our plan once reaching New York.

My injury is on the mend, but I can only walk for short times. Hunger is my biggest enemy now. We have not encountered anybody else from the Sharpshooter regiment. I hope our secret remains.

August 30, 1863

Long Island at last! It has been a long, long trek. Benny is weak but keeps going. As do I. We got leave by the regiment commander in New York. He did not hesitate when we arrived to the place they sent us and gave the names of the soldiers we took the clothes from. I guess the regiment is too big for him to remember all the men. That is a stroke of luck in our favor.

A kindly farmer gave us a ride as far as his homestead. From there we walked and made our way to our own home place. It is taken over by another, but we will do our best to complete our task and be on our way.

September 2, 1863

Night is close, and weariness takes over me. The fever is worse. I fear it will keep me from getting home to you, Mama, and my darling Becky.

I got some good fortune today. Evading the owner of this land I slipped through a hole in the ground, like a rabbit. It landed me in a small cave. Could be from an animal. I hope the owner will not return this night.

My heart is heavy with news I have yet to tell. Last night Benny went home to be with our Lord. The sickness from his hand spread over his body. At the end he was wild with fever. I know I promised to keep him safe, Mama. I am sorry to break my promise.

Benny never should have come along. This was my sworn duty to Grandpa Peter. I am the eldest, and it was my burden to restore the family. Funny how all the wealth I was to retrieve could not help us now. I wonder if you will ever get this account. Will you ever know our fate?

Maybe when this war is ended our family can return to its rightful place. It is up to my sisters to live the dream Grandpa Peter had for us all. I am sorry. Mama, I failed you and the family. The worst is that your most precious treasure must remain buried on Yankee soil. Maybe one day this will change.

I sleep now. If I do not continue, maybe a kindly soul will return this diary to you. I want you to know of Benny's bravery and our journey together.

Your most precious treasure is to be found on home ground. Start from the northeast corner…

****

Only a jagged edge remained where a page had been torn out. The journal ended without the final passage. Tom was right about the missing page, but who tore it out? Was it stolen from Brian by the person who caused his disappearance? Did Brian tear it out and hide it himself? Maybe William tore out the last page, and it rotted away with the flesh on his bones?

Janie fingered the back cover, willing the missing page to appear. She drifted off to sleep with the book still in her hands.

The clatter of the book hitting the floor awoke her. As she peered over the edge of the bed, a glow illuminated the journal. *There must be a full moon seeping through the window*. Horror gripped her when she noticed a transparent pair of boots next to the bed. Her gaze went from the boots to the legs inside them, continuing up the body attached. Tracking her way from the bottom edge of a gray jacket past the buttons, the now familiar face of a Confederate soldier gazed back at her.

Stifling the scream rising in her throat, Janie took a deep breath. She mustered her vocal cords into service and croaked, "Are you William?"

The apparition stared at her. Their eyes locked as if neither had the ability to look away. Janie attempted to repeat the question, but her voice wouldn't cooperate.

After what seemed an eternity, the young man opened his mouth to speak. Mute, he formed the words, "Help me, Janie. Help me." Repeating his silent plea three times, he wore the same heart-wrenching look of agony as seen in the basement—one of sheer devastation. Then his image faded.

Janie swung an arm toward the nightstand to push herself up. Instead, she knocked the teacup off. She was unable to stop it. The china shattered on the floor, scattering pieces like the light bulb from the other night.

Moments later Tom burst through her door. "What's going on?"

"Nothing, I knocked over...the teacup fell...it's..."

"Get a grip, Sis. Are you all right?" He looked down. The pieces of china were strewn on the floor beside her bed. "You look as if you've just seen..." His voice trailed off. "I didn't mean...What happened?"

Janie sat up gulping air into her lungs. "I finished the journal."

"And you were...celebrating?" Tom tilted his head.

"He was here again."

"By he you mean..." Tom waved his hand in front of him.

"The ghost."

"Aw, Sis, I'm proud of you—finally saying it out loud. You've made a breakthrough."

She placed a hand over her racing heart, its ferocious beat pounding against her ribs. "Don't start the graduation ceremony yet."

Tom picked up the journal, gingerly brushing off the shards of china. "So, out of frustration, you threw the book and your teacup at him?"

"No. *No*. I finished the journal. At some point I fell asleep, because the book fell off the bed and hit the floor. The noise woke me. I'm surprised you didn't hear it. Anyway, when I looked toward the floor, beside the journal I saw it...him...standing there. Right where you are now."

Her brother jumped two feet to his right.

"Stop that. He's gone now."

"You believe you're really seeing a ghost?"

Janie's eyes narrowed. "I know what I saw."

"It's not that I don't believe you, but it all seems so...unbelievable, for lack of a better word. Though, I have seen history shows on television about hauntings. There are enough stories floating around, excuse the pun, for me to take this seriously. Why couldn't you have seen a ghost?"

Sitting up straighter, Janie said, "There's more. I believe the ghost is William."

"William? Like the guy who wrote the diary, William?" Skepticism tinged Tom's question.

"Yes, that William. How many other Williams do you know who could possibly be wearing a gray Confederate uniform?"

"You're sure he was wearing gray? According to his journal, he died wearing an outfit from the New York Sharpshooters, and those were green."

"Yes, it was definitely gray. I may have been scared out of my wits, but I know my colors. How do we know how the 'after-life' works? Maybe when somebody's spirit comes back, it's in a familiar form, not necessarily wearing what he or she actually died in?"

"True. I'll probably come back holding a beer even though I may go doing too many shots of tequila."

She flashed him a look. "Seriously?"

Tom shrugged then sat on the foot of the bed. "You're definitely seeing something. You wouldn't make this up. If you're seeing a Confederate soldier, it must be connected to the journal. It could be William. Another possibility is Benjamin. Do you think Brian saw him too?"

"Those last couple weeks before he disappeared, Brian did act strangely. Kind of jumpy, I'd say. Did you notice anything, Tom?"

"Well, he would go through phases of stress whenever he had a lot of deals at work. It's hard to say for sure."

Janie rested against the headboard. "There was one other thing about the ghost; let's call him William. It seems saner, well, less crazy anyway, if we give him a name." Rationality. Her first step toward recovery, she mused. "He didn't actually speak, but it looked like he mouthed the words 'Help me, Janie. Help me.' He repeated it three times before disappearing."

"Anything else you want to add," Tom asked, "or are those all the details so far?"

"He still had a pained look on his face, but that's it."

"So, you finished the journal?"

Janie reached over and took it from Tom's hand. "Yes, I did. You're right. There is a page missing at the end. Now the question is, who removed it?" She opened the back cover and ran her finger along the rough remains.

"I've been thinking about it," he said. "In my mind, there are only three possibilities. The first being Brian, in case anybody stole the journal from him. The second might be the person or persons after him. The third, obviously, being William himself."

"Now you're scaring me."

Tom furrowed his brow. "Why's that?"

"Because those are the same conclusions I came up with," Janie stated.

"Well, you know great minds…"

"*Don't* say it. It's way too late for dumb clichés."

Tom smiled.

"I think we can rule out William. He wanted his mother to have the journal. Why not send it complete? It sounds like he may have found the treasure but had to rebury it. He knew he wouldn't make it home. The boy could have used a code of some kind to finish the instructions so anybody delivering the journal wouldn't figure it out."

"That's a valid thought which leaves us with two options. If Brian removed it, the problem is finding where he put it. If it was the people he mentioned in his letter, we'll never solve this mystery short of digging up all the land around Brassel Field."

"If that hasn't been done already," pointed out Janie. "Honestly, I don't see how that could help us find Brian. I don't care about treasure."

Tom took his sister's hand. "No, Sis, we both agree that's not our focus."

Her vision blurred. "I know."

"It's late. We both need rest. Maybe we could get a fresh perspective on this in the morning. Do you think you could sleep?"

"No," Janie said, "but I'm sure I will anyway. It's a good thing the girls' rooms are farther down the hall. They slept through this whole thing."

"That's kids for you. They wouldn't let a little thing like a visiting spirit keep them from getting their full eight to ten hours of beauty rest," Tom added with a wink. "I'll see you in the morning."

"Okay, Tom. Good night."

Janie followed her brother to the hallway, closing the door behind him. Thinking better of it, she propped it halfway open. Before climbing into bed, she took a magazine and swept the broken pieces of teacup into a neat little pile against the nightstand. She didn't want to forget about the mess and step on it in the morning. She crawled under the covers and turned off the light.

Her thoughts were no longer on the night's events, but of her husband. There was the time Brian had surprised her, Natalie, and Jenny by taking them to a cabin in upstate New York. It was Labor Day weekend, and she and the girls were thinking their summer had ended when they got to go on one more trip. The woods were peaceful as they sat on the deck the first evening, looking across Sanders Lake and breathing in the scent of the pine trees. Janie drifted off to sleep to the memory of wavelets lapping against the dock.

CHAPTER 12

Janie sat at the kitchen table drinking her morning coffee. The hot liquid helped her focus as she laid things out logically in her mind, hoping to discover clues about Brian.

Footsteps pounded down the stairs. A moment later Tom came into the kitchen. Janie got up and grabbed the other mug from the counter.

He held up his hand. "Sorry, Sis, they just messaged me from the worksite. There was a '911' tacked to the end, which means I need to head straight over there. So much for a leisurely morning off."

Janie shrugged and sat back down. "Life's tough when you're the boss, ain't it? I think I need time alone to work on this puzzle anyway. Maybe I can make some sense of it."

"I'll do the same, and we can compare notes later," Tom replied. "I'm busy all day and have a corporate thing with Cassie this evening at her company—unless you want me to come back tonight?"

"No. I don't need a babysitter."

"If you don't want to be alone, I can cancel with Cassie. She'd understand."

Janie sat up straight. "Wow! She would understand your sister is seeing a ghost and wants you to join her for the next possible sighting? Cassie is open-minded. You had better marry the girl before she gets away."

"Yes, Mother. I'll get around to it."

"Don't cancel your plans. We'll be fine. How does your schedule look for lunch tomorrow? That should give us enough time to ponder this mystery on our own."

Tom looked at her sideways. "Now you're getting poetic. Do people really use the word 'ponder' anymore?"

Janie chuckled. "All the time. Where've you been?"

"Then I shall ponder this dilemma and see what I can come up with on the morrow. See, I can do this too." Tom grabbed his jacket from the hook by the door and tossed it over his shoulder. "Catch you later."

****

At the office Janie plowed through the work on her desk. There was something therapeutic about accomplishing so much at once. Treating herself to lunch at the diner would be the perfect reward. The last time she'd been there was with her sister-in-law after court, and she wanted some happier memories of one of her favorite eateries.

Janie offered to have Meg join her, but her assistant begged off, this being her night out with the girls. Meg said she wanted to duck out a half an hour early and wouldn't accept an offer to take lunch and still leave early. That woman's work ethic amazed her. Once again Janie counted herself lucky to have such an incredible person juggling the day-to-day grind of their office.

The restaurant had a busier crowd than usual, but Janie waited for a table anyway. As she asked the hostess at the podium about the wait time, her eye caught a hand waving from a booth across the room. She turned and looked behind her, then back, and gave a sheepish grin when she recognized the owner of the hand—Tom's handsome friend from the deli. What was his name, she thought?

He called to her over the din of the crowd. "Janie, over here."

Waving back, she wove her way around tables packed with customers. The cacophony of silverware scraping on plates and loud conversations overwhelmed her senses. Before reaching him, his name finally came to her. "Hello, John. It's nice to see you again."

"Pleasure's all mine. I'm glad to see you're not dragging that dead weight around with you like you were at the deli."

She stopped a moment, then grinned. "Oh, you mean Tom. I can't hold his hand at every meal. He needs to venture out on his own sometimes."

"I'd love for you to join me. Please, sit down." John gestured at the seat across from him.

"Seeing how crowded it is today, I guess we should share."

"Now don't get all mushy on me. I had hoped my dazzling personality might be reason enough."

Janie gasped. "Sorry. I didn't mean…I'll sit down so I can take my foot out of my mouth. Let me try again. I'd love to join you."

"Did you get your family business wrapped up the other day?"

"Most of it," Janie answered. "There really wasn't much. Tom and I get together regularly."

John sipped his water. "I wish I had a brother or sister to do things with. Being an only child, I missed out on that family closeness. I was about to order. Do you need a couple minutes?"

"No, I'm ready." She got a whiff of fresh apple pie, and her stomach grumbled. "I've been here several times and know the menu by heart. You come here much?"

John pursed his lips. "Maybe a couple times a month. Usually I don't get a chance to go out for lunch, but I had a big gap between jobs today, so I decided to treat myself. And this turned out to be an even bigger treat than I'd planned." He winked.

A blush warmed her cheeks as she cast her gaze at the table. Maybe the time had come for her to start thinking about men in a romantic sense again. Starting slow like this fit her pace. "I consider this a treat myself. Usually I lunch alone."

"I heard about your husband—Brian, wasn't it? Sorry for what you've been through."

Janie appreciated the sincerity in his voice, but not the pity. She'd have to get used to this as many people knew Brian and would once again offer condolences with this new development. "Thank you. I suppose it is time to start living again. I owe my two girls that much."

"I have to admit, about a year ago I asked Tom to introduce me to you."

Janie's eyes opened wide at his thinking of her in that way. "You did not."

"Yes, it's true. You were out with Tom and Cassie one night at Luigi's Bistro. When I asked him who you were and if I could get an introduction, he said you weren't ready. I thought I'd make my own opportunity when you came into the deli."

The waitress approached the table to take their orders, relieving Janie from coming up with a response. While his admission flustered her, it also sent a tingle dancing up and down her spine. He seemed like a nice man. Why not take a plunge? It could be a much-needed distraction from all the turmoil going on.

After ordering lunch, conversation flowed easily. Before they realized it, an hour and a half flew by.

Looking at her watch, Janie said, "I can't believe the time. My lunches normally last no more than thirty minutes. My assistant will be sending out a search party for me."

Glancing at his own watch, John replied, "I've got fifteen minutes to make it to my next job."

She reached for the check, but John was quicker. "Lunch is on me. And, as I said earlier, it truly was a treat. Have dinner with me Friday night."

His last sentence stunned her into silence. She forgot to thank him for lunch before sputtering out, "You mean...like a date?"

"I believe that's the accepted term for such an occasion." John raised his brows.

In a quiet voice, almost a whisper, she said, "It's been so long."

"If I'm being too forward—"

"No!" Janie's face brightened, the corners of her mouth raising. "I mean, no. I'd love to."

Grinning from ear to ear, he replied, "Great. I'll pick you up at six-thirty, if that's good for you."

"Yes. Do you want directions?"

"Just an address will do. And maybe a cell number."

Janie nodded, and they exchanged information.

John took care of the bill and walked her out to the parking lot. "This was fun."

"Yes. It was a welcome break to a busy day. Thanks for lunch."

"My pleasure. I'll see you Friday then?"

"See you Friday, John."

Janie floated to her car while fumbling for keys. She glanced back after opening the door. To her delight, John stood watching. Giving a quick wave, she hopped in and drove away, unable to quell the gentle fluttering inside of her.

****

Back at work Janie sashayed through the front door and straight to her office.

Meg didn't say a word but stared after her with a smug smile plastered on her own face. Mission accomplished, she thought.

CHAPTER 13

"Finally, you achieved contact with the merry widow. It took you long enough!" Meg paced her living room like a caged lion.

"You know I've been trying for the past year, Mother. Short of knocking on her door and introducing myself, I had to wait for an opportunity," replied John. "I thought something would pan out with her friend from the salon, but she wasn't as helpful as I thought she'd be."

"It appears you've spent quite a bit of time cultivating that angle. Now you've gotten to Janie, you should extricate yourself from that other woman. Of course, what you do on your own time is none of my business, and frankly, I don't want to know. Just don't jeopardize your connection with Janie."

"I'll hold up my end of the bargain, but you're right about one thing. What I do with Carol is none of your business. I can handle her."

Meg stopped, facing her son. "I hope you're right. The last thing we need is for her to grow a conscience and spill everything to her friend. All these years enduring that repulsive little realty office has taken its toll on me, not to mention getting you into town without anyone discovering our family tie. I want what's rightfully mine, so I can leave here in style," Meg spewed.

John hated when his mother worked herself into a manic state. There was no reasoning with her then. Gesturing with his hands, palms down, he said, "Relax, Mother. What could she tell Janie? You don't think I told her the real plan, do you?" Sucking up to his mother always put her in a better mood. "I do have to admit you were a genius calling me when she left for the diner at lunch."

"Yes, it was quick thinking on my part, wasn't it? And the performance I gave her about not taking lunch since I'd planned to leave early. I should have been an actress with the way I portray the meek little mouse at work while Janie suspects nothing." Meg's eyes glazed, basking in the glory of her own brilliance.

John snapped his fingers in front of her. "Earth to Mother. You with me?"

"How dare you gesture to me like a dog." She glared.

Through gritted teeth, he said, "I'm sorry. You drifted off somewhere."

"You do realize I am doing all of this to secure your birth right, don't you, Johnny?"

"Of course, I do. Please stop calling me Johnny. You know I hate that name." He threw himself onto the couch like a sulky teenager.

Meg frowned. "You used to like it when you were little."

"Even then I hated it. Morty called me Johnny, but it was never used affectionately when it came from him."

"Morton was very good to you, despite you not being his real son. Don't forget it." Meg sighed.

"How could I, Mother? He reminded me every

chance he got. Look, I don't want to fight. Things are starting to move in the right direction. Let's focus on the future and all the wealth you and I will have to spend." If he didn't cut his losses and reason with her, he'd never escape this conversation.

"You're right, Johnny." Meg ignored his grimace at the endearment. "Now, on Friday, when you meet Janie for your date—"

John stiffened his back. "Mother, let me handle it. I certainly know how to smooth-talk a lady—and this one truly is a lady."

"Yes, but you have to convince her to invite you inside the house. That will be your chance to search for the missing page of the journal. She's got to have it!"

"I can tell you it won't happen on the first date."

"Why not? From the sounds of it, you were back at Carol's place within hours of picking her up." Meg wrinkled her nose as if catching a whiff of something rotten.

"Yes, Mother, but as I said, Janie has class. There will be no first date invitations back to her house. I guarantee it. Besides, she has two daughters. She's not going to ask a strange man to spend the night with her kids home."

Meg expelled a breath. "On this point, you are right. That slut Carol has no ties and obligations—or morals. Janie will need more time. Maybe you can convince her to cook for you. At least it would get you inside the house. What do you think?"

"I'm way ahead of you, Mother. I've thought of a few different ideas to have our second date at her place. Leave it to me." John gloated, spreading his arms across the back of the couch. He did his best to ignore the overwhelming smell of disinfectant and carpet freshener. "If nothing else, you know I always have a plan where the ladies are concerned."

She raised her arms. "All right. Do your best. I want this to be over. We've waited long enough." Meg left for the kitchen, talking as she walked. "You'd better go. The neighbors will get suspicious if you spend too much time in here. They'll assume you're settling up the landscaping bill, but any longer and it won't look natural."

"Mother, contrary to your beliefs, the neighbors couldn't care less how long my truck is parked at your curb." He pointed out the front window, despite not having an audience. "I need to leave anyway. There are real clients requiring my services in order to keep up this façade." He went to the front door. "After all, it was your idea to set me up in a business requiring manual labor."

Returning to the living room, she replied, "Now, Johnny, it was the only thing I could think of to get you into people's houses. You really don't have the qualifications for anything technical like an electrician or plumber, nor do you have the skills." She clacked her tongue. "Everyone needs their lawns mowed. It's a perfect cover."

His eyes narrowed. "Thanks for the vote of confidence. You're not the one doing all the backbreaking work."

"Look at it this way, you've got a great tan." Meg softened her tone.

Giving his mother a peck on the cheek, he remained silent.

She walked back toward the kitchen.

Before going, John yelled down the hall, "Oh, by the way, Mother, I forgot to tell you—"

A knock interrupted him. Madeline Weiss from next door stood on the other side of the screen holding an envelope. John forced a smile and greeted her. "Hello, Mrs. Weiss. How's the grass growing?"

Confusion covered her face, her lips pursed. "It's growing fine, as you well know, since your man cut it last weekend," she answered in a curt tone. "I received a piece of Mrs. Zutterman's mail by mistake and wanted to return it to her. Is she around?" She craned her head, as if trying to see past him.

John reached over and opened the screen door.

Meg stalked back into the living room at a fast clip, her face twisted in annoyance. "You know you need to be careful with..." She stopped abruptly. "Oh, Madeline, I didn't know you were here."

"I'm sorry, Meg, have I come at a bad time?" Her gaze shifted between Meg and John as she stepped into the entry.

"No. Not at all. John was collecting his lawn fees." Addressing her son, she said, "That'll be all, thank you. I'll see you next time."

He scowled at being treated like a common servant. "Right. Until Saturday." He looked to the other woman. "See you Saturday also, Mrs. Weiss."

****

The neighbor stepped aside to let John by, staring after him a moment before speaking. "I'd almost forgotten, Meg. This ended up in my mailbox by mistake. I tell you those postal rates keep going up while the service goes down. This is the second time in a week I received a neighbor's mail. Makes me wonder how much of my own I'm not getting."

Meg extended her hand and took the envelope. "Thank you, Madeline. I'm glad someone honest received it." Thankfully this busybody only got a piece of junk mail.

"Have you had any problems with the mail lately?" The woman glanced at the couch.

Madeline must be angling for an invitation to sit down. Not buying into the old gossip's tricks, Meg stated, "No." She smiled for an uncomfortable moment remaining silent.

Her neighbor shifted from foot to foot with her lips pursed.

"If there isn't anything else?" Meg motioned as she escorted her toward the front.

"No. Of course not. I wouldn't want to hold you up." Madeline sniffed before turning around and pushing the screen open. "You know..." She stopped and faced Meg again, "I may be getting old and a little hard of hearing, but I could have sworn I heard John call you—"

"Oh, there goes my phone." Extending an arm to hold open the door, she added, "I can hear it vibrating on the kitchen table, and I'm expecting an important call. Would love to chat, Madeline, but I'm sure you understand." She herded the woman onto the cement stoop.

"Certainly. It was nothing anyway. Bye, Meg. Perhaps we'll see you at the neighborhood block party in two weeks?"

If an answer was given, Madeline didn't hear it as the screen door sprang shut behind her and the inside door slammed. What a snob, Madeline thought, crossing to her own front yard. Meg would never show up at the event. While her next-door neighbor acted courteous most of the time, she kept to herself.

Madeline couldn't let go of what she'd heard when walking up to the door. John had referred to Meg as Mother. Why would they hide their relationship? Maybe Meg felt ashamed knowing how successful her own children were. With Sylvia a partner in a law firm and Myron the vice president of a bank, John could hardly compare, even if he did own a business. He probably didn't live up to his mother's expectations.

Meg peered out the front window from behind the curtain as her neighbor walked home. *Sometimes John doesn't think*! At least she stopped talking before saying more herself in front of Madeline. This had better not end up as another problem she'd need to handle. Releasing the curtain, she allowed it to slide back into place.

Back in her kitchen, Meg opened the refrigerator and removed the fresh salmon she bought for dinner. She chuckled to herself about the ongoing deception she pulled off on Janie. There wasn't a group of ladies she met with on Wednesday nights, but she wanted her boss to believe she had an active social life. It helped keep her cover as an aging widow. Janie was so wrapped up in her own personal life she would never discover the sham.

Meg almost got found out by Brian years ago. One Wednesday evening, he called her at home. Not thinking, she picked up the phone. Brian appeared surprised, as he only wanted to leave a message about an update for the office the next morning. Quick on her feet, Meg claimed to have developed a headache and come home early. She had assured him it was nothing to worry about, and she would be at work the next morning.

Brian genuinely cared and wanted her to take the next day off. She convinced him it would pass, and he agreed to let her come in, but she needed to leave early if her headache returned. What a sap.

Leaving so much in her son's hands rattled Meg's nerves, but she had no choice. Larry completely fell apart and was useless—not unexpected. After the disappearance of his partner, none of their threats would work. All their hopes were now pinned on Janie and the fact she might have the final page of the journal.

Befriending the secretary of Janie's lawyer had paid off. The woman let slip how Sam gave Janie an envelope Brian left for her in case of his death. It was unsettling, she'd said, especially since Brian disappeared shortly after giving the envelope to Sam eight years ago.

The package had to contain the journal and final page. What else could he possibly pass on to his wife in such a clandestine manner? Soon John would get his hands on it. Hopefully it wouldn't take as long as it did for him to get a first date with the woman.

CHAPTER 14

Distracted with thoughts of her lunch time encounter, Janie lost track of which spices she'd already added while preparing dinner. She coated the pork chops and popped them into the oven. With a glance toward the kitchen doorway, she took a deep breath then exhaled slowly. The time had come to tell the girls about her upcoming date. How would they take it? Would they be angry? Less than a week after declaring their father dead, she wanted to bring another man into their lives. Maybe not yet. It was only a first date, not a marriage proposal.

"Jenny, Natalie, would you please come in here for a moment?" She took a seat and squared her shoulders, bracing for resistance.

The kids shuffled into the kitchen with puzzled looks.

"What's going on, Mom?" Jenny spoke first.

"Yeah, Mom," Natalie added, "what's up?"

Both girls sat down in unison, eyes riveted on their mother's face. "Girls." Janie struggled to find the right words. "I have news I'd like to share with you. Now, I want you both to keep an open mind."

"Oh, no," Natalie groaned, "you're changing our summer vacation plans again, aren't you? I told you, Jenny, she didn't want to go on that schooner cruise in Maine. Where do you want to go now?"

Wrinkling her brow, Janie asked, "Schooner cruise? No, Natalie, this doesn't have anything to do with our vacation plans. But if you want to change them…"

"No! No, I don't. We don't. I mean…okay, Mom, what?

"I had lunch with a friend of your Uncle Tom's today. We hadn't planned it, but the diner was crowded and the wait kind of long. And…well…we shared a table for lunch." Janie cringed at the way she stumbled over her words.

"So, the big news is you had lunch with a friend of Uncle Tom's?" asked Jenny, scrunching her face.

"Kind of, but that's not everything I wanted to tell you." She massaged her temples. "I'm not explaining this well, am I?"

Flicking her eyes upward, Natalie quipped, "Not really, Mom."

"Thanks for the support." Sarcasm laced Janie's voice. "Let me try again. The short version is John, that's the friend's name, asked me out on a date this Friday night."

They stared at their mother, faces expressionless.

"And I said yes. Okay. There it is. I'm going on a date Friday. With a friend. With a man."

Both girls looked at each other. Natalie sprouted a grin, but Jenny leaned back and crossed her arms.

"Really, Mom? That's great!" Natalie nodded.

"You don't mind my going out with another man?"

"Mom, it's been eight years." Her older daughter repeated back what Janie had only recently said to her. "Like you told us when you had the legal papers done on Daddy, you're entitled to a life."

"What about you, Jenny?" She clasped her hands in her lap. The lack of approval from the younger girl carved a guilty hole in Janie's gut.

Jenny grabbed her elbows and hugged herself. "It feels weird. You said you wouldn't replace Daddy."

Janie moved around the table to kneel beside Jenny. She wrapped an arm around the girl's shoulders and pulled her close. "It feels weird for me too, but I'm not replacing Daddy. Remember how I said he would want us to move on with our lives and be happy?"

A pout remained on Jenny's face, but she nodded.

"This is part of it. If you really don't want me to go, I'll cancel."

Her daughter shuddered beneath Janie's embrace. "But you don't want to cancel. Do you?"

"I would like to have dinner with John. Will you be okay with that if I do?"

Jenny glanced at her sister, who nodded and smiled, then up into her mother's eyes. "Okay, Mom."

Relief washed over Janie. Putting both hands flat on the table and leaning in, she said, "I couldn't do this if both of you didn't agree."

"Are you asking our permission?" Natalie taunted.

"No, but I wouldn't feel right about this if you guys hated the idea."

"We think it's great, don't we, Jen?" Natalie nudged her sister with a shoulder.

Jenny's lips curved up into a small smile. She shoved her sister back "It's okay. That all, Mom?"

"I guess so."

"When's dinner? I'm starving," Jenny said, her eyes bright once more.

"In about thirty minutes."

"Great!"

Both girls bolted from the room and up the stairs. Janie suspected a private discussion was about to take place.

As she walked toward her office, the telephone rang. She strode back across the kitchen and grabbed the cordless phone from its charger. "Hello?"

"It's about time you joined the living, Janie," Carol squealed.

"Carol, what…how did you hear?"

"It's all over town. I think the local paper ran it as the lead story." Her friend chuckled on the other end of the line.

"I'm not amused. Seriously, John just asked me this afternoon. How did you find out?" The panic rose in her voice. *Who else might know?* Not that she minded people knowing, but she had hoped to have an adjustment period.

"Calm down. I ran into John at the grocery store on my way home from work. You'd be proud of this single man; he had fruit and vegetables in his cart. He's quite the healthy eater."

She gripped the phone. "All right, enough about his shopping habits. What exactly did he tell you?"

"That he ran into you at the diner and had a very nice lunch. Let me say that again, a very nice lunch."

"Okay, okay, cut to the chase."

"He told me about asking you out this Friday night. Now, we've got plans of our own to make."

Carol appeared to enjoy her discomfort. Her friend's last statement sounded ominous. "What do you mean by plans?"

"A little touch up and brush up by yours truly."

"Come again?"

Talking in a professional tone, she said, "Now, I have an opening at three o'clock on Friday afternoon, so I reserved it for you. You'll be my last appointment of the day, and I can do some coaching on dating etiquette."

"Dating etiquette? We're not going to the prom. He asked me out to dinner." Janie laughed. "Don't blow this out of proportion or you'll scare me off, and I'll have to cancel."

"Calm yourself, woman. I'm kidding. But you're coming in so I can spruce up your hair. Agreed?"

She leaned back against the counter. "Actually, it sounds perfect. I guess I could use a little help and advice—but only a little," she added.

"Great, I'll see you Friday."

"See you then." Janie ended the call and dropped the handset into its charger.

With a mischievous sparkle in her eye, Carol set her phone on the counter. Strong arms grabbed her from behind. She spun around, slipping into an embrace.

"How was I? Do I get the top acting award?" Carol asked.

"Absolutely," cooed John. "You were fabulous, kid. Is she nervous?"

Carol huffed. "Of course, she is. The woman hasn't dated in years. I still don't get why you wanted me to tell her I knew."

"Strategy. This way it's harder for her to back out if someone else knows—especially a friend who'll give her grief if she cancels."

"You're so clever. And to think, my first attraction to you was your muscle-bound body." Carol planted her lips firmly on John's, and he pulled her closer.

Pushing him away, she asked, "Now, you're sure you have to do this to get the journal? There's no other way? I don't understand why you can't break into her house and take it."

"Relax, baby. You're the one I want to do wild and passionate things with inside and outside the bedroom. This is the only way without arousing her suspicion. If she sees a break-in, she'll be looking for what could be missing. If I take it while I'm there, she may not even notice the book is gone. It's only a couple of dinners. Scout's honor." He held up three fingers pressed together. Her body relaxed in his arms.

With her eyes shining, she said, "Tell me again about this rare book dealer friend of yours. Does he really think that old journal is worth as much as you say?"

"No telling for sure until he inspects it, but he's sold other Civil War journals for thousands. We're talking six figures." John grazed his fingers down her arm.

"You're positive Tom was right? Why would she even have such a thing?"

"He definitely said Janie had some journal from a Confederate soldier. She found it in her husband's desk at home. Tom and I were throwing back a few beers one night, and he blabbed on about it. Probably doesn't even remember telling me." John spun the lie to better lure the blonde in and eliminate any doubts in her mind. Tom had no respect for Carol, despite her being his sister's friend. If the two ever did have a chance to compare notes, John would be long gone by then.

Carol's voice escalated. "Hopefully, Janie doesn't

know what it's worth and leaves it sitting around."

"Are you sure you two are friends?" John goaded her. "Sounds like you have no problem swiping this out from under her."

"All's fair in love and war, baby—and wealth! Besides, I'm not taking anything from her that jeopardizes her family's well-being. That woman's got plenty of dough to live on. She told me herself, or should I say bragged about it?"

"I'm sure Janie never bragged about having money. She doesn't seem the type."

Carol scowled. "Why are you taking her side? Don't forget—one word from me and this whole deal is off." She pulled away and crossed her arms.

Carol could quickly become a liability. Maybe his mother was right about Carol's getting too involved. He needed to locate that last page fast, then slip out of town. Time to sugar her up. "I'm not. What I am thinking about is what we'll be doing once we land this big payoff."

Carol's face lit up anew. "Tell me what we could be doing with that money."

"I'm thinking a vacation somewhere warm requiring very little clothing. How about the Côte d'Azur?"

"Someplace warm sounds delicious." Carol licked her lips. "But where is the Coat of what?"

"Côte d'Azur. It's the French Mediterranean. You know, Cannes, Monte Carlo—France, baby." John punctuated his last statement by tugging her close.

Carol pouted. "Even with warm weather, I'll still need a new wardrobe."

"Anything you want, baby, anything you want," he

murmured in her ear.

The blonde melted into his body, picking up where they'd left off earlier. With one swift move, John swept her off her feet and carried Carol to the bedroom.

My work is never done, thought John as he salivated over his current chore.

CHAPTER 15

Apprehensions about Friday night frayed Janie's nerves. Just the jitters, she told herself. At least there were no more sightings of William. Maybe, since she finished the journal, he'd moved on. Janie didn't believe this theory but had more immediate things to think about—like what to wear on her date tomorrow.

I should have asked where we were going, she thought. Having been so shocked when John asked her out, Janie counted herself lucky to have retained the power of speech.

After sending the girls off to school, she carried her coffee into the home office and reviewed the customer file for her nine o'clock appointment. She would go to the office afterward, since she was showing a house in her own neighborhood.

When she finished reviewing her next showing, she moved on to scan through other upcoming properties they had on the market. Engrossed in study, she almost missed her cell phone ringing on the kitchen counter. Janie jumped out of her chair. With a file still in hand, she went around the desk and stopped dead in her tracks. William had returned.

He mouthed the same mantra as the other times, "Help me, Janie. Help me." With an accusing finger, he pointed at her.

Janie retreated until she hit the desk. He'd never

materialized in broad daylight before other than a reflection. The file she held slipped to the floor. Reaching back with her left hand to steady herself, she knocked a photo off the corner. The crash of the frame hitting the wood laminate went unnoticed. Recovering her breath, she shouted at the apparition, "What do you want from me? I don't know how to help you."

William continued to point and mouth the same phrase as he faded from view. Sweat beaded on her neck, and her feet stayed cemented in place.

Knocking on the back door startled her out of her fugue. On shaky legs, she hobbled out of the office. Before Janie reached the kitchen, her brother's voice carried down the hall.

"Hello, Janie?" Tom poked his head around the corner.

She threw her arms around him. "I'm so glad you're here."

"I called the office, and Meg said you were working from home until your nine o'clock appointment. When you didn't answer your cell, I thought I'd swing by and check in since I was in the neighborhood." He held her at a distance. "What's going on? You're white as a..."

Holding up her hand, Janie said, "Please, don't say it!"

Concern clouded Tom's face. "You don't mean..."

"Yes. A few minutes ago. In the office." Janie gasped for breath.

Tom helped her to a chair in the kitchen. "Hold on; have a seat. You're sounding like that mystery board game. A few minutes ago? In the office? Did your character have a pipe?"

Janie flashed a harsh look as her breathing stabilized and her pulse slowed. "There's the door if you're going to be a clown. I'm not up for jokes right now. William appeared again. As I worked on some paperwork, my phone rang. I got up from the desk, and he blocked the doorway."

"Did he say anything this time, or is he still a mime?" Tom smirked.

Her eyes blazed again, but not as severely.

"Okay, I get it." Tom held up his hands in surrender. "Seriously, any new developments?"

"He pointed at me while mouthing the same words."

Tom tilted his head. "Like he accused you of something?"

Janie thought a moment. "More like he pointed to me saying I'm the one."

"The one, what?"

"I don't know! I'm still an amateur at this whole ghost whispering thing."

"Calm down." Tom rubbed her shoulder. "Where exactly were you when you saw him?"

Rising, Janie went into the hallway. "Come on. I'll show you."

He followed her to the office.

"As I came around the desk, William stood in my path. I backed up until I felt the edge behind me." Janie looked down at the floor where the frame had landed face up with the glass now cracked. It had been Brian's favorite of her and the girls at the beach. Gently picking it up, she placed the remains back on the corner. Add a new frame to the shopping list, she thought.

"Okay, you were walking around the desk toward

the door. Show me. Where did you stop?"

Janie demonstrated.

"You were standing where you are now, and I'm standing in William's spot, right?"

"Yes. I took a couple steps backward after he surprised me. That must've been when I knocked the picture off."

Raising his hand, Tom asked, "So he pointed at you like this?"

She nodded.

"Maybe he wasn't pointing at you."

"What do you mean?"

"Could he have been pointing at your desk, or possibly something on your desk?"

Tom walked forward as she turned around. Nothing was out of the ordinary.

"Is the journal in a drawer?"

"No. It's upstairs in my nightstand. The only things here are real estate files. None of them could be related to Brian or the book. They're all new listings."

Raising his arms in the air, Tom said, "Then we're back to square one, unless he meant you."

"Doesn't make sense." Janie leaned against the edge. "Why were you calling me?"

"What?" He crinkled his nose. "Oh, yeah, I called to see if you wanted to get together for lunch and compare notes. But I think we just did that."

"I guess so. Did you come up with any brilliant ideas on how to solve this mess?"

"Nope," Tom replied. "You?"

"Nope." Janie leaned in the doorway. "Our next step should be to check out the Brassel Field property. Looking through all of the files, I've narrowed it down to one possible estate."

"What would be the point? We don't have all the clues."

"You mean the missing page?"

He nodded.

"We may not need it to find out what happened to Brian. If there's nothing there, we can at least rule the property out and concentrate on other leads."

"Do we have any other leads?"

She hung her head. "No."

"Sis, the police checked out the estate eight years ago when Brian first went missing, along with other remote properties on their listings. If there was anything there, they would have found it."

"At the time," Janie gained momentum, "there were a lot of renovations going on. They could have missed something."

"And there's a clue sitting around waiting for us to stumble over? Think about what you're saying. There's nothing there."

She crossed her arms. "I suppose you're right. Maybe I thought...it's silly to say...but I thought I might feel a connection to Brian if I went to the property."

Tom's mouth popped open. "Oh. You mean like a...ghostly connection?"

Janie flashed a sheepish grin. "Why not? If William has been appearing to me because of the journal, why couldn't Brassel Field have some connection to Brian, if that's where he went the last morning? I don't know how any of this works or why, but I'm willing to try whatever it takes to figure it out."

"I understand, Sis, I really do, but slow down a

minute. Eventually, we need to check out the Brassel Field property. First, we should try to find where Brian put the last page of William's journal."

"What if it wasn't Brian who removed it?

"The journal would have been of no use to William's family if they didn't get it back intact. It wouldn't have been logical for him to tear it out. That leaves Brian. A bit of a stretch," Tom admitted, "but it's all we have to go on right now."

"Don't forget it could have been the people threatening him," Janie added.

"It's a possibility." He took a step forward. "Nobody's contacted you, have they?"

"No."

He moved closer and grasped her arm. "You would tell me, wouldn't you? None of this heroine stuff, right?"

"Believe me, you would be the first one I'd call."

"Okay. I need to head off to my next job site. It's eight forty-five. Don't you have a showing at nine o'clock?" Tom pointed at his watch.

"Yes. I had better go too. Good thing it's around the block. Let's get together and go over Brian's letter again to see if we missed anything. How about coming over for breakfast on Saturday?" Janie asked, putting her briefcase together with all her files.

"Well, I was hoping to get another dinner out of this deal. I'll even barbecue if you provide the grill. How about tomorrow night?"

"I can't." Janie fussed with the latch on her briefcase. "I have a date."

"That's great," Tom said, a little too enthusiastically. "Wait a minute. Who is this guy?"

She glanced at her brother. "Actually, he's a friend of yours."

"Is old Charlie stepping out on his wife again? I told that bugger to keep it in his pants."

"Charlie Alders? The tile guy? He's gotta be eighty years old. Is he the best you think your little sister can do?"

"You know those tile guys can be pretty…well…let's just say they know how to fit things together."

With hands on her hips, Janie said, "You're sick. No, you're more than sick. There's got to be a name for what you have, and I hope somebody is working on a cure. I happen to be going out with John Cooper."

"Really? So, I'm to blame for introducing you?"

"I think there were other forces at work. Carol told him about me too. Apparently, he was too old for her."

Tom did a double take. "Isn't he around the same age as you, me, and Carol?"

"Yes and no. Yes, he is about the same age. In Carol's world of men she dates, he's about fifteen years too old."

"Got it. Your basic cougar. Kidding aside, I'm happy for you, Sis. It's about time."

Waving her arms in the air, Janie asked, "Why does everyone keep saying that?"

"Probably"—Tom batted her on the shoulder—"because it is. I hope you have a great time. Honestly, I only know him in passing from job sites and the pubs. Maybe I should do some checking around?"

"You will do no such thing. We're only going out to dinner. He's not proposing marriage and doesn't need the third degree from you. Besides, I'm sure

Natalie and Jenny will do you proud when he picks me up," she said with a laugh. "Oh no. Look at the time. I'd better run. I'm taking the journal and Brian's envelope with me to work. Maybe I can study them a bit more." Janie ran upstairs and slipped everything into her briefcase beside the client files.

Downstairs, Tom waited for her in the kitchen. "You sure it's a good idea to carry that stuff around?"

"They'll be safe. I won't let this case out of my sight. Promise. Lock up on your way out." She ran out the door, grabbing her purse and phone off the counter as she flew by.

After starting her car, she glanced in the rearview mirror then tapped her fingers on the wheel watching Tom saunter to his truck behind her. Backing out of the driveway and shifting his vehicle into gear, Tom tooted the horn and waved. Janie zipped onto the street and drove the opposite direction. She arrived at the property with five minutes to spare.

Due to her ghostly encounter, Janie had a nervous edge the rest of the day. Talking with Tom before meeting her clients helped calm her enough to work on the sale. The husband acted aloof, but the wife's eyes glistened with longing. Her every caress of the cabinetry and tiling telegraphed how much she loved the house and already envisioned herself living there. An offer would come within the week.

Her fragile state of mind as she replayed William's recent visit continued to distract her once she arrived at the office. The rest of the morning and afternoon crawled by with her achieving very little. Every time she glanced at her briefcase containing Brian's packet of papers, she flinched and couldn't bring herself to drag it out for another review.

By evening the documents remained untouched. She required distance from the situation if only for one night. With her confidence buoyed, she snapped off the light to sleep.

CHAPTER 16

Nightmares disrupted Janie's slumber denying any hope of a peaceful rest. She awoke several times in a cold sweat, the sheets sticking to her damp skin. Finally giving up at five o'clock, she went downstairs to make coffee.

Her fingertips touched the puffy bags beneath her eyes. Janie didn't require a mirror to know she would need some touch-up from Carol. Maybe she should call John and cancel until this mess got resolved. What if it dragged on though? Janie didn't think she could go through weeks, let alone months, of this nightmare.

She rolled into work early still unsettled from a restless sleep. With her head cradled in her hands, she stared at the paperwork on her desk, not reading what sat on the blotter in front of her. When Suzie's Salon opened at nine, she would call Carol and cancel her appointment. Then, she'd call John. If she postponed their date rather than cancel, he might be open to trying some other time.

A shadow fell across her desk. Janie screamed, and her eyes shot up. Larry leaned back against the door jamb looking about to have a heart attack—face pale and hand on his chest.

"Larry." Janie jumped to her feet. "I'm so sorry."

"You looked so intent on what you were reading, I wasn't sure whether to interrupt or not." The color gradually returned to his face. "Are you all right?"

"Yes, I'm fine. There's been so much going on lately. I guess I'm a little on edge. What're you doing in so early?" she asked, sitting back down.

"Oh...well...my client changed to this afternoon. Thought I'd come in and get a head start on the day. What...what're you doing here?"

"Kind of the same thing."

He eased into the chair opposite her desk, the wooden joints protesting beneath his bulk. "You look tired, Janie. Everything all right?"

"I'm fine. Just a late night is all."

"Really? You seem a little...distracted. Kind of...jumpy, the way Brian was before..." He didn't finish the sentence.

Janie shot up like a rocket. "Like what, Larry? What're you trying to say? You'd tell me if there was anything I should know, wouldn't you?" She walked around the desk, glaring at him.

"I don't know anything. Never mind. I should never have brought it up." Larry pushed himself up and retreated.

Janie bit her upper lip. This could be a critical moment. Her next comment might help move her search forward or be the worst mistake she'd made thus far. Swallowing, she blurted out, "Larry, do you believe in...ghosts?"

He stopped, his hand returning to the door frame for support. His head turned to look at her; beads of sweat formed on his forehead. The man didn't utter a sound, as fright covered his face like a mask.

Janie had hit a nerve.

The front door slammed, and both jumped. Larry's

head snapped toward the entryway.

Walking past, Meg stopped at Janie's door. "Good morning. My, you two look as if someone walked over your graves. Everything okay?"

They nodded in unison.

"Well then," Meg said and went to the kitchen carrying her lunch tote.

Larry set a steely gaze on his partner. "Burn it," he hissed, his voice so low she strained to hear. The veins in his neck throbbed. "Burn it, Janie. Forget you ever saw the damn thing. Please. Don't ask me about it again." He spun around and pounded off to his own office, slamming the door.

Janie couldn't move, as if gravity dragged her down. She wanted to run after Larry and shake him by the shoulders until he told her everything. Maybe that was all there was for him to tell. The sheer terror on the man's face confirmed the trouble Brian referred to in his letter had to have been William. They both must have seen the young soldier.

Meg's voice broke her spell. "Are you waiting for me?"

"Huh?" Janie stuttered. She hadn't heard Meg approaching from down the hallway. "No. Yes, actually," she recovered. "Would you please bring me the Brassel Field property file when you have a moment?"

"Has there finally been a nibble on that old place? We've had it listed for ages." Meg tilted her head.

Janie kept her voice steady. "Yes. I don't know how serious they are, but it wouldn't hurt for me to brush up on the details."

"I'll bring it right in."

"No hurry. Get settled first."

Always the model of efficiency, Meg offered, "Shall I bring you a cup of coffee?"

"I already have one, thank you." Janie pattered back to her desk. She stared at the paperwork, her mind racing a mile a minute. Larry knew she had the journal. The sheer terror on his face told her he was as frightened as Brian had been when he wrote that letter. She wouldn't get anything else from him. Her next step would have to be a visit to the property.

"Here you go." Meg handed her the file. "Anything else?"

"No, thank you. Would you please close the door on your way out?"

Meg nodded as she turned and left, pulling the handle behind her.

Janie sat in her office with her palms pressed to the closed file on her desk. It contained papers identical to the ones she had at home from Brian, with the addition of the property keys. This way, both she and Tom had a copy to look through. It also eliminated anyone else getting hold of the paperwork. If someone was watching, it might slow him down. Janie tucked the folder away in her briefcase.

As nine o'clock rolled around, Janie picked up the phone, dialed Suzie's Salon, and asked to speak to Carol.

"Don't tell me you're cancelling, Janie Holgram," Carol chastised, as if they were already in the middle of a conversation.

"Are you developing psychic powers now?" Janie joked. How could she have hoped to fool Carol? She probably waited by the phone expecting the call.

"Yes, as a matter of fact I am. That'll be twenty dollars for the reading."

"Okay, so you knew I'd try to bail. Maybe I hoped you'd talk me back into it," Janie said.

"What do you want to hear, the list of a dozen reasons why you should go on this date? Or do I have to resort to flattery to prove you're worth it?"

"Never mind. I should have known you wouldn't let me squirm out of this. Forget I called. I'll see you at three."

"Now that's more like it. See you then."

Janie hung up the phone. That went well. Okay, maybe she did want to go on this date, if nothing else, to take her mind off the current dilemmas.

****

Carol stood in her shop twirling a lock of hair around her finger. John owed her yet one more favor. Perhaps she would get him to pay up tonight, after his date. Knowing Janie, it would be an early evening. Maybe she should start building her wardrobe at the mall tomorrow. You can never begin too early finding the right outfits when you're with a wealthy guy.

The delicious daydreams were interrupted with the arrival of her first customer, whom she ignored until she finished setting up her station. Soon, there would be no more customers for her. She would be the pampered client.

CHAPTER 17

Janie struggled with even the smallest task at work. Her mind couldn't get past the blow up she'd had with Larry. Mid-morning, when she stepped out of her office to refill her coffee, Larry's door remained closed. By noon it stood open and the office dark.

"When did Larry leave?" Janie asked.

"It must have been around eleven-thirty. Did you need something? I can call him on his cell." Meg reached for the phone.

Walking toward the kitchen to grab her lunch, Janie said, "No. I'll catch him this afternoon."

"I don't think he'll be back until Monday. He wished me a nice weekend on his way out. Do you think he's ill?"

Not turning around, she battled to keep the concern out of her voice. "That's probably it. He did look a bit peaked when we spoke this morning. We'll catch up after the weekend. Thanks, Meg." Her stomach lurched, eliminating the hunger pangs. She returned to her own office and closed the door.

More like frightened out of his wits, thought Meg, as one side of her mouth rose into a smirk. Larry had sworn he wanted nothing more to do with the journal. Maybe Janie went fishing, and he wouldn't bite. Her money rode on Janie leading them down the right path. Johnny had better come through tonight. This incessant back and forth of pleasantries drove her insane.

At one-thirty Janie carried her briefcase and left, wishing her assistant a nice weekend.

Meg smiled and wished her a good one too—the same as every Friday. Janie had an appointment with that slut hairdresser to prepare for her Johnny. He played a dangerous game sparking one of Janie's best friends, which put their whole plan in jeopardy.

As soon as she was alone, Meg went on her habitual search of the office. Rarely did Janie leave behind any clues, but it never hurt to check.

She started with the trash can. A couple of times she'd found notes Brian had made then discarded. He wasn't nearly as cautious as Janie until he'd been approached by an interested party. After that, pickings became scarce. Meg sorted through crumpled papers and found a sticky note with the words, "Get keys from Brassel Field original file." Janie must be getting closer to finding the treasure if she wanted access to the property.

Next, she riffled through the stack on the desk and found the Brassel Field file missing. *Janie has got to have that final page.* Beyond her discovery of the file being gone and Janie's needing the keys, Meg netted a big zero. Another waste of time. Before leaving, a flash of metal caught her eye.

On the floor beside the desk, lay a ring with two keys on it. One was a postal key. All the neighborhoods in this area had switched to centralized mailboxes for every ten or twelve houses on a block. The other looked like a house key. Now that could come in handy. Meg mentally congratulated herself on a spectacular find. She would stop by a hardware store and have a copy made before returning them. This kept their options open if her son failed.

The keys jangled when she dropped them into her purse. It would be a waste of time searching Larry's office. The man turned into a spineless wimp after his partner disappeared. Guess you can't blame him for being spooked, she mused.

****

Janie parked in front of Larry's house. She sat with her hand resting on the briefcase in the passenger seat. Despite his refusal to speak of anything connected to the journal, other than to burn it, she needed to try again. He knew something. There must be a way to get him to talk about the events leading up to Brian's disappearance. If he didn't help her, who would?

Jaw set, her fingers wrapped around the handle of the case as she dragged it across the seat and got out of the car. The heels of her pumps echoed on the cement as she strode to the front steps, the smell of freshly mowed grass tickling her nostrils. She rapped on the metal frame of the screen door, then waited patiently. After a few moments with no response, Janie rang the bell.

Heavy footsteps approached from the back of the house, then hesitated. Janie recognized the plump silhouette of Margaret, Larry's wife, through the dark mesh.

The woman's shoulders slumped as she moved closer. "He's not here, Janie."

"Hello, Margaret. I know he's home. His car is in the driveway, along with yours. Please, I wouldn't have come if it wasn't important."

After glancing behind her, she moved her face

closer, almost whispering. "I'm begging you; leave him alone. He can't help you." Her hands fidgeted with the cross hanging from a chain around her neck.

"I believe he can." Guilt swept over her at bullying the distraught woman, but she saw no other way.

"We want to put this behind us. You should too— for Jenny and Natalie, if for no other reason."

Anger strengthened Janie's determination, and her voice rose. "Margaret, you know this hasn't been easy on any of us. Help me find closure."

"Let her in, Maggie." Larry's bulk blocked the light from the kitchen doorway at the end of the hall.

His wife spun toward him shaking her head, her blonde ponytail bobbing from side to side.

He approached, kissed her cheek, and rubbed her shoulder. "It's okay. I'll talk to her."

Margaret stifled a cry with her hand and fled to the left off the entryway. She ran upstairs, her footsteps muted by the carpeting.

Larry reached over and unfastened the latch, stepping back to allow her entry.

Janie squeezed past him, emotions playing across her face as she chewed her lip. Remorse nagged at her for having intruded on their lives coupled with relief at being let inside. From her conversation with Margaret, it was obvious Larry had told his wife about the situation. If only Brian had done the same, she wouldn't be here now for anything other than a social visit.

The stout man, his business attire replaced with khaki shorts and a yellow polo shirt, led her through the kitchen and onto the back porch. On the way, he grabbed a glass from a cabinet.

Janie followed silently. Two half-full glasses of

iced tea sat beside a pitcher on a table shaded by an umbrella.

Larry gestured to a seat, filled the glass in his hand, and set it in front of her. Easing his large frame onto a cushioned chair, he waited for her to speak.

Setting the briefcase on the table, she sipped, clearing her parched throat. "Thank you."

He nodded and crossed an ankle over his knee. His khaki shorts rode up over his pasty white legs.

"I wouldn't have come if I wasn't desperate. You know that, don't you?"

"You won't take my advice, will you?" he asked in a resigned voice.

"Would you, if it was Margaret who disappeared?"

He bolted up straight, his elevated foot now slamming onto the floorboards while he pressed into the back of his chair. "That's unfair."

"Is it? Larry, I didn't come here to cause trouble, but this needs to be finished—for all of us." She unzipped the case and retrieved the journal, along with the envelope containing Brian's letter and newspaper articles.

Color drained from his face at the sight of the leather-bound book. He spread his hands flat on the table, fingertips turning white as he pressed them onto the acrylic surface.

"What happened to the final page?" she asked, battling to keep her voice even. If she pushed too hard, he would shut down and turn her away like his wife had wanted.

His eyes flashed at her. "I don't have it. Put that thing away. I can't do this again."

The shade in the kitchen window behind him

dropped back into place. Janie focused on her partner. "Do you know where it is? Was the journal complete when you found it? This is important, Larry."

With his breathing labored, Larry wrapped his hands around the glass in front of him. Sweat trickled down the sides of his face as damp tendrils of blond hair plastered to his forehead. He took a long gulp. The glass clattered on the table when he set it down. "Yes. It was there when we found it. What difference does it make? This mess got your husband killed. It won't bring him back."

Janie winced.

If Larry felt any remorse for his callous words, he didn't show it. His face remained pale and expressionless.

"Please," Janie controlled her tone, "tell me what happened before Brian disappeared. Who threatened you?"

"How do you know about them? Brian told me he didn't say a word to you."

Pulling her husband's letter from the envelope, Janie studied the worn paper. She'd read it so many times, it looked crumpled. Extending her arm, she offered the note to him.

He stared at the paper, unmoving. Looking back at Janie, he asked, "What is that?"

"Just read it." She extended her arm farther. "This is how I know."

With shaking fingers, he grasped the paper and unfolded it. From the taut expression on his face, Janie could tell Larry recognized the handwriting.

She drank from her glass while studying Larry's expression as he read.

Several minutes later, he folded the letter along its well-worn creases and slid it back across the table. Hanging his head, he muttered, "I never knew who threatened us. Nor did I bring anyone else in."

"What did you do?"

Larry remained silent, his fingers plucking at the hem of his shorts.

Pounding her hand on the table, Janie demanded, "Tell me what happened." Her nostrils flared, and her face warmed from the heat of her words.

He shrank back into his chair. More sweat trickled down his hairline, dripping off his cheeks.

"You're the only one who can fill in the gaps. Help me. Please."

"I don't know who contacted us. All I know is, whoever it was said they'd kill Margaret, you, and the girls if we didn't surrender the journal. I told Brian to give it up. He insisted it wouldn't end, even if we handed the book over."

"When did this happen?"

Larry swiped his forehead with the back of his hand. "Right after we were awarded representation of the Brassel Field property. We knew it used to belong to Jacob Pelter and thought all we had to do was locate the treasure and live off its riches. We were idiots to think it would be that simple."

"How could anybody even know you had the journal and what that property meant?"

"I...I don't know. Since Brian wouldn't give in, I told him I wanted nothing more to do with it. He was on his own." Compassion echoed in his voice. "I'm sorry, but I couldn't risk losing Maggie. No wealth is worth more than the people you love."

Slumping back in her chair, Janie pitied the man—and herself. If only Brian had done the same, she would still have him in her life. "Is there anything you can tell me? A clue the police didn't know about. Where he went?"

"The last page. When we'd first been contacted, Brian tore it out and hid it but wouldn't tell me where. He said that was his 'bargaining chip.' "

Janie leaned forward and placed her hand on Larry's. "Tell me what it said."

Pulling away, his eyes moistened. "All I recall is there were coordinates, steps from the corner of the barn. Don't ask me what they were. I don't remember."

"Where did he go that day, Larry?"

Looking down, with a deep breath, he said, "To Brassel Field. Brian told me he had a meeting with whoever contacted us and would give them the journal but not the last page. I told him not to go. He wouldn't listen. Brian must've changed his mind about handing the journal over since you have it." He raised his head, and his eyes grew wide.

She opened her mouth to ask why he let Brian go alone, but he wasn't looking at her. A chill slithered down her neck. Whipping her head around, she found that William hovered beyond the edge of the deck. She could see the expanse of yard through his transparent body.

The apparition looked the same, except this time he reached out and mouthed the words, "Help me, Larry. Help me."

"*No*. Not again. I won't go through this again." Bolting up, his body shoved the chair across the deck, and it smashed into the wall. As he stumbled toward the back door, he shouted over his shoulder, "Don't come back here, Janie. Don't ever bring that damn thing near me again. I can't help you. I won't help you!"

The door slammed behind him, and the bolt slid home. When she turned back toward the young soldier, he was gone. "Oh, William," she said aloud, "how can I ever help you—or me?"

Picking up Brian's letter, her fingers caressed the paper for a second before she slipped it back into the envelope. She grabbed William's journal and placed everything inside her briefcase. Janie walked down the steps to the back lawn and let herself out the side gate. From her car at the curb, she looked at the house. The front door and all the curtains were closed. She wondered if Charger Realty still retained two business partners but couldn't worry about work now. While not learning much from Larry, she had discovered the last place Brian had been—Brassel Field.

CHAPTER 18

The call waiting cut in on John as he primed Carol for her appointment with Janie. He ignored the beep in his ear. Making sure his date didn't back out of their dinner was more pressing. "You're sure you convinced her to go through with tonight, babe?" John cooed into the phone.

"Let's just say you owe me big time," Carol boasted. "You're cutting in and out. Are you getting another call?"

John tightened his grip on the phone as his mother's office line appeared on the screen. *Would she ever give him credit for having a handle on the situation?* "Yes. It's a high-maintenance customer. She can leave a voicemail. You're my priority."

"I love it when you say that." Carol sighed. "Now, remember who your priority is when you're out with 'you know who' tonight. After all, if it hadn't been for my help, Janie never would have gone out with you in the first place."

"It's you and only you."

"Maybe we could get together later?"

"I'll be out, remember?"

Carol lowered her voice, giving it a sexier tone. "I know. I mean later, after your date."

"Rain check. I don't want to do anything to ruin tonight. We need that journal."

"You're not going to get it tonight. Janie's a good girl. She'll make you have her home by ten." Disappointment shown through Carol's tone. "Oooo, gotta go. She just pulled up in front of the shop. Tell me what I wanna hear."

"Tell you what?" John toyed.

"You know. Don't make me beg."

He murmured. "But I love it when you beg, baby."

"Pleeeeease," she pleaded.

"Oh, I can't resist. I love ya."

"Mmmmm…gotta go.

John's voice feigned hurt. "Nothing for me?"

"Bye." She ended the call.

He threw his phone across the cab of the truck where it bounced off the passenger seat and landed on the floor. Between Carol's smugness and his mother's needling for quick results, he couldn't imagine a worse hell to be in. At least spending time with Janie would be a bright spot in his life. His finding the treasure would be the ultimate pleasure, of course. No need to lose perspective.

****

Janie parked in front of the salon. Her pulse raced from the confrontation with Larry. Taking a moment to calm her breathing, she watched Carol through the window as she spoke on the phone. Given her posturing and body language, it appeared her friend had another future ex-husband dangling on the line. They knew each other too well. She'd have to grill Carol about him and steer the attention away from her dinner tonight. She chirped the remote for her car and walked into the salon.

The stylist ended her call and motioned for Janie to

come back.

She gave Carol a hug then slipped her purse onto the hook underneath the beauty station.

"You're really excited about tonight. I don't usually get hugs," Carol fussed.

"Thank you," Janie said, her expression serious.

Her friend tilted her head. "For what?"

"For not letting me back out. You knew I'd try."

"In that case, you're welcome. This is a huge step you needed to take. Now, let's start with a wash." Carol led Janie back to a sink and draped a cape over her.

Neither said a word until they were back at Carol's station.

Picking up scissors, she said, "I'm going to freshen up the layers, then blow dry your hair into a spectacular 'do."

"Great," Janie said with a little more enthusiasm than she felt. "Who were you talking to on the phone when I drove up?"

"On the phone?" Her eyes widened as she dropped the comb from her other hand. "Oh…a client wanting to change an appointment." She scooped it off the floor and tossed it into the sanitizing jar before selecting another one to use.

"Don't even try it. I could tell by the way you moved a man was on the other end—and not a client," she added. "Spill. Who's your next candidate?"

"Okay," Carol said. "I…I didn't want to say anything yet. I've met someone new." She resumed clipping hair, her tight grip on the tools whitening her knuckles.

"That's it? You met someone new? You think I'm going to be satisfied with that answer? You're going to have to do better. Come on. I want details."

"Uh-uh," Carol said in a no-nonsense voice.

With a huff, Janie asked, "What do you mean 'uh-uh?' "

"Today is about you—and only you. My dating habits are nothing new. Yours, on the other hand, are an absolute novelty and the only topic up for discussion."

"I'm not sure I like this."

Carol used a clip on the upper parts of Janie's hair and snipped at the under layers. "Well, that's the way it is. Now, what are you going to wear tonight?"

Admitting defeat and embracing how it was her turn to feel special, Janie conceded. "All right, we'll continue this conversation next time. Agreed?"

"Agreed. What did you say you were wearing tonight?" Carol persisted.

"I thought I'd wear this. What do you think?" Janie indicated the business suit she wore.

"You've got to be—"

Holding up her hand, she said, "Yes, I'm kidding. I thought I'd wear my summer paisley dress in yellows and blues. You know, the one I wore at the Jackson boy's graduation last year?"

A smile spread across Carol's face. "That'll be perfect. It's casual, yet feminine."

"Really? You don't think the outfit is too frumpy? Maybe I should wear something a little flouncy, you know, with more flair." Janie's jaw tensed.

"Nope. I think it's a good choice. You don't want to overdo it on a first date," Carol answered with enthusiasm. While they chatted, she snipped and styled, ending with the blow dryer. "Okay, what do you think?" She held a mirror so Janie could see the back of her hair.

"I love it!" She touched the edges. "You've outdone yourself. If he doesn't ask me out on a second date, it will all be on me to have spoiled it."

"Listen to you, already thinking beyond tonight." Despite her teasing tone, Carol's eyes flashed.

"Carol, what's wrong?" Janie asked.

Her jaw tightened as she busied her hands with the brush. "Oh, nothing. I saw a spot I missed. Hold on." She smoothed and prodded the back of Janie's head. "There, now you're perfect."

"You're a true artist—and a great friend," Janie added with a serious note to her voice. "Thank you for helping me through this."

"You're going to wow him, girl. Now remember, no sleepovers on the first date."

"Carol, I'm not even sure I should kiss on the first date." Janie's cheeks reddened at the thought of being intimate with a man she barely knew.

"Here's a tip. Always leave them wanting. I expect a full report tomorrow."

"Okay." Janie pulled the wallet from her purse.

The stylist shook her head. "Oh, no. This one's on me. Go get him."

"No, I can't."

"Yes, you can. Now go home and get dressed."

"Thanks." Janie hugged her friend one more time. "I'll call you tomorrow."

"Sounds good." Carol waved. "And Janie?"

She stopped and turned.

"Relax. It'll be fine."

Janie's chest puffed out with confidence, as she strode outside.

Jealousy gnawed inside of Carol as she watched the woman drive away. This better be worth it. John was hers and hers alone! She'd make Janie realize that soon enough.

CHAPTER 19

Pulling into her driveway, Janie got out of the car and reached for her house keys. That's strange, she thought. I remember putting them in my purse after locking up this morning. She went back and checked the front seat and floor of the car. No luck.

As Janie raised her fist to knock on the kitchen door, it magically opened. Natalie awaited, a big grin on her face. "You look great, Mom. John is going to love your hair."

"Do you think so?" She patted the bottom edges. "I don't want it to look too fancy. After all, it's only a first date."

"So, you're supposed to look ugly?" Natalie poked fun at her mother's discomfort.

"No…well…oh…you know what I mean. I don't want to look too anxious."

Natalie goaded, "Too anxious for what?"

"You know, sometimes you have way too much of your Uncle Tom in you. Have you and your sister eaten?"

"Mom, it's only four thirty."

Setting her purse and car key on the counter, she said, "Right. By the way, you didn't happen to find my house keys on the ground near the door, did you? I can't find them."

"Nope. Did you check your car?"

"Yes. They're not there. Probably fell out of my purse at the office. I remember rummaging around in it a few times. Get me the spare from my desk, will you?"

"Sure, Mom. I'll bring it upstairs to you."

Janie narrowed her eyes. "Upstairs?"

"Go to your room. Jenny and I have a surprise. She's waiting."

Janie wasn't sure whether to be excited or scared. Her first thought jumped to her nightstand with Brian's package. The tension in her shoulders eased as she remembered everything was secured in the briefcase she held in her hand.

Upstairs in the bedroom her daughter stood by the dresser laying out turquoise earrings and a necklace. "Surprise," Jenny shouted. "Nat and I thought we'd take the pressure off your deciding what to wear."

"Yeah," Natalie added as she walked in carrying the spare key. "We picked an outfit for you. What do you think?"

With a catch in her voice, she said, "I think you two have grown up quicker than I realized."

Jenny quavered, "Does that mean you like it?"

"Let's see what you've chosen." Inhaling to banish any impending tears, Janie set her valise by the closet then strolled to the bed, her hands clasped behind her back. They'd laid out a teal blue dress with a deep vee neck in the front and back. A bit more revealing than she'd planned to wear, but still tasteful enough for a casual dinner. Not wanting to disappoint the girls, she cried, "It's perfect!"

"Really?" Jenny asked, her fingers fidgeting as they laced and unlaced. "You don't have to wear it if you don't want."

"But we picked out matching shoes, and Jenny even found the right jewelry," Natalie added, anxiety obvious in her voice. "So?"

"You girls did a great job and saved me hours of deciding. I really like it. Thank you." She fussed over the outfit a moment longer and gave each girl a squeeze. "I guess this means you're okay with my going out with John."

Jenny bit her lip then said, "Mom, it's fine. We know this doesn't mean you're forgetting Daddy. It means you're continuing to live your life. He'd want you to."

"Now you're going to make me cry." She dabbed at the corner of her eyes with her fingertips. "The two of you skedaddle so I can shower and get dressed."

Natalie's eyes bugged wide. "But your hair."

"Not to worry. I won't get it wet. I've done this a time or two before, you know."

Handing the key to her mother, Natalie said, "Okay. Here's the spare key. What happened to our picture on the desk?"

"I completely forgot. Yesterday morning I knocked it on the floor. I'll pick up another frame next time we go shopping."

"Don't bother," Jenny said. "Grandma gave me a couple of nice frames last Christmas, but they don't match my room. Why don't you use one of them? I think they're the same size."

"That would be great, honey. Leave one on the desk when you get a chance, and I'll change it tomorrow."

Jenny grabbed her sister's arm. "Okay. Let's scram, Nat."

"Yell if you need help, Mom," Natalie offered before being dragged from the room.

Her daughters' preparations helped calm the butterflies in her stomach. Having their support eased Janie's mind more than they realized.

****

At five o'clock Meg went through her evening routine of locking up the office. All paperwork got straightened and put away in secured cabinets. The cleaning people came on the weekend, and she certainly didn't want them snooping through anything. Who knows what those people do when the occupants weren't around? When Janie hired those foreigners, Meg had objected, but after all, she wasn't the boss. Lucky for Janie Meg found those keys first. If it came down to using them, she would only take what was rightfully hers.

After work she'd planned on going to her favorite butcher three towns over. The substandard quality of meats at the local shop made it worth the thirty-minute drive. On the way she would stop at the hardware store and have a copy made of the house key. The duplicate needed to be done before Saturday in case her boss stopped by the office looking for her missing keyring. Meg could slip in early on Saturday morning and place it beside Janie's desk where she'd found it. With the slipshod job those janitors did, it would be easy to believe they'd missed finding it.

Beaming at her ingenuity and thoroughness, Meg locked the front door and walked to her car. As she drove away, her cell phone rang. Meg touched the screen and spouted, "It's about time you called me back."

"Mother, I wasn't in a position to talk until now," John responded, slinging the same amount of sting he received.

Meg stemmed her frustration and lowered her tone. "I wanted to make sure our plan is straight for tonight." Meg stuck to the right lane while she talked. She didn't want to miss her turn since the roads were busy this time of day.

"Like I told you before, I have everything under control. Stop nagging."

"No need to get snippy. By the way, I have a little insurance policy for us in case things don't work out the way we hope." Stopped at a light, she patted her purse sitting on the passenger seat.

John sounded wary. "What kind of insurance policy are you talking about?"

You never know who might be listening with all those fancy devices people have these days. "Not over the phone. I'll tell you tomorrow when you come to take care of my lawn."

"Can't wait," John said.

"Now, are you sure that little hussy is under control because—"

"Mother, enough already. Everything is fine with Carol. Couldn't be better."

"You can never be too careful. We've come too close, Johnny."

"I know, Mother. Let me go so I'm not late picking up my date. I'll see you tomorrow."

"Okay." Meg ended the call and slipped the phone into her purse. Just in time too, as she drove past a police car facing her way. She knew about the hands-free law while driving but could never get used to those things hanging on her ear. The last thing she needed was a ticket.

****

John pulled away from the curb after hanging up with his mother. He pounded the steering wheel. When would the woman learn to trust his actions? Actually, he'd grown tired of being caught between Carol and Janie, but his mother didn't need any more fuel for her crusade.

Tempted to stop by the pub for a quick one, he decided not to risk running into Carol. He didn't need the third degree from her too. The fridge at home had beer. With him finally hooking up with Janie, Carol's usefulness waned. He'd have to do something about her sooner or later. Right now, avoidance seemed the best plan.

As he showered and dressed for the evening, his mother's words niggled at him. What kind of insurance plan had she schemed up now? Knowing her, he wouldn't like it.

CHAPTER 20

The kitchen smelled of garlic and tomato sauce where the Holgram sisters dined on leftover pizza and root beer. Natalie twisted open the half empty bottle of soda and poured herself another glass. The ice crackled as the soda fizzed around the cubes.

"Do you think Mom's nervous?" Jenny asked, her mouth full of cheese and crust.

Natalie finished chewing and swallowed. "Of course. She hasn't been on a date since Daddy."

"True. She does seem pretty excited, don't you think?" Jenny worked on her slice.

"Yeah. She must really like this guy," added Natalie. "But still…"

Their mother's heels clacked down the hallway. Both turned.

"How do I look?" Janie stepped into the kitchen and threw her arms out in a modeling pose.

"Great!" They answered as one.

Her hands twitched as she smoothed the seams of her dress and fingered the necklace she wore. "Not too dressy, right?"

"Mom, you look fine," Jenny said. "Just relax. John is going to love you."

Almost on cue the front doorbell rang. Panic shone in Janie's eyes; her body frozen in place.

Jenny bolted toward the front of the house. "I'll get

it. You stand there looking beautiful."

She opened the front door and spoke with a forced maturity beyond her twelve years. "Yes?" Her face remained still, giving away no sign of emotion.

John lifted his brow. "You must be Jenny."

"Good guess," she replied. "Although you only had two choices."

Just as he feared, the kids might be a tough sell. "I'm John," he said, breaking the ice with a laugh and eliciting a huge smile from Jenny. "I'm here to pick up your mother." His charm oozed from every pore.

"Come in. Mom's almost ready." Jenny held the screen door. "Have a seat. She'll be out in a minute."

John followed her instructions, making himself comfortable on the couch. After Jenny walked down the hall, he surveyed the front area of the house. Tastefully decorated, he thought. The scent of roses permeated the air complementing colors of muted greens and mauve. He could appreciate a place with a woman's touch without it being too feminine. Nothing like the austere furnishings his mother strategically placed about her house as if it were a minimalist display in an art gallery. This was a home—comfortable without being overdone.

Back in the kitchen Jenny walked up to her mother and quietly said, "You didn't tell us how handsome he was. Where did you meet him?"

"Shhhh, he'll hear you." She glanced toward the living room. "But, yeah, he looks nice, doesn't he?"

Natalie jumped up. "I want to meet him."

"Girls, calm down. We don't want to overwhelm the guy. Okay, Natalie, come with me, and I'll introduce you."

"I'm coming too." Jenny followed.

They trooped into the room. "Hi, John," Janie said, tightening her stomach muscles to quell her nerves. It took all her reserve not to gush like a teenager at seeing him again.

"Hello, gorgeous." John stood. "You look great."

Both girls wore big grins while a blush rose on their mother's cheeks. "I had some help from my two fashion advisors. One, you've already met."

John nodded at Jenny.

"This is my oldest, Natalie."

"It's nice to meet you, Natalie," John responded, pouring on more charm.

"Hi," Natalie almost whispered.

Janie tilted her head at her daughter, squinting her eyes before gesturing toward the couch. "Please, John, sit down."

He retook his seat, and Janie settled onto the settee off to the side. Jenny parked herself on the other end of the sofa, while Natalie perched on the arm of her mother's chair. Anyone observing the group would think they watched a standoff from a western with nobody speaking.

John shifted on the cushion and said, "You have a beautiful home. Did you decorate it yourself?"

"Thank you. Yes, I did. It probably needs some updating, but I haven't had the time."

"It looks wonderful. Why change it?"

Butterflies flitted around her belly as she gripped the arm of her chair, surreptitiously wiping her sweaty palms on the smooth fabric. "Thanks."

"Where are you and Mom going, Mr. Cooper?" Jenny asked.

"Please, call me John. I hear Mr. Cooper, and I look around for my father. If that's okay with you, Janie?"

"No, that's fine," Janie responded, a little too quickly. She hadn't put any thought into an appropriate way for the girls to address him. Dating as a parent added a new list of protocols.

Jenny shot a quick side-glance at her mother before continuing. "Okay...John," she dragged out, pronouncing the one syllable of his name. "Where're you and Mom going?"

"I thought we'd drive over to Kelsey's on the north shore. It's not too far from here, and they have a beautiful enclosed patio overlooking the beach. I hope you like seafood." John directed his last comment toward Janie.

She did her best not to show surprise at his choice. The girls were too young to remember, but Brian always took her to Kelsey's for their anniversary. This evening may turn out to be harder than expected. Focus on the positive, she chided herself. "Yes. Kelsey's used to be one of my favorites, though I haven't been there in a long time. I wonder if the menu has changed?"

"Depends on how long it's been since you've eaten there. I know they have a different special each week." He casually glanced at his watch and added, "We may want to head out. I made a seven o'clock reservation, and you know how Friday night traffic can be."

"Oh...sure. I'll just grab my purse." Janie stood and walked down the hall.

A few moments later, Jenny raced after her. "Mom, I forgot to show you something." She found her mother sitting in a chair, dabbing at her eyes with a tissue.

"Mom, what's wrong? Are you mad because I called him John? I can call him Mr. Cooper if you want me to."

"No, I'm not mad, honey." Janie heaved. "I guess this is suddenly going too fast. Maybe I shouldn't have accepted John's invitation."

Jenny threw her arm around her mother's shoulders and squeezed. "It's okay. Daddy would want you to be happy."

"I know. Doesn't make it any easier," she sniffed.

"You better stop, or your mascara will run and ruin the whole outfit," Jenny joked.

She giggled. "As always, my twelve-year-old knows best. Hand me my purse." Janie dabbed the remaining moisture from the corners of her eyes.

"Oh, yeah, I almost forgot. Do you like this frame?" Jenny picked it up off the counter. "I already put the picture in."

"It looks wonderful. You were careful with the broken glass when you took the old one apart, weren't you?"

"Nothing a tourniquet couldn't handle." She shrugged.

John poked his head into the kitchen. "Everything okay in here?"

"I'm sorry, John. I didn't mean to take so long."

"You had me worried. I feared you bolted out the back door. Not having second thoughts, are you?" He winked.

"It crossed my mind, but Jenny talked me down off the ledge." Janie rubbed her daughter's shoulder as she stood. "She put one of my pictures into a new frame. What do you think?"

He gazed at the photo of her and the girls. "Looks like a beautiful family."

Reaching into her back pocket, Jenny said, "Mom, I found this behind the picture. Natalie wouldn't let me open it because she said it might be private—like a love letter you wrote to Dad, or something. I think she was just being bossy." Jenny stuck her tongue out at her sister, who stood behind John.

Janie saw the folded parchment in her daughter's hand and gasped. She recognized the old, yellowed paper immediately. All this time it had been in plain sight on her desk. That's what William had pointed at yesterday morning.

"Jenny," Natalie scolded, "I thought it might be personal between Mom and Dad. You have to respect people's privacy."

John wore a hungry expression on his face as he drank in the sight of the paper. *What must he be thinking?*

"Mom? Mom?" Jenny prodded her. "Can I read it? What is it? Mom?"

Shuddering, she came out of her trance. "Sorry, Jenny. What?"

"Can I open it? Or is it personal like Natalie said?"

All eyes in the room were set firmly on Janie. It took all her restraint not to snatch the folded parchment from her daughter's hand and tear it open. She and Tom had been searching all week for this missing piece, and now here it rested in her daughter's innocent grasp. The agony of not reading it immediately tore at her insides.

"Sorry, Janie, but is this going to take long? We really do need to shake a leg, or they'll give our reservation away." John tapped his watch. "Is it something important?"

His impatience poked at her, causing stabs of guilt for dragging him into her personal drama. "No. Well, yes, but only to me. It's silly, really. It's just…just…" Her mind raced. She had to come up with something believable yet trivial so neither he nor the girls would think it important. "It's a note I wrote to Brian after we first met. Let me have it, Jenny. It is kind of personal. Something I would prefer not to share as it's a little embarrassing. I thought your dad had kept it, but I never knew where."

Jenny offered it to her mother, her lower lip sticking out in a pout.

Janie silently thanked her older daughter for having the presence of mind to make Jenny wait. What would they have thought? And what about John? Did it embarrass him witnessing this family scene? A first date was awkward enough without the drama of discovering a love letter to a deceased husband. The intensity of his stare jangled her nerves even further, making her believe he had second thoughts about dinner with her.

"John, I'll only be a minute." Janie scooted upstairs to her bedroom. She needed to be quick before her date ran screaming from the house. The final part of William's story would have to wait. Retrieving Brian's envelope from her nightstand where she'd placed it after her shower, she slipped the paper inside and put the packet back.

Hurrying out of the bedroom, she found John waiting at the bottom of the stairs, his lips a thin line. She couldn't decide if his eyes conveyed anger or concern.

As she descended, his face brightened into a grin. "Life must be very interesting in your house, Ms. Holgram."

Her tension eased, and she added a slight bounce to her step. "Never a dull moment."

Both girls stood by the front entry like a receiving line of maids. Natalie held Janie's purse, and Jenny proffered a sweater. "Here you go, Mom," Natalie said.

Janie took both items and allowed John to escort her outside.

"Don't stay out too late," Jenny yelled as John held open the passenger side door of his truck.

Blushing, Janie got in. As an afterthought, she cracked open the door and yelled, "Don't forget to lock up, girls."

Natalie waved as she shooed her sister into the house and closed the inside door. The bolt slid home.

****

John walked around the front of the truck, opening and closing his fists. It had been right there. Right in front of him! And he did nothing but watch it get whisked away. If only the girls hadn't been there, he would have acted differently. He needed that information. At least now he knew for sure Janie had it. That dolt, Brian, must have hidden it and not told her. The surprise on Janie's face looked genuine. The room she ran into must be the master bedroom—her bedroom. The home office sat off the back hallway. Walking to the kitchen gave him a better idea of the layout of the place. They really didn't need to hurry, but it gave him the excuse he needed to see more of the house. He lucked out walking in when he did. Why couldn't she be more like Carol? He'd had no problem getting into the bedroom after dinner with the blonde. There would be no bedroom invitation anytime soon from this woman. He'd have to find another way. John opened his door and slid behind the wheel while forcing the corners of his mouth to rise. "I hope you don't mind my work truck. I haven't had much use for a personal vehicle."

"Not at all." Janie's voice had softened, closer to normal. She buckled her seatbelt.

"Most of my equipment gets pulled behind on a trailer, so the truck stays clean. Are you all right? You acted pretty distracted back there." Maybe he could ease her into a conversation where she might slip and mention the journal.

Wringing her hands in her lap, she said, "I'm fine, thanks. Just a few butterflies. This really is my first date since losing Brian. I'm a little on edge." She met his gaze.

"You were fine when I first arrived. Jenny's finding that…note upset you." John fished.

"Well," Janie said, "I've been searching a while. I thought Brian had gotten rid of it. What a shock to find it's been sitting on my desk all this time."

"I see," John said. *Time to stop before she completely shuts down.* "Honestly," he chuckled, "I was being selfish and hoping it wasn't something you'd dwell on all evening. Childish, huh?" He looked sideways at her.

Placing a hand on his arm, she said, "You'll have my full attention tonight. I promise."

His body stirred below the belt at the touch of her cool fingers pressing gently against his flesh. This evening didn't have to be all work. "I'd guess you're the type of person who keeps her promises, which puts me in a great mood." A genuine smile covered his face. "Now, let's get down to business. What's your favorite seafood dish?"

"I don't even have to think about that. Pretty much anything with shrimp, hands down. How about you?"

"Shrimp is my favorite too. Maybe we can get two different dishes and share?" He watched her bristle when he suggested sharing. His mother had been right on the money telling him about Kelsey's and what he should order. With these coincidental similarities, she might relax and welcome him into her world, and home, sooner.

John drove out of the neighborhood, then took a right onto Route 48 toward the north shore of Long Island. The twenty-minute ride turned to comfortable conversation as the two discovered other things they had in common.

CHAPTER 21

"Thanks for making time for me this evening, Mrs. Weiss." Tom accepted a glass of iced tea from his customer. "I hope I didn't disrupt any dinner plans." He scanned the kitchen, but the only smells present came from cleaning fluids not cooking.

"Not at all. Ever since Mr. Weiss passed away, I don't have many plans. With my Sylvia and Myron living their own lives in the city, I usually stay in at night."

"Come on, Mrs. Weiss. A hot number like you? Home on a Friday night? I find it hard to believe this happens very often." Tom winked, causing a slight blush to rise in her cheeks.

She feigned insult. "Now, stop that, young man. You know the only man for me was Mr. Weiss." Placing a hand to her chest, she looked up.

"If you say so." He winked again. Tom knew how to butter up a client—especially one that would be a royal pain in the you-know-what once the job began. After the last time she hired him, Tom swore he'd never work for her again. Despite her complaining, he did end up getting additional work from her referrals.

"Actually"—she tapped her chin—"I do have shopping to take care of tomorrow morning, so this worked out perfectly when you mentioned your sister inviting you for breakfast. Spending time with her and the little ones is so important. Especially now with this nasty business about her husband coming up again. I can't imagine going through that myself, declaring a missing husband dead. How is she?" The woman settled back into her chair, as if expecting a detailed account.

He wouldn't be sharing any juicy details to stoke her curiosity for a good story. "She's doing fine. Janie's a trooper. Now"—he cut the gossip off at the chase—"why don't you show me where you'd like the addition built so I can take some measurements?"

"Certainly." Her lips pursed into a frown. "Along this wall." She pointed at the corner of the dining nook. "What I want is a small solarium. You know, something glassed in so I can have a nice, bright area to drink my morning coffee? Having only one small window makes it quite dim and dank. What do you think?"

Tom looked around, taking out his tape measure. "I think it would brighten this room a lot. How far out were you thinking of going?"

"Twelve feet."

"Hmmm…"

"Will that be a problem? If you can't do it, I can call Jeff Filcher. He's always anxious for work."

She's already angling to cut the price, and I haven't even given her one, thought Tom. "No. I can do the job. I'll need to measure for sure, but it may have to be shortened to ten feet."

"Why? That extra two feet would bring it right up to my property line. I measured myself." She puffed out her chest, as if she'd renovated a whole house single-handedly with nothing more than a nail file and a spoon.

"That's just it. There needs to be a two-foot clearance from the property line."

"Why? It's my land. I can do whatever I want with it." Mrs. Weiss crossed her arms.

Tom winced. "Not according to the town."

"What?"

"It's a zoning requirement. When we apply for the building permit to make the addition, it can't be less than two feet from the property line. The only way around it is to get your neighbor's permission. Meg Zutterman lives there, if I'm not mistaken. We could ask her."

Defeat in her voice, Mrs. Weiss replied, "I don't think so. I know she works for your sister, and far be it for me to pass judgment on anybody"—she placed a hand over her heart—"but Mrs. Zutterman can be a little, how can I say this politely…difficult."

"Really? Janie always speaks highly of her. Would you like me to talk to her?"

"No. I don't want to be beholden to that woman." Her enthusiasm deflated, she sighed. "Ten feet will be fine."

Curious about her reaction, he asked, "Are you sure? I've always found her to be polite and proper whenever I've spoken with her at Janie's office."

" 'Proper' hits the nail on the head. She won't even admit that young man is her son. The poor boy." She made a clucking sound with her tongue.

Tom tilted his head, his curiosity piqued. Mustering every ounce of diplomacy, he said, "Mrs. Weiss, I don't mean to disagree with you. After all, the customer is always right"—he flashed a toothy grin—

"but Meg doesn't have any children. She and her late husband, Morton, never had kids."

She shook her head with another cluck. "I'm sure that's what Mrs. Zutterman told you, being she's ashamed of him. I could see her not wanting to tell me, with my children achieving such success. But to lie to her employer?"

"Meg has worked at the realty office for fifteen years. I'm sure she would have mentioned if she had a son. What makes you think she does?"

"I heard him with my own ears two days ago when the postal carrier put a piece of her mail in my box. No matter how much the post office raises its rates, their service continues to go down. I don't understand when people take no pride in doing a job right. Just the other day—"

Keeping this woman on topic proved to be a full-time occupation. "Mrs. Weiss, you were telling me why you think Meg has a son?"

"Oh, yes. Sorry. Sometimes I get sidetracked. Where was I?"

After sipping from his glass, Tom prompted, "You got a piece of Meg's mail by mistake."

"Right. Being a good neighbor, I waited until she got home from work to deliver it. When I saw her car in the driveway, I walked over. That's when I noticed his truck parked out front. It seemed strange he didn't have the trailer with lawnmowers and tools."

"What truck?"

She waved her arm in front of her. "You know, the landscaper who mows her lawn. He takes care of mine too."

"Which landscaper?" Tom's grip on the glass

tightened as he quelled his frustration at her dragging out a simple story. He swore she lollygagged on purpose, only doling out crumbs at a time to keep her audience hanging on.

"The one with the lawnmower on the side. It looks like a cartoon with a face."

Tom took his client a little more seriously. "You mean John Cooper's truck?"

"Yes, that's the young man's name, John Cooper. Anyway, as I approached the house, he looked about to walk out the screen door, then turned and yelled to Mrs. Zutterman."

He scrunched up his forehead. "How does that make him her son?"

"Because he called her 'Mother.' When the man noticed me, he looked as if he'd gotten caught with his hand in the cookie jar." She bobbed her head, accenting her last comment.

"Are you sure?"

With a hand on her hip, she spouted, "Of course, I'm sure. I may be getting old, young man, but my hearing is perfect. He called her 'Mother.' "

Tom put up his hands in surrender. "I'm sorry. I didn't mean to be disrespectful. It just seems strange she's never mentioned him."

"Like you pointed out before, she is very proper. It must bother her to no end having a son who is only a simple landscaper." She cast her eyes downward, as if John's occupation offended her too.

He attempted to view this from another angle, but the seeds of doubt took hold. Why would Meg not say anything to his sister? Yet, if John was Meg's son, he wouldn't have needed an introduction to Janie through her brother. As much as this old lady in front of him loved a good gossip fest, why would she make this up?

"So, what do you think?" Mrs. Weiss broke his concentration.

"I really don't know what to think."

"I mean about my solarium. Can you do it? And how much are you going to charge me?"

Tom shook his head at the sudden change of subject. "I'll have to go back to my office and do some calculations. Can I stop by Tuesday with the estimate, and we can go from there?" All he wanted to do now was hightail it out of there and talk to Janie.

"What time Tuesday?"

"How does nine o'clock sound?"

"Can you make it eight o'clock? I have my hair appointment every Tuesday at nine o'clock, and I never miss it." She patted her locks as if they were made of rare jewels.

Tom walked toward the front entry. "Eight it is. You have a nice evening."

"Thank you. You too." Mrs. Weiss followed Tom to the front doorway as he let himself out and hurried across the front lawn to his truck at the curb.

****

Once they reached Kelsey's, John pulled into a parking spot in a dark back corner.

"Don't tell me," Janie said as John helped her out, "you're one of those guys who can't stand to get a dent or ding on his truck?"

"What makes you say that?" John asked as they walked by several vacant spots. "This place fills up fast. I wanted to give those older folks a shorter trek to the restaurant." He gave her a wink.

Inside the entry John gave the maître d' his name. Relief flooded through Janie seeing old Roger wasn't at the podium. He'd been a fixture when she and Brian dined there but had probably retired by now. If he'd recognized her, it would have been awkward, as if she cheated with another man. This host said their table would be ready shortly and suggested a drink in the lounge while they waited.

John escorted Janie to a quiet corner of the bar with comfortable armchairs. He took a seat across from her. She ordered a glass of Summer Harvest White from one of the local vintners while John chose a draft.

They sat in silence until their drinks arrived. "So," Janie ventured, "not to sound too cliché, but do you come here often?"

"Actually, I've been here a few times. Usually when I have friends from out of town."

"Oh?"

"What you really mean is, do I bring other women here?" He smirked as she shifted in her seat.

Janie pressed her lips together. "That's not what I meant." She crossed her legs and leaned back into the cushion. "You're enjoying this, aren't you?"

"Immensely," he laughed. "To put your mind at ease, however, you're the first woman I've brought here on a date. Happy?"

"Immensely."

Five minutes after their drinks arrived a waiter approached. "Sir, madame, your table is ready. Please follow me. Shall I take your drinks?" he offered as he brought around his tray.

"Thank you," John said, allowing the young waiter to take each of their glasses off the table.

Janie followed with John close behind, guiding her with his hand on the small of her back. She stiffened. Brian had escorted her the same way. Stop it, she chided herself. Stop comparing.

The waiter led them toward the back of the restaurant. Plates loaded with pasta dishes and finely grilled meats tantalized Janie's taste buds. One server carried a whole lobster on a platter with buttered corn and coleslaw. Another had a bowl of steamers swimming in wine sauce. The couple were led onto an enclosed patio and seated at a table overlooking the beach.

How perfect, Janie thought. They couldn't have asked for a more spectacular view of the shoreline with the waves lapping onto the sand. John outdid himself setting up this romantic scenario. What if she didn't live up to his expectations?

Couples dotted the beach walking arm in arm. The night had a chilly nip to it but not for those willing to get in close and share warmth.

As Janie leaned down to set her purse on the floor, she heard her phone vibrate. Not the girls already. "I'm sorry," she said, taking out her cell and checking the caller ID. Tom's name lit up the screen, and she scowled. He knew she had a date tonight. She wouldn't allow him to ruin it with any of his shenanigans. With a press of the button on the side, the call went straight to voice mail.

"Everything okay?"

"Yes. I thought it might be the girls, but it was Tom. We're supposed to have breakfast together in the morning, but he probably has to cancel," she lied. "He can leave a message."

"Good thing, because I thought we'd be having breakfast tomorrow." He waggled his eyebrows.

Putting a hand to her chest, Janie emoted, "Excuse me? What kind of a girl do you think I am?"

"Certainly not that kind," he chuckled. "You do know I'm kidding, right?" His fingers pressed flat on the table as he leaned closer.

"I should hope so, sir." She continued to feign indignation.

"Now we've gotten the sleepover issue cleared up, what shall we talk about? Maybe what to do on our next date?" He tilted his drink her way then took a sip.

Her cheeks warmed. "Don't you think we should get through this one first?"

John acted as if he'd been jolted by lightning. "Get through it? You make it sound like a chore."

"I have to admit," she lowered her voice, "it does feel like work. As I might have told you, I'm new to this dating stuff."

He mimicked her pose and spoke in a hushed tone as well. "You may have mentioned it once or twice. How's it going so far?"

Janie sat up straight and flashed her best smile. "Quite nice, actually." She picked up her menu, and John followed suit.

They discussed the merits of the various seafood entrees before agreeing on two. Once they'd closed their menus, the waiter approached. John suggested Janie select a bottle of wine, deferring to her greater knowledge on the subject. She chose a Syrah she knew would pair nicely with the meal.

"So, who're these out-of-town guests you've brought here? Are they relatives?" Janie didn't know much about John other than his occupation and some likes and dislikes. Despite his knowing Carol and Tom, the man sitting opposite her remained a stranger. A moment of doubt filtered in as she thought about Brian's ominous warning of not trusting anyone. Surely, he didn't mean to include her social life.

"No, I don't have any family."

"What do you mean you don't have any family? Were you an orphan?" She sipped the last of her white wine.

"Nothing that dramatic. My parents died in an accident when I was twenty-three."

Janie put down her glass. "I'm sorry. I didn't mean to make light of it." While curious about the accident, she didn't want to pry. She watched the couple sitting behind John, jealous of their intimacy as their faces almost touched while they spoke in murmurs. Would there ever come a day when she would feel as comfortable on a date as the pair of them?

"How about you? Anyone else in town besides Tom?"

"Yes. My whole family's here." She regaled John with stories about her brother Jeremy and life with Ruth. She even threw in a few about Tom. Not wanting to monopolize the conversation, she tried to bring John into it by asking questions. Instead of answering, he encouraged her to keep talking about her relatives, as if he couldn't hear enough.

Throughout appetizers and the main course, Janie chatted happily about her life. Every time her wine glass came close to empty, John refilled it. She pointed out how he nursed his own drink, but he deflected her comment, saying he was the designated driver. Her comfort level elevated once their conversation flowed into an even exchange and not a one-sided monolog on her part. John continued to skirt around expressing too many details of his upbringing, yet his participation gave her confidence he enjoyed her company.

CHAPTER 22

When Tom heard his sister's voicemail greeting, he didn't leave a message. What could he say? "Hey, Janie, you know your date? He may be your secretary's son. Have a great time!" She would never take him seriously without hard proof. What if John really was Meg's son? Would it matter? Still, why not mention it?

As much as he wanted to leave this alone, something at the back of his mind urged him to dig deeper. Too many coincidences were cropping up, and he couldn't ignore them.

He tried calling Janie at home on the off chance she'd gotten cold feet and cancelled her date. No such luck. Jenny answered and sounded more excited than her mother about the date. She confirmed Janie had taken her cell phone.

According to Jenny, John took her mom to Kelsey's for dinner. That surprised him until he found out it was John's choice. One coincidence too many, Tom thought. Meg would have known about his sister's anniversary tradition with Brian. Maybe he didn't have to see a dead guy to know some force guided them.

He reluctantly settled for waiting until he met with Janie for breakfast in the morning. Meanwhile, he could do a little digging on the internet and see if he found any connections between Meg and John.

****

With the meal finished and the bill paid, Janie's anxiety returned. The beckoning of the final page had too strong a hold on her, and she found it hard to stay in the moment with her dinner companion, regardless of his charm. Having held the missing information in her hand without a chance to read it made her crazy. Her heart raced as she speculated on its content.

When she stood to leave, Janie swayed as she felt the effects of the wine. She gripped the edge of the table to steady herself. Another wave of nostalgia swept over her as John placed his hand on the small of her back again while they walked toward the exit.

"Why don't we go for a stroll on the beach before we leave?" John suggested, angling toward the sand.

"It's a little chilly for me. Do you mind if we head home?"

Sidling closer and putting his arm around her shoulders, John whispered, "I'll keep you warm."

The fuzzy effects of the wine taunted her to go with him and not analyze the scene. However, the lure of the final journal page, the memories of Brian, and the guilt of being out with another man weighed in heavier than the alcohol. "Maybe on our next date?"

"Then I won't take this as the brush off." Bowing and extending his arm with a flourish, he said, "As requested, I shall deliver you home." Halfway to the truck, he slowed his pace. "You know, I'd really like a chance to get to know Jenny and Natalie. I bet they're dying to check me out too."

"Oh?" Janie stopped. Wasn't it a bit soon to be spending time with her kids? Did she really know enough about this new man to involve her children? Jenny had needed time to warm up to her mother going on a first date. "What did you have in mind?"

"How about I come over on Sunday and barbecue?"

She mentally weighed the pros and cons of the offer. "That sounds nice."

"Just nice?" he joked. "I would invite you to my place, but your girls might feel more comfortable on familiar territory."

He did have a point about the girls wanting to check him out, as he put it. "You've put a lot of thought into this, haven't you?"

"I always like to have a plan." He held up both hands. "Now, I don't want to push you into anything you're not comfortable with. Though the girls did warm up to me before we left. What do you think?"

Another huge step of moving on from the loss of Brian loomed before her. She waffled on whether including the girls so soon would be appropriate. Rubbing her arms as if she felt a sudden chill, she tilted her chin up and said, "I think the girls would love it."

"And their mom?"

Her pulse quickened. "Their mom would love it too. How does two o'clock sound?"

"Great. I'll bring the meat and wine. Can you handle the rest?"

"Absolutely." She smiled.

Approaching the truck, he stepped ahead and reached for her door. Janie stumbled on the rough pavement. John caught her in one smooth move and pulled her in close. Without hesitating, he kissed her. Her lips lingered a moment before Janie pulled away.

"I'm sorry," John murmured. "I didn't mean to take advantage."

"You didn't." She pulled her sweater closer onto her shoulders, wrapping the open front around her waist. "We had better go."

John helped her into the truck. As he drove out of the parking lot, an odd silence settled between them. Neither spoke while they rode back to Janie's house. The radio poured out classic rock music from the seventies. He waited for his date to re-start the conversation. After stealing a kiss, he needed to tread carefully by not overplaying his hand and scaring her off. Her response had conveyed interest though.

Now that he had confirmation Janie possessed the last page of the journal, he wanted to schedule their date for Saturday but didn't want to come off as pushy. His mother would rake him over the coals for waiting two days, but it was his turn to handle things. She would have to trust him.

Mother should be happy at his discovering the missing page so quickly. It would also eliminate wasting time searching the house from top to bottom. All he had to do was figure out a good excuse to be upstairs. That shouldn't be hard. Granted, Janie could move the parchment between now and Sunday, but she seemed adamant her girls not read it. Her actions made it obvious she hadn't shared this business with Natalie and Jenny.

John pulled his truck into the driveway and parked behind Janie's car. Turning off the ignition, he drank in the beguiling sight beside him. Once more, he regretted she wasn't more like Carol. He would have loved to have taken her into the bedroom and continued before searching for the missing page. Life didn't always have to be all business. "This was one beautiful evening."

"I had fun. Thank you for dinner."

"The pleasure was all mine. Look—" He glanced down before meeting her eyes again. "—about what happened in the parking lot..."

Janie put up her hand. "Don't spoil it," she said gently. "It was sweet. Really. Let's just enjoy the memory of our first kiss."

"Since you put it that way..." He perked up. John walked around to the passenger's side, helped her out of the truck, and they strolled to the front stoop.

Janie pulled opened the screen door and unlocked the deadbolt. As she turned to John, he risked one more advance. Slowly he leaned his head down, stopping just short of her lips. Not disappointing him, Janie raised up to meet his mouth. He enjoyed another sweet kiss. They parted, and she put her hand on his chest. He covered it with his own.

"I'll see you Sunday, John."

"Can't wait."

He sauntered to his vehicle, resisting the urge to turn around. If she's still watching, he thought, I've got her hooked. Reaching for the handle, he glanced up before getting in. She remained on the cement steps. With a quick wave, Janie disappeared into the house. The deadbolt slid home before he got in behind the wheel. In a wave of unexpected emotion, his chest tingled at the spot her hand had been, and he felt her touch once again.

Driving back to his place, he savored the memory of their parting kiss. Maybe if he played this right, he and Janie could have a future together. His sudden wealth would be explained away as an inheritance from a long-lost uncle. The only bump in the road, besides

Mother, would be Carol.

****

Janie leaned against the front door, eyes closed, heart racing. Unprepared for her reaction, a humming sensation coursed through her body. When she and John had talked about simply "getting through tonight," it wasn't far from the truth. Now, bouncing up and down on her heels like a schoolgirl with a crush, she looked forward to Sunday.

Someone standing in front of her cleared her throat. Opening her eyes, Janie found two grinning kids staring at her.

"Are you okay, Mom?" Natalie asked.

"I think Mom's in love," proclaimed Jenny.

Poking her sister in the arm, Natalie chastised, "You don't fall in love that quickly."

"How would you know?" Jenny shoved her back. "Like you have so much experience."

"Kids." Natalie rolled her eyes at Jenny. "Mom, how was it?"

Shaking off the tranquil haze she'd lapsed into, Janie said, "Nice."

"Just nice?" they asked in unison.

She pushed off the door, and they followed her to the kitchen. "Okay, maybe a little more than nice."

"Does that mean you'll be going out with John again?" Jenny asked.

Janie sighed. "Actually, it's funny you should mention that." She set her purse on the counter and draped her sweater over a chair.

"Why?" Natalie narrowed her eyes.

"John wants to get to know you."

Jenny pulled at her mother's hand in excitement.

"Really? Does that mean we get to go on your next date?"

"Yes and no."

Natalie's voice remained suspicious. "What's that supposed to mean?"

"He's coming here for dinner on Sunday. John offered to barbecue but wanted to do it here so he could get to know the two of you. What do you think?" Janie now had second thoughts about the idea.

Jenny jumped up and down. "I think it's great. Can I make dessert? I can make brownies or cookies. Would that be okay?"

"Whatever you want, honey. Natalie, you haven't answered." Her warm feeling of only minutes ago waned.

"Honestly, Mom, it might be kind of weird. But it's okay. Is that what you want?"

"Yes. I'd really like you to get to know him."

"You like him, don't you?"

"Of course. I wouldn't have gone out with him if I didn't."

Natalie folded her arms over her chest. "That's not what I meant."

"I know. Yes, I do like him. It's too early to know how much. Does that answer your question?"

She nodded. "Yes. I like the smile he put on your face. And I think Sunday sounds like fun. Would you like me to make a salad?"

"That would be great," Janie said, the tension in her jaw easing. "I know it's not late, but I think I'll go to bed. All this excitement has worn me out. Good night, girls."

"Good night, Mom," Jenny said following her

upstairs as she went to her own room.

Natalie stopped in the living room. "I'll lock up down here. Good night."

"Thanks, honey. See you in the morning," Janie called from her bedroom before closing the door. She walked to the closet and kicked off her shoes, leaving them where they landed. Removing her earrings and necklace, she placed them in the jewelry box. Her hand lingered on the lid after closing it.

Examining her reflection in the mirror, she almost didn't recognize herself. She had a glow about her as she beamed, despite feeling a slight chill. Her mind wandered to the restaurant parking lot and their first kiss then flashed forward to the second at the front door. Lost in those private moments, she turned and stifled a scream.

William floated before her. The glow she thought came from her emanated around the young man in uniform. Composing herself, she thought, Oh, William, you couldn't give me one night off? Aloud she asked, "You know I found the final page, don't you William?"

He looked at her, imploring the same silent request. "Help me, Janie. Help me."

"Maybe I can help you now," she said, excitement building in her voice. "I know now you were trying to show me where it lay hidden that day in the office, but I didn't understand. I can find your treasure and return it to your family so you can rest."

The soldier looked even more forlorn while still mouthing the same words over and over as he faded away.

Wrinkling her brow, Janie wondered why he still acted upset. With the found page, she and Tom should be able to figure out exactly where the treasure lay buried. The mystery was finally coming to an end and, hopefully, they would find Brian's...Janie hesitated at even thinking the word.

Slowly, she went to the nightstand. Pulling open the drawer, she retrieved the envelope, then sat on the bed clutching it to her chest. Even if she could help William, would she be able to put Brian to rest? Locating this information didn't assure her of finding her husband.

With a deep breath, she carefully slid the papers out of the envelope. The loose page rested on top. Gently, as if it would disintegrate before her eyes, Janie unfolded the parchment. She recognized William's handwriting.

...walk ten paces. Turn right and walk eight paces more. You will be at a flower bed. Here lies your most precious treasure. The owners of the home were away, so I was able to bury your treasure here. Please know I tried my best to return it to you and the family. It was not meant to be. Give my regrets to Becky and know I will always love her.

Mama, please do not think poorly of me for failing. My broken body was not up to the task. I pray you will still be alive to receive this journal. I hope it gives you some comfort to know what happened to your sons. God be with you.

All my love,

William Pelter Carver

Janie reread the page three times. After all this waiting, the last passage was simple—and heart wrenching. So much loss had been connected to these few lines. It appeared William had dug up the treasure, then buried it again when he knew he wouldn't survive the journey back to Virginia. No mention of Benjamin beyond his succumbing to fever puzzled her. William didn't say anything about giving his brother a proper burial. Putting it down in words must have been too painful for him. He had let his mother and whole family down by not bringing back the treasure or his younger brother.

No wonder William looked in agony each time she saw him. The overwhelming guilt followed him to the grave.

Janie resisted the temptation to call Tom with these new revelations. Tomorrow would be soon enough. He would want to read it himself and rush right over the second she told him.

Her brain shifted into overload between her date with John and this new discovery. The anguish Brian had to have felt while attempting to extricate himself from this mess and protect his family must have been unbearable. No man should have to go through something like that alone. Had he confided in her, they might have been able to figure it out safely, and he would still be here with them. The more Janie learned convinced her Brian was dead.

She returned the papers to the envelope and tucked it away in the drawer. Changing into her pajamas, she crawled under the covers. For the first night in a week, she drifted off to a peaceful sleep.

CHAPTER 23

John cruised home replaying their parting kiss in his mind. Despite the evening ending sooner than expected, he'd made progress. It surprised him when he couldn't coerce Janie into a stroll on the beach. His charms rarely failed.

He pulled into his garage and hit the remote closing the door. He fingered his keyring until he found the one for the house. Beyond the den, he walked into the front entry. The tri-level house was just the right size for a bachelor—two spare bedrooms and a large master suite. A smirk spread across his face. Brian had shown him the house and closed the sale for the previous owner.

The chandelier, usually left off, illuminated the area. He must've flipped the switch absentmindedly when he left earlier. John whistled as he dropped his keys into the valet on the table, turned off the light, and mounted the five steps to the living room.

Striding up the final flight to the bedroom hallway, John hesitated, and his whistling stopped. The bathroom light on the far side of the master was on; he'd turned it off before leaving. The scent of lilacs hovered in the air. Stepping inside the room, he hit the switch.

Carol lounged on the bed in a skimpy black negligee. "Surprise," she purred.

"What're you doing here?" John held back his

anger. His date with Janie was supposed to have been a chore as far as Carol knew.

She pouted and turned over to give him a full view of her backside beneath the sheer mesh. "I thought you might enjoy a little company. Plus, I wanted to take your mind off any lingering thoughts of Janie."

"Who?"

"Good answer." She flipped onto her back again, allowing her left breast to slip out the front opening. "Maybe you could come here and give me a little attention."

John tugged off his shirt as he sauntered across the room. Wadding it up, he playfully tossed it at her.

Carol grabbed the garment, inhaled the fragrance, then hurled it back at him. "It smells an awful lot like Janie." She jumped off the bed and stormed toward the bathroom. "I'm getting dressed."

John cut her off and wrapped his arms around her. "Come on, babe, why so mad? I had to get close to her. After all, we were on a date." If he didn't do some major damage control, she would get completely out of hand—and unpredictable.

"How close?" Carol steamed, trying to wriggle free of his embrace.

"Just a cuddle here and there. Nothing more. You know I thought of you the whole time."

Her lips pursed. "Sure."

"Honest. Come back to bed, and I'll show you my appreciation for the part you played in all this. How 'bout it?" he coerced, sliding his hands down her backside and cupping the cheeks.

Carol sulked. "I don't know. You seemed to be in a great mood when you came home. Too good of a mood to have had a rotten time."

"You're the only one I want to be with. You should know that by now."

Her eyes blazed with jealousy. "You're falling for her." She stiffened to his touch.

"Why would I want someone like her when I've got you?" The more John tried convincing this bimbo of his fidelity, the more he wondered what he ever saw in her. Still, he glanced down at her cleavage. She did have her assets. He smothered her lips with his own—until she shoved him away, escaping his grasp.

"I can smell her on you. You kissed her." Carol stomped into the bathroom and slammed the door.

"Of course, I did. A good night peck, nothing more," he called from the other side of the door. "I rode in the same car with her, how else would her perfume get on my shirt? Believe me, this date was tamer than any time I've spent with you." He opened and closed his fists at his sides, the veins in his temples pulsing. Keeping his voice calm, he said, "Baby, don't be like this. You knew I had to do this to get near the journal—which, I might add, I caught a glimpse of when I was there." He could allow that much without giving his whole hand away. Not being on her good side would put him in a dangerous position.

The door flew open, and Carol stormed out fully dressed, forcing him to back up. "To think I agreed to help you in this scam."

"Think of the payoff. Janie will be no wiser, and we'll be off to the French Riviera in style." John grabbed her by the arms. "Put that sexy negligee back on, and I'll show you my undying gratitude. After all, if it hadn't been for you, my date never would have happened." He pulled her against him.

"I don't know." Her voice quieted, but her body remained rigid.

"Better yet," John said slipping his hand inside her shirt and gently caressing her breast, "forget the negligee—and the rest of the clothes."

She allowed him to pull the shirt over her head. Next, he reached down and tugged on her pants.

Instead of protesting, she unbuttoned his jeans and started to slide a hand down the front but got swept off her feet and carried to the bed. Her enthusiasm led him to believe all thoughts of Janie and the evening were forgotten.

John, however, wished the full head of hair in front of him was brunette not blonde. He made use of Carol's presence but imagined how good it could have been if it were Janie in his bed.

"Oh, Janie," he whispered.

Carol shoved him off and jumped out of bed. "I knew you couldn't resist her. You had sex, didn't you?"

"No. It was just a good night kiss."

Jabbing a finger in his direction, she yelled, "Don't lie to me. Sweet, innocent Janie, my ass. You pulled off the road and screwed her right there in your truck."

John crept toward her. "Babe, think about what you're saying. You know she wouldn't do something like that. Besides, it wasn't the objective."

"Well, I think you lost sight of your objective!"

"Carol, get hold of yourself. Nothing like that happened."

Searching the room, she retrieved her clothes and put them back on. "To think I came here to surprise you. What was I thinking? The deal's off." Fully clothed, she reached for her purse and slipped the strap over her shoulder. "Tomorrow I'm going over to Janie's and making a new deal. Your friend can't be the only one out there looking to acquire rare Civil War journals. I'm sure Janie will be more than happy to split the profits with me as a finder's fee."

"I wouldn't do that if I were you. In order to let Janie know how much the journal is worth you'll have to fess up to your part in this whole scheme." All the time he spoke, John inched nearer. "Friendship might not cover deception. Come back to bed, and we'll talk about this rationally."

Pushing his chest, she yelled, "Get out of my way, you bastard. I'm leaving."

"Sorry, babe." A menacing calm descended on him, and his expression grew cold. "It's too late for that."

She hesitated. Fear shone in her eyes. The trapped woman frantically looked for an escape route, but he blocked the only one. Carol took a breath. "Okay, baby." Her voice quivered. "Maybe I...you know...overreacted. How else should I act? You were out with another woman."

John edged closer. She stepped back.

"Baby"—Carol held up her hands—"let's sleep on this, and we'll talk in the morning. Yeah, that's what we should do. We'll both get a good night's sleep, then I'll come back, and we can make up." Her body trembled. "Making up is always the best, right?"

John encircled her waist and cracked a smile. "You're right. We both overreacted." One hand traveled up and palmed the back of her head, pulling her closer.

Carol's frame relaxed as he kissed her gently on the lips until his hands wrapped around her neck and squeezed. Her eyes bulged as she struggled for breath, pulling at his hands.

"Please," she rasped.

He stared into her eyes, his gaze never wavering. "Sorry, babe. Your price got too high. You understand, don't you?" He watched the terror glisten in her eyes until it went out.

When her head lolled to the side, he loosened his grip. Carol's lifeless body crumpled to the floor in a tangle of arms and legs like a rag doll.

Leaning back against the dresser, John slid to a sitting position. His arms rested on his knees with his head atop them. After several moments, he looked at the broken body beside him and emitted a guttural yell, pounding the floor with his fist. Mother would not be pleased. He knew what he had to do.

John hadn't seen her car when he came home. To keep up the façade of his being unattached, she rarely came to the house. She must have used the hide-a-key to let herself in. Rising to peek out the front window, he located her red sportster down the street. He'd wait a couple hours until he was sure the neighbors were asleep. Meanwhile, he went downstairs then returned with a pair of rubber gloves, cleanser, and a rag. He wiped down the bedroom, bathroom, and anywhere else in the house she might have touched. Retrieving the spare key from under the porch mat, he rubbed it with the rag as well before putting it back. When finished, he placed everything inside a plastic bag and left it by the front door.

John wrapped Carol's body in a blanket and carried

it down to the front entryway. When one a.m. rolled around, he pulled her car into the driveway without turning on the headlights and loaded her into the trunk. Before leaving, he scanned the master bedroom and bathroom one more time, making sure all her belongings were removed. He grabbed the bag with the cleanser and gloves on his way.

The drive to Carol's took fifteen minutes. She lived in a four-bedroom colonial on a quiet street. Who was he kidding? All the streets in this town were quiet. Pulling into her driveway, John pressed the button on the remote and drove into the garage. He clicked the button again and waited for the door to close before exiting the car.

He prided himself on remembering to pull the seat back to its original position, so it looked like Carol had been driving. These cops may be small town, but some of them were sharp. Everything here would need to be wiped down thoroughly too.

It should be easy to stage a scene looking as if she'd brought home the wrong guy for a tumble. With Carol's reputation, it wouldn't be a far stretch for the authorities to conclude. He went to her bedroom in the rear of the house and closed the blinds before turning on the light.

Back in the garage, he had just enough space to get behind the car and open the trunk. Lifting the corpse, he carried her to the bedroom, dropped her on the bed, and removed the blanket. John thought about putting the negligee back on but settled for stripping her and leaving the clothes scattered about the floor. Returning to the car, he grabbed her belongings and the bag of cleaning tools.

The lingerie got dumped into the hamper, already filled with similar clothing. He reminisced about all the seductive outfits he'd taken pleasure in peeling off her. Setting her purse and keys on the kitchen counter, John began a thorough cleaning, concentrating on the bedroom. They hadn't spent much time in the rest of the house, except morning coffee in the kitchen. A maid service came twice a week, so hopefully any evidence there had been wiped away.

Before leaving, he took one last look at Carol's lifeless figure. She really was a looker and great in the sack. Too bad it had to end this way, but like his mother always said, no sense leaving loose ends lying about. In this case he'd have to make an exception, he smirked, carrying the blanket as he left.

As an afterthought, John returned to the garage and ran the rag over her car one more time, being sure to clean off the button on the remote. He wiped the door handle to the house, went inside, and bumped it shut with his elbow. Carrying the cleaning bag and blanket, he used the tail of his shirt to cover his hand as he opened the back door, twisted the lock, then pulled it closed behind him. The lock clicked in place.

With any luck, the body wouldn't be discovered until Monday when the cleaning girl came. Carol hated having the house cleaned while she was home. This meant her housekeeper wouldn't arrive until after the salon opened. By then he and Mother should have the journal. He might be well on his way to a lasting relationship with Janie after Sunday's barbecue too.

John slipped through the open gate and hurried down the street and out the neighborhood. Tempted to call his mother for a ride, he decided the night air would help clear his mind. While strolling, he composed an alibi, just in case, but his date should cover most of the time.

The walk home took almost an hour and a half. John did his best to stick to the side streets. Passing through an alley behind a row of businesses, he tossed the bag into a dumpster. It was full, which meant it would be emptied in the next day or two. When he arrived at his own neighborhood, he appreciated how devoid of life the street remained this time of night.

Letting himself in through the front door, John dropped the blanket in the laundry room, then went to the bedroom. This time there would be no surprise visitors. Wearily, he undressed and crawled into bed. As he slid under the sheets, the scent of Carol's perfume assaulted him. He'd do something about that in the morning.

CHAPTER 24

Tom arrived at Janie's back door by eight. After a quick knock, he let himself in. "Hello, anybody home?"

Janie carried her mug into the kitchen. "You're up early."

"As are you," he said. "How was your date?"

"It was nice."

"Just nice?"

Lifting her arms in the air, she asked, "Why does everyone keep asking me that? Can't I say a date was 'nice' without people reading more into it?"

"Okay, so it was nice." Tom poured himself a cup of coffee. "That's nice."

"Stop it. Besides, I have exciting news." Janie bounced up and down on her heels.

"Me too, but you first. When's the wedding?"

Smacking her brother's shoulder, she said, "Can you focus for one minute?"

"I'll try my best."

She set her mug on the counter and hurried out of the kitchen, saying over her shoulder, "I'll be right back."

Returning with her hands behind her, she asked, "Remember I told you about William appearing in the office and pointing at me?"

"Yeah."

"He wasn't pointing at me, but at this." She held up

the picture of her and the girls.

"And?" Tom prompted.

"It was sitting on the desk."

Taking the picture from her, Tom repeated, "And?"

"When William startled me, I accidentally knocked it off, cracking the glass. Later, Jenny found it, and said she had a frame I could use."

"If you don't make a point soon, the next time I'm alone with your kids I'll pump them full of espresso and give them each a puppy. Now, what does this picture have to do with William?"

"I'm sorry." She held out the final page of the journal. "When Jenny replaced the frame, she found this behind the picture. It explains so much."

Tom's eyebrows shot up as he plucked the paper from her hands, sloshing his coffee over the edge of his mug onto the floor. "William actually pointed at—"

"—the picture," Janie finished. "This is what Brian meant when he said the secret lies with the girls and me. By the way, I got another visit last night." She grabbed a paper towel and mopped up the spill.

"Was he doing a happy dance?"

"Not exactly. I'm sure he knew I found this and can locate the treasure. I told him as much. Who knows if he can even hear me? His face still contorted with pain, and he mouthed the same words."

Tom sat at the table. "Maybe he's stuck in a loop."

"He's not a video."

"I'm making suggestions, given neither of us has had any experience with the supernatural—at least until now. Are you going to start your own reality show?"

"Not amused."

He examined the page. "All we have to do is find

the south corner of the original barn, and we've got the treasure."

"Yes. Can you believe it? It shouldn't be hard for us to figure out."

Tom jumped up and hugged his sister. "So, what's our next step?"

"We go to the property. I have the complete file here, so we can go over the original plans and compare them to the way the place looks now."

"Great." Tom sat, gesturing to the seat across from him. "Before we do that, I need to talk to you about something else."

Janie's enthusiasm fizzled as she eased onto the chair, her lips a straight line.

"Last night, did you and John talk about his family?"

Wrinkling her forehead, she asked, "That's a weird question. Why would you ask?"

Putting up his hands, he said, "Humor me. Did you talk about relatives?"

"As a matter of fact, we did." She tilted her head. "He said his parents died in an accident when he was twenty-three and he had no siblings. Why?"

"You sure?"

Agitation crept through her voice. "What do you mean am I sure? Tom, what's this about?"

"Last night I stopped by Mrs. Weiss' house to do an estimate for an extension on her kitchen." He paused.

"Are you going to tell me what's going on, or do I have to play twenty questions?"

Leaning back, he sipped his coffee. "Trust me, there's a point. I know she's a busybody and likes getting into everyone's business. Last night…well…she said something odd about John and his mother."

"What're you talking about? Mrs. Weiss lives next door to Meg, right?"

"Exactly." As if this should make it clear.

Janie pushed for information. "And?"

"And Mrs. Weiss said John was Meg's son."

"What?" She bolted up straight. "Meg doesn't have any children. I think I'd know if she did."

"That's what I said, but Mrs. Weiss sounded sure of herself." Tom related the story the woman told him. Finishing, he added, "Like I said, she's nosey but not senile. She was adamant about hearing John call Meg 'Mother.' "

Walking across the kitchen, Janie turned. "Why would John lie? For that matter, why would Meg lie? All these years she led us to believe Morty, her late husband, died, leaving no other relations. It doesn't make sense. They don't even have the same last name."

"I know, but that's what Mrs. Weiss told me. Besides, it's possible John isn't Morty's son. Maybe Meg had a prior marriage. That's why I tried your cell last night—and I know you sent my call to voice mail."

"Don't take it personally. I assumed you were calling to give me a hard time."

"Come on, you know me better than that."

Sitting back down, Janie smirked. "Yes, I do. That's why I didn't answer."

"Touché. I called to see if you could get it straight from the horse's mouth, so to speak."

"Here I thought our biggest challenge would be figuring out which of the Brassel Field properties belonged to the Pelter family and the location of the original buildings."

Tom tilted his mug toward his sister in a toast. "Never a dull moment, huh, Sis?"

"This whole thing is absurd. Why would either of them lie? Mrs. Weiss is off her rocker and trying to stir up trouble."

"I don't know. She seemed pretty certain. Last night I thought about doing an online search to see if I could find any connection between Meg and John, but my internet wouldn't work."

Janie refilled her cup. "Can we focus on the final journal page for right now?"

"Sure. Just promise me you'll be careful about John. He seems like a good guy and all, but if this has any truth to it—"

"I know." She cut him off. "He'll be over here tomorrow."

"Tomorrow? Doesn't that man know about the three-day rule?"

She wrinkled her nose. "Three-day rule?"

Tom shifted in his chair. "Yeah. A guy is supposed to wait three days before calling a girl after getting her number and after the first date. What an amateur." He snorted.

"Guess he doesn't abide by all those guy rules. He's coming over for barbecue and to get to know the girls."

He put his hands to the sides of his head, looking like the figure in Munch's painting The Scream. "Are you trying to scare him off?"

"By his spending time with my kids?" Janie asked warily.

"No. You can't barbecue. Do you want to poison

him?"

She slapped her brother on the arm. "Very funny. Besides, he'll be working the grill."

"Maybe your brother Tom should be invited to this little soirée." He bristled.

"Thanks, but I think I'll fly solo on this one. Can we please focus on Brassel Field? I have the file laid out in the office."

"All right."

Topping off his java, Tom followed her out of the kitchen. Janie took a seat behind the desk while he sat in the chair opposite. She had the original and a copy spread out so they each could look one over.

"I spoke with Larry on Friday morning," Janie mentioned.

"You work with the guy. Doesn't that happen daily?"

Her eyes narrowed.

"I'm sorry. What did you talk about?"

Janie told him about her discussion at the office and his telling her to burn the book.

"Did he admit to seeing the ghost?"

"He never said the words, only hinted at seeing something. I took it to be William."

Tom shrugged. "Sounds like you're right, but there's no point exploring further. If he was willing to come clean, he would have by now."

"There's more. He left early before we could talk again, so I went by his house. I figured he must think we're in trouble since he told me to burn the journal," Janie continued.

"Did he say anything else?"

She nodded. "He knew Brian was…was dead. At

least he assumed since he never came back after his meeting at Brassel Field with whomever threatened them. Larry also told me these people said they'd kill his wife, my kids, and me. That's why he backed off and wanted nothing more to do with it when Brian wouldn't surrender the journal. My husband didn't believe they'd leave us alone if he gave them the book. That's why he removed the last page."

"Did Larry know where Brian had hidden it?"

"No. Before I could get any more out of him, William made an appearance. From Larry's reaction, it wasn't his first sighting of the young soldier. The man ran into the house, slammed the door, and our discussion was over."

Tom's chair creaked as he leaned back. "Wow. What a party killer. That ghost needs to work on his timing. I guess we'll keep plugging along with what we've got here then."

Indicating the paperwork in front of them, Janie said, "This lot consists of three properties. I guess at one time the same person owned all of them. Right now, they're up for sale separately. Even years ago, property taxes were high, so the land got split into three parcels. This one in the middle at 483 Lake Road seems the most likely."

"Why?"

"See these notations along the edges of the original plot map? That's Brian's handwriting. He must have researched it. There's a lineage included too. One of the owners during the Revolutionary War was Jacob Pelter. In the journal, William stated his full name as being William Pelter Carver, a direct descendent of Jacob. This must be the property."

Tom nodded. "Sounds logical to me. Look at the current layout though. There's the main house, but the barn is newer. Can you tell if it stands on the original location?"

They studied the map of the original property compared to the new buildings and discovered the location of the barn had changed. Originally, it lay south of the house. The new one stood directly behind and a little to the north. They must have cleared land to make room for a larger one since the dimensions were twice the size of the old structure.

"This went a lot quicker than expected," Tom said. "I thought we'd have to spend the day tearing your house apart looking for the missing page. Good thing you're clumsy."

"I guess I got a little distracted with a ghost standing in front of me." She chuckled. Looking up at her brother, a gasp escaped her lips.

Jenny stood in the doorway. "What ghost, Mom? Did you see a ghost? Did you see Daddy?"

Janie waved her hand. "No, honey, Uncle Tom and I were joking."

"Uncle Tom!" Jenny ran over and threw her arms around his neck. "Why were you and Mom talking about ghosts?"

"What about ghosts?" Tom opened his mouth wide.

"But Mom said…"

He broke into a grin. "I told her about a dumb television show I saw. Don't worry, there aren't any floating about here…at least that I've seen." He winked at his sister.

Janie raised her eyebrows.

"So," he changed the subject, "what's for breakfast?"

"Do you want me to make some bacon and eggs?" Jenny offered.

"Sounds delicious. Why don't I help?" He followed his niece to the kitchen. "Should we make some for Natalie?"

Jenny shook her head. "It'll be cold by the time she gets up. You know her."

"Okay, just for the three of us then."

Janie sat back in her chair surveying the papers as a flush of sadness ran through her. Everything had fallen into place, and they could go to the property. She had the keys from the original file. Regardless of what they'd find, her heart knew the inevitable fact—Brian would still be dead.

As a precaution, she locked the real estate files and keys in the office cabinet. Next, the papers from Brian, including the completed journal, got tucked into their envelope and stowed in her bedroom nightstand.

She now regretted her barbecue date with John. Their mid-afternoon lunch didn't allow enough time to go out to Brassel Field tomorrow. In case it took them a while to look around, she didn't want to risk getting home late. It would be awkward finding her guest sitting on the front stoop waiting. Today was out of the question. They had back-to-back soccer games for both girls this afternoon. She would ask Tom if he could get away mid-week.

****

John lingered in bed remembering the previous evening with Janie. A smile crept across his face thinking about their good night kiss—the softness of her hair, the scent of peonies, and the gentle teasing of her touch on his chest before they parted. He wanted more.

Inhaling as if he could conjure up her fragrance, the harsh scent of Carol's perfume scorched his nostrils. She wore heavier, floral tones, more overpowering than enjoyable. John dove out of bed and tore the sheets from the mattress. Pulling off the pillowcases, he carried the load downstairs to the washer.

He thought about stuffing the blanket in too but decided to do two loads so all traces of the blonde got eliminated. John had done his best to be discreet while seeing her, but he couldn't know who might have noticed them together. He needed to have his ducks in a row should a clue lead to his doorstep.

Carol's body wouldn't get discovered until Monday, giving him a little breathing room. Good thing she didn't work on Saturday.

He went to the bedroom and donned a pair of work jeans with one of his landscaping T-shirts. Back in the kitchen, he pulled out bacon, eggs, and a roll of biscuits from the refrigerator. John leisurely set about making breakfast while the coffee brewed. More than once he imagined what Janie might be doing. He knew her brother would be there having breakfast. She was a very family-oriented woman—something he never had. Mother hated family get-togethers when Morty's family invited them over. What would it be like to wake up next to somebody, the same somebody, every morning? If he played his cards right, he would find out.

After cleaning up the kitchen, he scoured the rest of the house. While he'd done a thorough scrub down the night before, John wanted to check once more for any traces left by Carol. He found her black lace bra on the floor between the sink and tub in the master bathroom. Scrunching the delicate fabric into a ball, he stuck it in a rag bin in the garage. Trash didn't go out until Tuesday, and he didn't want to chance stowing it in a drawer.

Shortly before ten, he grabbed his truck keys. Mother expected him over to mow the lawn. His curiosity gave him pause, afraid to know what she had meant by having an insurance policy. That woman never fell short on schemes.

CHAPTER 25

Meg transferred her groceries from the cart to her car. She preferred shopping early, before all the coupon-toting mothers bogged down the lines at the checkout stands. Most of those teenaged cashiers had no idea how to spell customer service, let alone practice it in getting patrons rung up quickly. Anything out of the ordinary and they flipped the switch on their register light, popped their chewing gum, and waited for a manager to stroll over and save the day.

Her plans to shop the night before were replaced with a trip to the hardware store to have a copy of Janie's house key made. Still relishing her discovery, she splurged at the butcher shop on a fresh T-bone. With her superb barbecue skills, it would be a nice Sunday treat. Meg wanted to invite John to join her, but with nosey Mrs. Weiss sniffing about she couldn't take the chance.

When Meg swung into her driveway, John's truck and trailer sat parked by the curb between her property and Mrs. Weiss'. He mowed the neighbor's front yard. Hers would be next.

She pulled inside the garage, then carried the bags into the house. Grabbing the last two, she hit the garage door button, closing off the outside world. She couldn't wait for the day when she could afford a home far away from the prying eyes of neighbors. The only people she needed around for miles were servants.

An hour later she answered a knock on her front door. Meg opened it to find John holding a paper in his hand. She insisted he do that moving forward so it looked as if he brought her a bill. He wore an ear-to-ear grin.

Barely inside, he announced, "Mother, I saw it!"

"Hush," she scolded. "I don't need that busybody next door eavesdropping like she did the other day." Meg slammed the front door after him, grazing his elbow. John winced but said nothing.

"That old bat didn't hear a thing. Stop obsessing."

"Obsessing? Obsessing! One wrong move, and all my hard work will go spiraling downward. Remember, I've been at this a lot longer than you." She jabbed her finger at her son.

"And you've never been closer," he said with a smug grin.

Catching his tone, Meg's eyes glistened. "What do you mean? Did you get it? So, Janie is as much of a slut as that dumb hairdresser, huh?"

"No, Mother. Janie is a lady."

Meg scoffed at his comment.

"I saw it."

"The journal? The page? What?"

"The last page."

Meg anxiously wrung her hands. "Are you sure? What did it say?"

"I didn't get to read it, but I know where she's keeping it." John related the events of the previous night.

Each time he tried to mention how the date went, his mother cut him off. Those details should be kept to himself, she insisted. She gave no reaction when he said he'd be back at Janie's house on Sunday.

"No need for further exploration," Meg said. "I told you I have an insurance policy, and now would be the time to put it into action."

"You mentioned that yesterday. What're you talking about?" John followed her to the kitchen where the scent of freshly brewed coffee lingered.

She picked up her purse and retrieved a small plastic bag with a key in it. Holding it out, she said, "I've made a copy of her house key. Now you don't need to keep seeing her. You can slip into the house while she and the kids aren't home. No more entanglements, and we get the final piece of information."

"Mother, slow down." John's eyes grew wide as his mother ripped the dream of being with Janie from his grasp. "I can't pull away from her without looking suspicious. If I keep seeing Janie, I may win her trust, and she'll take me into her confidence. It would come full circle with no need for further deception."

Meg's jaw dropped toward the floor. Recovering her powers of speech, she asked, "Please tell me you're not saying what I think you're saying?"

"If you hear me saying I want to continue dating Janie, then yes, you've got it right."

She stormed across the kitchen, her loafers squeaking on the tiles. Turning around, she spat, "What on Earth are you thinking? Your delusions of domestic bliss are going to sabotage my plan. Do you intend to tell her what's really going on?"

"Of course not. Don't be daft. I don't plan on being that honest with her. All I'm saying is if I get her to trust me, I might not need to steal it from her."

"Johnny." Meg applied sugar instead of vinegar as she relaxed the muscles in her jaw. "You told me you know where she put it. All I'm saying is you can slip into the house, retrieve the page, and nobody will know." She held the key out to him. "Take it. Keep your date with the woman tomorrow, but use it if you see fit."

"Fine." John snatched the bag out of his mother's hand and stuffed it into his pocket. "How did you get this anyway? Did you steal it from her purse at work?"

"I found it on the floor near Janie's desk after she left Friday. This morning I'd planned on returning it, but I saw Larry's car parked in the lot. He couldn't possibly be working, but who knows with him. The man is afraid of his own shadow. You know if you hadn't pushed that moron so hard, we might have gotten him to take care of this."

Waving his arms in the air, he said, "Mother, must we relive that again? I enjoyed it so much the first time we went round about the topic."

"Don't get smart with me, Johnny. You know he might have given it up."

"As it turns out, he didn't have the final entry. Treading lightly with him wouldn't have mattered."

"Brian might have confided in him, but you scared Larry so badly." Meg's voice escalated again. "I'm surprised he didn't pick up and leave town when his partner disappeared."

He raised his hands in surrender.

In a controlled voice, she said, "Okay. Keep your date. If you can't get the page tomorrow, then use the key when she's at work on Monday."

"All right. I can live with that plan, but I don't think I'll need it."

Meg broached another concern. "Now, since you have gotten to Janie, what are you going to do about that blonde tramp? You need to extricate yourself from her as soon as possible."

"Funny you should mention her," John said with a mirthless chuckle.

"Did you already dump her?" Meg asked. "I knew you would come to your senses and send her packing."

"Let's just say, she's out of the picture." He squared his shoulders.

Her brows arched in alarm. "What do you mean by that?"

"All you need to know, Mother, is I handled it."

Meg gripped the back of a chair, her knuckles turning white. "What did you do?"

"For once, believe me when I say I took care of it. She won't be a problem."

"I hope not. The moment you took up with her, I knew she would be trouble."

Through gritted teeth he sneered, "As you've mentioned—many times."

Walking to the sink, she picked up a sponge and fastidiously wiped the counter. "You better get out of here. We don't want—"

"I know, I know." Exasperation filled his voice. "So Mrs. Weiss doesn't start peeking in the windows."

"Don't take this lightly."

John leaned over and gave her a peck on the cheek. "I'll talk to you tomorrow."

Without turning, she said, "Let me know as soon as you have the page." His footsteps echoed as he headed toward the front door. It bothered Meg the way he wouldn't share details of how he had handled Carol. Whatever Johnny did, she hoped it wouldn't come back to haunt them.

****

The line rang several times before going to voicemail. The greeting began, "Hi, this is Carol. I'm sure I'm out doing something fun. And guess what? You probably aren't. So, leave me a message, and next time I might include you." The device beeped.

"You must be doing something fun," Janie said, "since you didn't call me first thing this morning to find out how my date went with John. It's two o'clock, and I'm in between soccer games for the girls. I left a message on your cell, which you obviously didn't answer. Where are you? Call me. And by the way, it went great!" Janie disconnected. How strange. Carol had been all over her to go out with John, and now she couldn't reach her to tell her about it. Knowing her friend, she had an encounter of her own and might still be on it. That woman led such a wild life.

"C'mon, Sis, the game is about to start." Tom didn't have anything planned for the day, and his nieces had begged him to watch them play soccer. The season was almost over with the playoffs next weekend. He'd become a huge presence in their lives since his brother-in-law's disappearance.

"I'm coming. I've been trying to reach Carol."

Elbowing her, he asked, "To tell her about your nice date?"

"Men will never understand how some things must be shared with a girlfriend."

With a crooked grin, he said, "Knowing Carol,

she's probably out doing the wild thing with her latest pick-up."

"Tom! Quiet before the girls hear you." It bothered her more because he had the same thought as she did.

Motioning to the field, he said, "With all this shouting, I'm surprised you can hear me."

Janie tucked her phone into a back pocket, slipped under the canopy, and settled onto a camp chair. The girls' games were on the same field, so they'd set up their little encampment early to enjoy the afternoon.

"You know," Tom said as he stretched his arms up and backward, "I could get used to being a soccer mom. What do you think?"

"I'll let Cassie know. I'm sure she'll be thrilled to know the part you aspire to play in child rearing."

With a playful slap on his leg, Natalie squealed, "Uncle Tom, you can't be a mom."

"I didn't say mom; I said I want to be a soccer mom. There's a difference."

"Your uncle's funny," giggled Natalie's teammate, who also had a sister on Jenny's team. Both girls looked at Tom then at each other before rolling around on the blanket laughing.

Janie pointed at the two girls while looking at Tom. "That's your doing, you know."

"I do good work, don't I? Now, shhhh, the game is about to start." Tom hunkered down with his elbows on his knees and stared intently at the field.

****

Driving home from his mother's, John considered sneaking into Janie's house using the key. If he found the journal page today, he could relax and enjoy her company while getting to know the girls. He always thought he'd be a good dad. Since he grew up without one—Morty never acted like a father to him—he knew all the things not to do. The girls could grow to love him, as would Janie.

If only it were a weekday. He knew for sure nobody would be home with work and school. Weekends were too risky. Even if he called and nobody answered, there would be no assurance they wouldn't return at any time. He'd have to be patient and wait until tomorrow.

John bought ribeye steaks at the butcher shop for Sunday. The irony of Carol's ex-husband owning the place didn't elude him. At the liquor store he picked up the perfect wine for the meal. He consulted the owner for a recommendation as his preferences leaned toward a good draft. For now, it had to be all about her. Not overlooking an opportunity to schmooze the girls, he included a bottle of sparkling cider.

Without a doubt, his second date would be another small victory.

CHAPTER 26

Janie awoke early and spent Sunday morning poring over the journal and Brassel Field files. Not discovering anything new, she stowed everything in her briefcase and left it under the desk. Monday she would confront her partner again. He may not want to deal with this mystery, but she needed his help. Larry must have some idea of who else was involved, despite denying any knowledge.

Her encounters with William still caused the blood to run cold in her veins. While getting used to his appearances, it disturbed her to think a boy who had been dead for almost two centuries hung about. Janie now understood the strain Brian had been going through, on top of the threat to his family.

****

Meg pulled into the parking lot of Charger Realty and muttered a quiet thanks at finding it empty. She couldn't imagine why Larry would have been here on a Saturday, especially after making it clear he was gone for the weekend.

A tabby cat crossed her path as she hurried for the entrance. Without a second thought Meg booted the pesky feline out of her way. The animal yowled and scurried off.

Unlocking the front door, she entered then turned the bolt behind her. She didn't want customers stopping in thinking they were open. Meg retrieved the keyring from her purse and went into her employer's office.

As she dropped the ring behind the back leg of Janie's desk, Meg spied a paper on the blotter that wasn't there Friday. So that's what Larry had been up to yesterday. The note stated he and his wife had an out-of-town emergency and would be gone for at least a week. "Hmmpf," she snorted. Nothing like slinking away without giving anyone a chance to ask questions.

He'd left a list of rescheduled meetings—all a week out or more.

Meg snatched the note, crumpling it as she stuffed the paper into her purse and left the building. At a brisk pace, she hurried to her car, got in, and fired up the ignition. She drove out of the lot certain nobody would have noticed her being there in the brief ten minutes she'd spent. Most people were either on their way to church or already sitting in their self-assigned pew.

Gloating at her success, she flipped on the radio. They carried an excellent classical music program on the local station. Tuning into the middle of a sonata by Schumann, she tried to place the title. As the piece ended and she neared her neighborhood, the station reached its top-of-the-hour news.

"Tragedy has struck the Suffolk County area," the announcer said. "A local woman has been found..."

A few seconds later, Meg slammed on the brakes. The tires squealed and left tread marks on the pavement as her car skidded to a stop on the side of the road. Struggling to reach her purse where it had landed on the floor, she unhooked her seatbelt, yanked up the bag, and snatched out her cell phone.

She hit the speed dial. Her free hand tapped on the

steering wheel while she waited for John to pick up. After several rings her call went to voicemail. When the message ended, followed by a beep, Meg yelled, "Call me immediately." Dialing his home number gave the same result. She didn't bother leaving another message.

Shifting the car back into gear, Meg flew down the street and turned into her neighborhood. As she drove past Mrs. Weiss' house, whose owner was outside on the front lawn, Meg didn't return the wave offered by her neighbor. She barely slowed enough to allow the garage door to go up all the way. As she poked the button to close it behind her, she caught sight of Mrs. Weiss in the rearview mirror. The woman shook her head with lips pursed.

Meg stormed into the house, cell phone in hand. Throwing her bag on the kitchen counter, she pressed redial. No answer. She resisted the urge to drive straight to her son's place.

****

Early in the afternoon, Janie fussed about the kitchen making sure all the fixings for the barbecue were in place. A nervous shudder went through her—which meant she wanted things to go well between John and the girls. The brief introductions the other night weren't the same as spending time together.

It would have been helpful to get a little insight from Carol about what all this meant. That is, if Carol would answer her phone. It must have been some date she went on Friday night.

The doorbell rang, and both girls screamed in unison they would get it then stampeded down the stairs. How could two thin girls make so much noise? John had arrived ten minutes early. If he wanted to play it cool, he would have been fashionably late.

As if she hadn't heard the commotion in the living room, Jenny yelled, "Mom, John's here."

Janie walked to the front of the house, resisting the urge to run and throw herself into his arms. "Hi, John. Right on time."

"I couldn't wait to get here. How often do I get to spend a few hours with three beautiful women?"

Natalie and Jenny giggled.

A warm tingle rushed across Janie's cheeks.

He extended a bottle, which Janie accepted with a slight nod. The label touted a cabernet from a local vintner—the same one she had cooling in the wine refrigerator. Small hairs on the back of her neck prickled.

"Why don't you show me to the grill where I can get these babies started?" John gestured toward the pan in his other hand.

She peeked under the foil and saw steaks marinating. "Wow, what a treat. We were expecting hamburgers."

"I could run out and exchange these, if you prefer."

"No," she exclaimed, a little too quickly. "Those look great."

Jenny piped in, holding up the sparkling cranberry-apple cider. "Look what he brought us, Mom. I love this stuff. Did Mom tell you?" she asked John.

"Just a lucky guess. Apparently, a very lucky guess." He snuck a glance toward his date.

Without another word, Janie led the way to the kitchen. She put the wine on the counter and escorted John outside to a large porch off the back of the house. A short staircase in the middle went to an expansive backyard currently boasting a volleyball net. The girls immediately ran down the stairs and began to hit the ball back and forth. Janie wasn't the only one wanting to make a good impression.

The barbeque sat on the far side of the patio underneath a metal awning. John placed the pan of steaks on the side burner and went to work igniting the gas. "It'll take a few minutes to heat up."

"Why don't I pour us each a glass of the delicious cabernet you brought?" offered Janie.

"Sounds good to me. Since you already know how delicious it tastes, I take it you've had that one before?"

"Actually, it's one of my favorites. Another lucky guess, huh?" She flashed a smile. "You have a seat while I get the wine."

John relaxed on one of the chaise lounges near the grill. He leaned back with his arms behind his head, enjoying the tranquility of the suburban backyard. I could get used to this, he fantasized. It made him smile as he watched the girls showing off with their volleyball skills. Maybe someday they would be his girls too.

He slipped his cell phone out of his back pocket. It had vibrated as he arrived at the front door. Assuming who the caller was, he hadn't answered. His suspicions were confirmed when his mother's number appeared— again. John hadn't listened to the message she'd left earlier, not wanting to deal with her condescension. Her doubting his confidence would only agitate him. Avoiding further interruptions, John pressed the power button until the device shut off. He could "report in" later. Better yet, he might drive straight over to her house and flash the prize in her face.

Janie fished out the wine opener from her gadget drawer. With a practiced hand, she popped the cork. Allowing the bottle to sit on the counter and breathe a moment, she retrieved two stemmed glasses from the cupboard. Reaching in again, she got down two more for the girls to use with their cider. This afternoon was about them too, and they deserved special treatment.

She gently placed the glasses on the counter. Besides missing Brian, she yearned for a complete family. No amount of get-togethers with her siblings or mother could take the place of this feeling. Guilt gave a twinge at her enjoying life without her husband. Physically shaking her head, she forced the melancholy away.

Picking up the glasses for John and herself, she turned around and almost dropped them on the floor.

"Sorry, Sis, I didn't mean to scare you."

"Don't tell me you're here to crash my barbecue with John." Janie lowered her voice, glancing at the outside door. Her brother could be a real card, but he'd taken it too far this time.

"No, I'm not here to crash your party," Tom quietly said, his tone out of character.

Janie's shoulders tensed. "Is Mom okay?" She could barely get the words out. *Not now, please dear God, not now.*

"No, Janie, Mom's fine. You should sit down."

Her pulse quickened at his somber mood. She shook her head.

"Please," Tom urged, holding out his hand, "come sit at the table with me."

She placed the stems beside the cabernet and eased down onto a chair. Her fingers twisted in her lap.

Sliding onto a knee, he grasped one of her hands. "It's Carol."

"Carol? I don't understand." Her brows furrowed, a million questions in her eyes.

"Sounds as if you haven't watched the news today. In case you hadn't heard, I wanted to be the one to tell you."

Her lip trembled. "Tell me what, Tom? What's happened?"

"They found her body this morning."

"Her…her body? Found her where? Is she okay?" Tears flowed down her cheeks. Her mind denied what Tom meant about finding her body instead of finding Carol.

"Janie, sweetie, Carol's dead. It looks like someone strangled her. Her body, I mean…she was found in her own bedroom. And they've taken Calvin in for questioning."

Her head shot up. "Her ex-husband? Why would he be involved?"

"The authorities believe he'd been angry about the divorce settlement."

Janie struggled to wrap her mind around this whole thing. "But he doesn't have that type of temper. He couldn't have done it. Why would they arrest him?"

"No," Tom continued, "they haven't arrested him, just taken him in for questioning. You know how those news hounds sensationalize everything. Shoot, he's the one who found her and called nine one one. He'd be pretty dumb to strangle someone then stick around until the cops arrived."

"My God, I tried calling her a few times yesterday and again today. Do you think all this time she was really...? I can't say it." Janie held her face in her hands, sobbing.

"Hey, did you need help with the wine?" John asked, stepping into the kitchen. "Oh, sorry, Tom, I didn't know you were joining us. There's plenty of steaks. I think I bought too..." He hesitated. "What's happened? Why are you crying?"

Tom stood. "One of Janie's best friends, Carol, uh...oh, that's right, you knew her." He stumbled over himself trying to get the words out. "She's been murdered."

"No. That's terrible." John put his hands to his cheeks. "How was she found?"

Tom did a double take. "How?"

"You know, I mean where did they find her? Who found her?" He jammed his hands into his pockets.

"The news said she'd been found at home. Her ex-husband, Calvin, found her."

"Did they still have relations? I was under the impression the divorce was final."

"The news said Calvin had stopped by to pick up some things he'd left stored in the basement. When Carol didn't answer the door, he used his key to let himself in. She apparently never changed the locks."

"So, she was in the basement?" John asked.

"No, the bedroom. The news reports speculated she brought home the wrong guy."

Janie pleaded, "Tom, please. Carol was my friend. Do you have to say things like that?"

"That's what the reporters are saying. Since the police took Calvin to the station, another speculation is they were having one more tumble for old time's sake, and he snapped."

"Calvin didn't hurt her. They may have been a mismatched couple, but he never could physically hurt her. Never." Janie broke down, wracked with sobs.

Tom stooped by his sister's chair putting his arms around her. "I'm so sorry, Sis. I didn't mean to spoil your afternoon, but it didn't seem right for you to hear about her on the news."

John shifted from foot to foot. He reached an arm toward her then pulled it back. "Janie," his voice gentle, "I'm sorry about Carol. I didn't know her too well but do know what she meant to you."

Looking up, her face a splotchy mess, she said, "Thank you."

"Maybe I'd better go." He looked back and forth from Janie to Tom.

"I'm sorry, John. Right now, I need to be alone with my family. Maybe we could do this...you know..."

"...another time," he finished.

"Yes. Do you mind?"

"Of course not. I'll turn off the grill before I go. Can I call you tomorrow?"

Janie smiled through her tears. "I'd like that. Thank you."

John extended his hand. "Tom, good seeing you again. I'm sorry about the circumstances."

Tom accepted the hand, and they briefly shook. "Right. I'll see you around the neighborhoods. You can show yourself out?"

He nodded. "Bye, Janie. I'll talk to you tomorrow." He walked out to the patio and turned off the grill. Exiting by the side steps onto the driveway, he shoved his hands into his pockets and strode to his truck parked at the curb.

CHAPTER 27

John had no doubts why his mother blew up his phone all morning and afternoon. He should've told her yesterday about Carol but thought he'd have one more day before it became necessary. If only he'd secured the missing page, it would've alleviated some of her ire. *Damn you, Carol! Why couldn't you have kept your big mouth shut?*

Facing the inevitable, he drove straight to his mother's. She wouldn't want to discuss this on an open line—as if authorities had nothing better to do than listen in on the private conversations of a secretary and a landscaper.

The truck rolled to a stop at the curb. Resting his head on the steering wheel, John braced for the storm ahead. His hand slipped back onto the keys still in the ignition. Driving away now wouldn't eliminate this discussion, only postpone it. If he waited, his mother's fury would escalate to gale force winds, pummeling him like a gnat.

Trudging to the front stoop, he rapped on the metal frame of the screen door. Glancing toward Mrs. Weiss' house, he saw the neighbor watching him from her driveway where she held a bulging plastic bag. Damn, he didn't even think to have a fake invoice in his hand. Another strike against him. "Hello, Mrs. Weiss. Nice weather we're having."

She bobbed her head then looked away and continued walking to the garbage can at the curb.

The inside door whipped open. "It's about time you showed up," his mother snapped, her face flushed.

Controlling his emotions, John looked back toward the neighbor and waved. "Have a nice day, Mrs. Weiss."

Meg retreated into the house.

"Nice performance, Mother," he growled in a low voice, "and you're always on me to watch what I say in front of the neighbors." He closed the door behind him.

"Don't you dare take that tone with me. For all she knows, I'm firing you for shoddy work—which this whole mess is! What were you thinking?"

John placed a hand on her shoulder. "Calm down."

Shrugging off his grasp, she spat, "Calm down? Now there's going to be police snooping around. When you said you 'took care of her,' I had hoped that meant you broke off relations. But this…this…how could you be so stupid? Her murder might set us back weeks." She paced in front of the living room window like a caged tiger. The shades were open, and nosey Mrs. Weiss watched from her post on the front driveway. Meg reached up and swished the curtains closed.

"How could this affect us? There's no connection between Carol and me, except a common acquaintance. Don't worry. I have all the angles covered."

"What have you done to cover this mess?" She held up her hand before he could answer. "You know what, never mind. The less I know the better. If the police find their way to your door or mine, I am not taking the fall for you. I told you to handle her, not kill her." Meg pounded down the hall to the kitchen where she refilled her half empty coffee cup on the counter. "I don't suppose you got the page, did you?"

Sometimes it scared him the way she switched gears so fast. "No, Mother, I didn't. I'd barely arrived at Janie's when her brother showed up with the news of Carol's death. There was nothing for me to do but leave. It would've been out of character for me to stay."

"Well, Johnny"—Meg ignored his grimace at the annoying endearment—"you know what you need to do now."

"I'm way ahead of you. Tomorrow, while Janie's at work and the girls at school, I'll sneak over and use the key to let myself in—providing she goes to work. She might be too distraught and stay home."

"Leave that to me. She wouldn't want the office to be unattended."

"Why would it? What about her useless partner? I don't think he knew Carol well enough to be all broken up about her passing."

Meg told him about finding Larry's note on Janie's desk. While talking, she pulled the crumpled paper from her purse and handed it to John.

After reading it, he asked, "Why did you take it?"

"Think about it." She smacked the paper in his hand. "Janie might get careless and let something slip if Larry suddenly vanished without a word. A lot like Brian, hmmm?" Expelling a breath, she glared. "Now I'll have to tell her he's out of town for at least a week. Another perfectly crafted plan ruined."

Handing back the crinkled paper, he said, "You can't give this to her now. She's going to wonder what happened to it."

"Don't worry. I'll call her from the office and say

Larry phoned in. She has no reason to doubt my word and will come to work."

Swallowing his pride, he gave her a peck on the cheek. "You're brilliant."

"You had better get out of here. I'll call you in the morning once I know the house is empty. Be ready, and don't take all day about it."

"Yes, Mother. I'll move like the wind."

"Don't get smart with me. Just get it done." Meg sat at the table and picked up the newspaper as if she were already alone.

Slinking out like a dismissed servant, John turned on his heel and strode to the front door. Walking across the lawn, he shifted his gaze toward Mrs. Weiss' driveway and found it empty. Hopefully she didn't take it into her head to sneak into Meg's backyard and press her big crooked nose against the kitchen window. John chuckled to himself picturing the scene.

****

Monday came, and Meg arrived at the office a few minutes before eight o'clock. Janie's car sat parked in its usual spot, and the locked door meant she'd gotten in early. The aroma of French roast hit Meg the moment she stepped inside.

Well, she thought, no need to mention Larry's whereabouts after all. She stopped at Janie's doorway on her way to the kitchen. "Good morning, Janie. Thank you for making coffee. What time did you get here?"

"Hello, Meg. About twenty minutes ago."

If Janie came in early, she might not stay long. "You look tired. Is everything all right?"

"No, actually, it isn't." Her breath heaved. She

took a minute to get herself under control. "Have you heard anything on the news about a local murder?"

"I did hear a snippet about a woman found strangled in her home. You didn't know her, did you?" Her eyes widened.

"Yes. Do you remember my friend Carol, the one who does my hair?"

"That's why her name sounded familiar." Meg feigned surprise, putting her hand to her cheek. "Oh, Janie, that's dreadful. Had you been friends long?"

"Since we were teenagers."

"I'm so sorry. Did your girls know her well? How are they taking it?"

"Yes, they did. Of course, they're upset. They didn't want to go to school, but I made them. I knew I had things to do here at the office and didn't want them home alone."

Another problem solved. Stepping farther into the office, Meg asked, "Why are you here? Larry can handle things when he comes in. Did your friend have family in town?"

"No. Her parents moved to Tampa years ago. Carol's father passed away, and her mother is in a nursing home. She has dementia and won't understand what's happened. Maybe that's a blessing. Oh, Meg, who would do such a thing?"

She clucked, shaking her head. "I thought they arrested her ex-husband. Nasty business that divorce stuff."

"Calvin didn't do it," Janie said in a defensive tone.

Meg tilted her head. "They've released him?"

"They never arrested him. He got taken in for questioning. Procedure, I guess." She paused, looking down at her desk with her head in her hands. "I know Calvin, and he's not capable of hurting anyone."

"I guess you would know him better than most." She hesitated, treading carefully. Time to wrap up this charade. "What's your plan for today?"

Scanning her desk, Janie said, "I have some papers I need to look over and will probably leave around noon. Once Larry arrives, we can get things squared away. Did he have any appointments today?"

"No, so he should be in any minute. I'll let you know the moment he arrives. Anything else you need right now?"

"No, Meg, thank you. I don't know what I'd do without you."

She forced a smile. "You would do fine, but thank you for the sentiment."

"Would you mind closing my door? I need to focus."

"Certainly," she said, pulling the handle until the door clicked shut. Grabbing her cell phone from her purse, Meg dialed her son.

He answered on the second ring. "John Cooper Landscaping. How can I help you?"

"It's me." Meg spoke quietly into the phone so Janie couldn't hear her. "She's here until noon, and the house is empty. Get over there and take care of business."

"Got it." He broke the connection.

In the privacy of her office, Janie pulled out the Brassel Field file and the journal. She still intended on confronting Larry when he arrived. This tragedy with Carol added to the urgency of getting closure. One had nothing to do with the other, but she didn't know how much more strife she could handle. For good or bad, she needed answers.

The one bright spot in her life lately was John. He genuinely had a caring nature. If Tom hadn't been with her yesterday, she would've snuggled into John's arms for comfort.

Since John left, it had been a relief having Tom there when she broke the news to the girls. He stayed most of the afternoon until she made him leave. There was nothing more he could do.

After forty-five minutes of poring over the property maps and making notes, Janie put everything back into her briefcase. As she zipped the valise closed, her pen rolled off the desk, and she bent to retrieve it. "Oh, for heaven's sake," she said aloud. "Here they are."

Meg tapped on the door and entered. "I'm sorry, I couldn't quite hear you. Did you call?"

"No. I didn't mean to disturb you." She dangled her keys from her finger. "I found my house keys beside the foot of the desk. I looked all over the place for these on Friday. Thank goodness I didn't lose them in the parking lot. They might have been long gone."

"Good thing the cleaning people didn't find them either," Meg groused.

"I'm sure they would've turned them in. I've known Carmen and her crew for years. Now I don't have to worry about making a spare." Looking toward the hallway, she asked, "By the way, is Larry here yet?"

"No, he's not. That's strange, isn't it? He's always on time if not early on Monday mornings. Shall I try his cell phone?"

"Yes, please. It's not like him to skip out and not call. Maybe he got a last-minute appointment." What

Janie really believed was she'd spooked him so badly on Friday he couldn't face her. She needed to talk with him while she had the real estate file in hand.

"I'll let you know." Meg closed the door again. Hurrying to her desk she picked up the phone and called John.

It took several rings this time. "Why are you calling on the office phone?"

"That doesn't matter, but it's serving a purpose. Are you there yet?" Meg whispered.

He sighed. "I'm pulling into her neighborhood now."

"Just be quick about it."

"I could be quicker if you'd stop calling," he snapped.

"Don't get surly with me," she hissed. "You should have had this wrapped up yesterday."

"I'll call you when I've got it." He hung up.

In a louder voice, Meg continued talking. "...so when you get this message, please give a call to the office so we can get your schedule. Thanks, Larry." She dropped the phone back into its cradle and went to the closed door. She gave a tap then stuck her head in. "Sorry, Janie, I got voicemail. He should call in soon. You know he doesn't answer his phone when he's trying to close a deal."

Janie ran a hand through her hair. He would have mentioned a meeting before leaving on Friday. She was sure he intentionally avoided her. He'd have to come around sooner or later with a business to run. "Thanks, Meg. I guess he'll call when he's done."

"Good enough. I could try calling his wife..." She paused.

Janie shook her head. "I don't want to disturb Margaret. We'll wait for Larry to call. In the meantime, did he have any other meetings today that you know of?"

"Nothing is on the calendar."

"Good. I mean, I don't think I'd be up to handling clients today."

"Very good. Shall I keep your door closed?"

"Yes, go ahead and close it. Thanks, Meg." Alone again, she dialed her brother's number.

"Hey, Sis, how are you?"

"I'm hanging in there. Thanks again for coming over yesterday. I don't know what I would've done if I'd heard about Carol on the news. Is there anything more about Calvin?"

"Only that he was released after a few hours. The police are keeping this one close to the chest right now. My buddy Eddie is on the force, and even he wouldn't throw me any tidbits. Maybe that's a good thing for her ex-husband. If they thought it was really him who did her harm, they would have charged him by now."

Janie leaned back in her chair and pressed her eyes closed. "You're probably right. Look, Tom, I've been thinking. Now that we have the final page and know where to look...Can you get free this afternoon?"

"Today? What's with the sudden rush?"

"I need to put this behind me. Can you go with me to Brassel Field today?"

"Actually, Sis, today is bad. Tomorrow I'm tied up with customers too. Can't get out of it. How about waiting for the weekend?"

Janie panicked, suddenly thinking this might not be a good idea. "Tom, I want to go sooner. I need to go.

You understand, don't you?"

"I know, sweetie. But with the stress of Carol's death on top of your seeing you know who, don't you think it would be best to let things settle a bit?"

"I don't think you know who," she mimicked her brother, "will settle down until we go out there. Even if we find nothing, maybe it will be enough to search the property. Please, Tom. What about Wednesday?" she pleaded, gripping the phone with one hand while balling the other into a fist.

"Possibly. I could probably move a couple of things around and make an escape."

"Good. It's settled." Relief washed over her.

"Promise me one thing," Tom urged.

"Anything."

"Promise you won't go out there alone."

She hesitated, having considered it. The drive there and back, plus a couple of hours to explore, would get her home before the girls returned from school.

"Promise me, Janie." His voice rose, punctuating the request.

She sighed. "Okay, I promise not to go alone. Happy?"

"Ecstatic. I'll talk to you later."

"All right. Take care."

"You too."

Janie held her cell phone a moment before putting it in her purse. She tidied up her desk, picked up her briefcase and bag, then walked to the door.

Meg looked up as Janie's door opened and she came out carrying her belongings. "Leaving already?" she asked. "It's only nine-thirty."

"I can't focus, Meg. Nothing will get done today,

so I might as well go home. Maybe I can take a nap before the girls come home. I didn't sleep much last night. You understand?"

"Of course. You probably shouldn't have come in at all, but it was noble of you to try. Any last-minute instructions?" Meg asked.

"No, nothing. You know you could probably leave early—"

"I'll do no such thing," Meg stated firmly. "The last thing you need is the stress of knowing the office is unmanned. You go along and get some rest, and I will handle things here."

"As always, thank you, Meg. I wish Larry would call in."

"The moment I hear from him I'll give you a call, okay? Now you run along."

"See you tomorrow." Janie strode out the front door.

The moment the car left the parking lot, Meg called her son. He had to get out of there before Janie arrived home. His phone went straight to voice mail, which meant he had it turned off. Now why would he do that? Hoping he would turn it on soon, she left a message. "It is nine-thirty and Janie just left the office for home. Get out of there now!"

CHAPTER 28

When John had received his mother's call earlier than planned, he'd quickly shoveled down his breakfast and jumped into his truck. Feigning car trouble, he rescheduled his first two customers of the day. They lived on the other side of town, so no chance of his being found out.

He pulled into Janie's driveway and parked by the side entrance. A grin spread across his face as the lock turned easily using the duplicate key. Slipping inside and closing the door behind him, John made for the stairs.

Leaping the steps two at a time, he started in the master bedroom. Just inside the door frame, he stopped to drink in every detail. If he were prone to such emotions, he believed his stomach would be turning somersaults at standing in Janie's sanctuary. This was where she got dressed in the morning, spent her evenings reading before bed, and slept. The faint scent of peonies hung in the air. Breathing deeply, he closed his eyes and envisioned himself part of her evening routine. It would be a natural transition to incorporate himself into this family. With time, he would make it happen.

Snapping out of his daydream, he went into action. At the dresser, he methodically searched each drawer. His hands lingered as they ran over her undergarments.

The silky fabric tickled his fingers with delight. Each item spoke of mature femininity—not one set of garters or fishnet stockings among the lot. Going through her pajamas, he caressed smooth negligees and soft flannels. The bedtime attire looked nothing like Carol's collection. While those tawdry nighties fit appropriately on a woman like the blonde, they had no place in Janie's wardrobe.

Finding nothing in her dresser, John moved on to the bed area. On a whim he bent down and moved the comforter aside to look underneath. Nothing, not even dust bunnies. Next, he searched the nightstands on both sides of the bed. One held a phone charger and a couple of books. This was obviously the side Janie slept on. Deeper toward the back were envelopes addressed to her. Slipping a page out, he discovered a love letter from her husband. John wanted to peruse the note more closely, but time was short. He reluctantly put it back into the envelope. Checking five more, he found none to be of parchment paper. The journal wasn't anywhere either. Rooting through the bottom of the closet and along the top shelf revealed nothing as well.

She had moved it. Maybe downstairs? Racing to the first floor, he turned toward the hallway that led to her office.

After rifling through the desk, he tried to open the filing cabinet. It was locked. He searched the desk looking for a key. Sitting back in the chair, he surveyed the surface and spied the paper clip cup. John dumped its contents into his hand, and the key spilled out with the clips. He chuckled to himself. Too predictable.

What he searched for had to be inside. Why else would she lock it? Giddy with excitement at securing his prize, he whipped open the top drawer and found real estate files. None were thick enough to hold a book. He sifted through them anyway. The second held personal files for household bills and such. Damn! Neither the journal nor the parchment sheet was anywhere to be found.

Huffing out a loud breath, John grabbed his phone from his back pocket and turned it on. Maybe Mother possessed a useful suggestion. Seeing a voicemail and a missed call from her cell, he listened first. Checking his watch, he saw the message came in twenty minutes earlier. Jumping out of the chair, he bolted through the kitchen.

Once outside, he made sure to lock the door behind him. Janie could be home any minute. He crossed his fingers, peeked around the corner of the house, and cursed. Her car cruised down the street. With a disgusted sigh, he sank onto the stairs and waited for her pull into the driveway.

Janie got out of her car with her face scrunched. "What a nice surprise. How did you know I'd be home?"

"I tried calling you at the office, and your secretary told me you'd just left for the day. Since I was in the neighborhood, I took a chance you were heading home. Hope I'm not being too presumptuous. You left work so early I thought maybe you were distraught over—" He hesitated. "—Carol…and might need someone to talk with. I could leave if you prefer to be alone," John said tentatively.

"I'm glad you're here." Janie jangled her keys. "Besides, your truck is trapped by my car. How about some coffee?"

"Coffee would be great," he said more enthusiastically than intended. His elevated pulse evened out.

John followed her into the house. Seated at the table, he watched Janie prep the coffee maker. Sitting in the kitchen stoked his fantasy about joining this family. *I could do this.*

His phone rang, and he pulled it from his back pocket. When would his mother relax and trust him to handle things? With a quiet grunt, he hit the side button sending the call to voice mail and stowed the cell away.

"Did you need to answer that?" Janie asked.

"No. It's a client, probably wanting to reschedule. I can call him back later."

Janie hit the brew button then grabbed her briefcase off the floor. "Back in a sec," she said walking out of the kitchen.

John gripped the edge of the table wishing she'd left the briefcase behind.

Upstairs, Janie closed her bedroom door and collapsed onto the bed, her body trembling. John had promised to call today not show up unannounced. Still, having him as a distraction would be better for her state of mind than brooding at home alone.

His presence showed genuine concern. How lucky she'd found another good man. She kicked off her pumps and carried them toward the closet. The warmth of a smile flushed across her face until she saw the door stood half closed, and her skin ran cold. A compulsive neat freak, she never would have left it open after getting dressed this morning. Then again, being upset over Carol coupled with very little sleep, she counted herself lucky to have left wearing matching shoes.

Slipping off her work clothes, she hung up her skirt and jacket, then tossed the blouse in the bathroom hamper along with her stockings. Janie put on a pair of blue jeans and her favorite blue, V-neck T-shirt. The soft cotton blend swaddled her body. Old comfortable clothes always calmed her. She probably should have worn them to the office, except Meg would have given a double take if she came in dressed so unprofessionally. Even with no clients scheduled, you never knew who might drop in unexpectedly.

Returning to her briefcase on the bed, Janie took out the journal with the final passage stuck between the last page and back cover. As an afterthought, she pulled out the office copy of the Brassel Field files and put the whole package into her nightstand drawer. Next, she went downstairs to her office with the intent of stowing the home copy, as well as a few work files, into her filing cabinet.

She stopped short in front of the desk. The paper clips had been spilled. Giving the office a quick scan, she saw the bottom drawer of the filing cabinet ajar. The key stuck out of the lock. Possibly one of the girls had knocked over the paperclips in a hurry, but neither would have any reason to go through the drawers.

Janie trembled. Whoever had been in her office might still be in the house. This meant they had also been in her bedroom. "John! John!"

He bolted down the hallway. "What's wrong?" The key stuck out of the lock in the filing cabinet. What a stupid move. Now she would figure out the real reason he waited on her doorstep.

She grabbed his arm. "Someone was in my house. I locked that cabinet before I left for work this morning.

And in my bedroom...I thought I'd shut the closet door but found it open."

Frozen to the spot, John surveyed the room to see if he'd missed anything else. Luckily, he'd only had his phone with him. No chance of his leaving any telltale personal items behind.

"We have to get out and call the police. What if they're still here?" Janie's shoulders gave another shiver as she cast a frantic look toward the doorway.

John wrapped his arms around her and rubbed her back. His mouth formed a smirk before he said, "Shhh, calm down. You're safe. I won't let anybody hurt you," he whispered. "Whoever did this is probably long gone."

"What if they aren't? What if they're still in the house?" A sob caught in her voice.

"Tell you what—you stay here and lock the door. Look around and see if anything is missing. I'll search the rest of the house."

"No, I don't want to be alone." Janie's eyes brimmed with tears.

He pulled back and rubbed the moisture away with his thumb. "Okay. Let's do a quick look around the house. There didn't appear to be anybody here when I drove up, and I'd been sitting on the steps about ten minutes before you got home."

"Are you sure we should do that? Why can't we let the authorities handle it?"

His voice remained calm. "Does it look like anything is missing?"

Janie swiveled her head. "I'd have to look. Why would anybody break into a filing cabinet?"

"Come on." John led her by the hand. "Let's start

upstairs. Stay behind me." They went to her bedroom even though she'd already been there. It took all his strength not to ease her onto the bed and embroil her in passionate kisses. He stirred below his belt.

John checked the bathroom and closet.

As he walked back into the room, John caught a flash of the leather cover in the nightstand drawer before she shut it again. The muscles in her face visibly relaxed, further confirming his suspicions. Janie had the journal with her in the briefcase then put it in the drawer when she came upstairs to change. "Everything okay?"

"Fine. Everything's here."

"Are you missing any jewelry, or did you have anything valuable sitting around?" John kept up the ruse.

The jewelry box on the dresser looked untouched. Janie opened it anyway and found everything in its place.

He'd obviously calmed her down, making her believe nobody remained in the house but them. Still, she insisted they check the girls' rooms but found nothing missing or disturbed. With all the electronics scattered about, it would have been easy to make a good haul had there truly been a break-in.

After giving the ground floor a cursory glance, they ventured into the basement. This was probably the messiest area in the house, yet Janie admitted it didn't look any different than when she had been down there last.

"Maybe I scared them off when they heard my truck pull into the driveway. Could be I foiled their thinking they had all day to peruse your house and scoop up loot. With nothing missing, it doesn't seem like there would be much for the police to do."

"I suppose you're right. The lock wasn't broken on the kitchen door. How could they have gotten in?" Panic shone in her eyes anew.

"You're right. The front entry looked fine when we did our walk-through. Is it possible somebody got hold of your keys?"

She put a hand to her cheek. "Funny you should mention that. I did lose my keys but found them on the floor at work. They'd slipped from my purse on Friday. The only people in there would have been Meg, you know my assistant, and the cleaning people. I've known Carmen for years, so if she had found them, she would've called me or left them on my desk." She ran her hand through her hair.

John's gaze shot to her face. "What? Did you think of something?"

"When Brian...my husband...went missing, his keys were never recovered. I wonder if they were found and somebody used them. It's been so many years though. Maybe one of the girls got careless with her set. How hard would it be to change the locks?" Her eyes searched his.

His ego soared at the way she leaned on him to fix the situation and allay her fears. Puffing out his chest and resting both hands on his hips, John swaggered. "It just so happens that I am an expert at lock replacement. Can you see the cape flowing down my back?" He glanced over his shoulder.

She laughed. "Come on, superhero. What do you say we take a trip to the hardware store? Unless you have to get to work."

"I have no place else to be for the next few hours. Let's go. Why don't you move your car, and we'll take my truck?"

Walking through the kitchen, Janie grabbed her keys off the counter then turned around.

John tilted his head. Had she changed her mind about who'd been searching her home?

She looked into his eyes. "Thank you, John."

"For what? I haven't done anything."

"Just for being here."

"In that case, you're welcome." He leaned down and kissed her. Resisting the urge to pull her closer, he drew back, and Janie turned and went out the door. John issued a quiet sigh then followed as they each went to their own vehicles and shuffled them around.

While Janie backed her car out to park it on the street, John gave Meg a call and a brief rundown of what had occurred. As usual, she was none too happy things didn't go according to her plans, but at least Janie wasn't suspicious of him. He cut the call short when Janie walked toward the truck. While she would assume he spoke with a client, he couldn't risk her hearing any of his conversation.

John hopped out and walked around to the passenger side. He opened the door and helped her in.

"You know"—she gazed at him—"I really can see that cape."

The morning and afternoon flew by. Locks were purchased and installed without a hitch. While the activity distracted Janie from her friend's murder, the sadness bubbled close to the top of her mind on and off. The reality of never seeing Carol again surged through her veins like venom from a snake.

John didn't need help replacing the locks, but Janie wanted to be involved if for no other reason than to have a sense of physically doing something to protect her family. With the chore completed, he insisted on taking her out to lunch. Despite her trying to treat him for the work he'd done, he wouldn't hear of it.

They didn't linger over lunch since Natalie's and Jenny's keys would no longer fit the locks in the doors. Janie feared they might panic if they couldn't get inside.

John told her he had clients scheduled for the afternoon, so he needed to hit the road.

She decided to tell the girls she'd changed the locks as a precaution, despite finding her keys at the office. No sense alarming them with the notion someone had been searching their house. It might lead to questions about why nothing got stolen and the real reason for the break-in. Withholding things from her kids had become hard enough. She didn't want to lie.

"I think I've said 'thank you' a million times today, but I really do appreciate your being here. You turned a horrible day into something enjoyable."

"It's unfortunate it all came about for a sad reason, but I'm glad I was here for you, Janie. When can I see you again?"

Janie already had a plan. After much internal debate, she allowed today's events to bolster her resolve of checking out the old Pelter farm sooner rather than later. This ideal solution allowed her to keep her promise to Tom. "Well"—Janie shifted her eyes sideways toward her hero—"what're you doing tomorrow?"

He tilted his head. "What did you have in mind?"

"It's a work-related thing." She explained the story she'd fabricated. "You see, I've been putting off visiting this one property a client has had listed with us. It's in a remote area about an hour away. Would you be interested in going out there with me? The property is called Brassel Field. Maybe we could make an afternoon of it. I pack a great picnic lunch." She halted and tapped herself on the forehead. "Oh, what am I thinking? I forgot it's mid-week. You must have clients scheduled."

"Actually, my schedule is clear tomorrow. That phone call I took while I waited for you to move your car was my customer canceling an all-day job. Emergency out-of-town business or something like that. How perfect is that?" He spread his arms wide as if hugging the world.

"Then you'll go with me?" Eyes glistening with excitement, her lips broke into a huge grin. She might finally get some answers. Pangs of guilt at lying to John tugged down on her, but it wasn't a complete lie. The owners of Brassel Field had engaged her office to list the property for sale years ago.

John leaned against the doorjamb to the kitchen with his arms crossed. "Wild horses couldn't drag me away. You provide the lunch, and I'll provide the chariot. Deal?"

"Deal. How does ten o'clock sound?"

"I'll see you then." John pulled her into his arms, but before he could lean down, Janie stretched up on her toes and matched her lips with his.

Passion seared through her before she pulled away, her body tingling with warmth. If she read his reaction correctly, he felt it too.

He gently brushed one more kiss on her cheek. "I guess that's my exit cue."

"See you tomorrow." She waved from the door. Janie watched the truck back out of the driveway and cruise down the street. Her gaze lingered a minute longer on the spot where he went out of sight, as if waiting to see if he would appear again.

Giggling like a teenager, Janie grabbed her keys and moved the car back to its usual spot in the driveway. She thought about calling Tom to fill him in on her trip tomorrow then thought better of it. He would try to talk her out of going without him, and she couldn't wait another day.

****

As John drove out of the neighborhood, he did somersaults in his head. He hit speed dial on his phone then held it to his ear. His mother picked up on the first ring.

"Did you get it?" Anxiety filled her voice.

"No. I couldn't sneak away without her seeing me."

"Then you'll just have to go back there and break in tomorrow."

Meg's curt tone should have made him angry, but with a solution already at hand, he wouldn't allow her to squelch his excitement. "I've got something better than breaking into her house. She invited me on a picnic tomorrow."

Meg screeched through the phone. "Let me remind you I do not want to hear about your sordid personal relations. If you don't have the final entry, we're nowhere."

"Mother"—he sneered through gritted teeth—"can

you control your temper for a moment? She wants me to take her to Brassel Field. You know what this means?"

"Finally." She sighed. "Progress. Don't screw it up."

"Give me some credit," he said as he ended the call. One of these days she'll acknowledge I know what I'm doing, he thought. Today obviously isn't the day. He pounded on the steering wheel as his good mood darkened.

CHAPTER 29

Eight o'clock Tuesday morning, Tom arrived at Mrs. Weiss' front door. Before knocking, he let out a deep sigh then forced a toothy grin.

"Right on time," she said, leading him to the kitchen. "So many young people these days have no respect for people's time."

"Yes, Mrs. Weiss. How are you today?" Tom gritted his teeth, hoping to avoid her latest gossip story. With her, the comments she made were always a lead into a complaint.

"Just fine, thank you for asking. Now, what have you got for me?" She motioned for him to sit at the table. "Coffee?" She swiped a mug from the counter and held it up.

"No, thank you." Tom wanted to be on his way as quickly as possible.

She curled her lips into a pout. "I hope you're not going to scare me with your prices, young man. Are you sure you don't want coffee? I made a fresh pot."

Tom took the road of least resistance. "You know, on second thought, I would love a cup. Thank you." He flashed another award-winning smile to further his good will.

Beaming, she filled the mug and placed it in front of him.

I hope she doesn't expect me to take that off my

bill. He smirked. *Let the negotiations begin.*

Mrs. Weiss slipped into a chair. Throughout the explanation of the estimate for her extension, she ran the gamut of emotions. Her favorite seemed to be the look of an impending heart attack.

She must practice that one a lot.

After a few concessions on Tom's part, and even less on hers, they agreed on a price that still didn't please the woman, but she accepted.

"More?" she asked, the pot poised over his cup.

Why not? It went for good public relations, and, he had to admit, she made a good brew. "Sure. Thank you, Mrs. Weiss. I must say, this is the best coffee I've had in a long time," he schmoozed. Even though she gave the go ahead, the old crone had yet to take pen in hand and sign the contract.

"You're too kind. I do make a point of buying quality grounds. None of that canned garbage you find all over the grocery store shelves. This is one of my few indulgences." Still glowing from the compliment, she poured herself another cup, replaced the pot on the stove, and took her seat again.

Tom got out a pen and placed it on the paperwork near the signature line. "Only one thing left to do," he prompted with a wink.

"Of course." She picked up the pen and held it poised over the contract. "Such a tragedy, the murder of that hairdresser. In her own home, no less. Nobody is safe these days, though I did hear she had a bit of a…risqué reputation." Her hand remained motionless with the signature line empty.

Tom inwardly groaned. At least the caffeine in his system would stave off fatigue from her lengthy sagas.

"Yes, very tragic." He withheld the knowledge of his sister's friendship with the victim. Such information would only prolong the conversation, despite her being on target about Carol's reputation.

"I wonder if that's what Meg, you know Mrs. Zutterman, was so upset at her son about."

Tom didn't want to get dragged into this conversation, but his curiosity got the best of him. What connection could Carol's death have with Meg and John? Already regretting his response, he dove in anyway. "You still think John is Mrs. Zutterman's son?" The question was barely out when he realized his poor choice of wording.

"What do you mean think he's her son? I know what I heard." She bobbed her head.

"I'm sorry, Mrs. Weiss. I didn't mean to offend you." Unless he made peace, Tom knew he'd never get her to sign any time this century.

"Well," she continued, "Meg appeared very upset with him when he came over this past Sunday afternoon."

Tom did a double take. "He was at her house on Sunday afternoon? What time?"

He could visibly see her hunker down, ready to dig into a juicy tale. The pen slipped from her fingers back onto the table. "Let's see…it was right before three in the afternoon," she said. "The birds had done something nasty on my car, and I had to clean it off. I can't abide those dirty pigeons."

"Yes, they can be a problem. Why was John at Meg's?" Tom led her back to the original conversation before she strayed onto another topic.

"Well, she answered the door and spoke to him like

a mother would to a son, not a servant. She was terribly angry about something. They hurried inside, but I could see her pacing in front of the living room window, waving her hands around. My guess is she was infuriated about his having associated with such a woman."

Tom's intrigue turned to concern as he narrowed his eyes. "You think he knew the woman who got strangled?" If there was any salt to what Mrs. Weiss said, then maybe he didn't know John as well as he should, especially with his sister being involved with the man.

"I'd say he knew her quite well from the looks of it! Driving home last Thursday night from my weekly mahjongg game at the Temple, you know the game that's played with tiles? It's like dominoes but a little different—"

Tom put his hand up. "I know what mahjongg is, Mrs. Weiss." He struggled to hold his emotions in check, otherwise he wouldn't hear the end of her story.

"Oh, of course, I just thought…anyway, I was driving home. I sometimes take a short cut through the alley behind the stores on Beach Street. You know, where it crosses Water Avenue? That traffic light is too long, and you wait forever. Five times I've called the city office about getting it fixed, but do you think they'd do anything? Each time they told me they'd look into it."

Tom gripped the edge of the table, close to shaking the rest out of his customer. "You were driving down the alley…"

She got a little testy at his interruption. "If you don't want to hear about it, just say so."

Breathing deeply, he said, "I'm sorry. Really. What happened next?" He leaned in as if he hung on her every word.

"As I drove through the alley behind the salon, there was a big white truck parked illegally near the back door, barely leaving enough room to get past without scratching my car. I had a mind to stop and say something when I realized it was John Cooper's truck. Since he mows my lawn, I didn't want to have an awkward scene, so I kept my thoughts to myself."

That was probably a first for you. Tom pressed the woman. "Since he's here once a week, I'm sure you recognized his truck."

"You bet I did." She gave a sneer. "He was completely oblivious to my car going by anyway with his focus on that blonde. The things they were doing. It may have been a dark doorway, but they were still out in public." She put her hand to her mouth.

"Do you mean to say..." Tom tried to think of a tactful way to put this into words.

She helped. "Let's just say her panties were on the ground, and they were doing a lot more than kissing. A lot more!" As if her words needed any more emphasis.

Tom sat up straight with his eyes bugged wide. He couldn't write this off as an over-exaggeration by a chronic gossip. Too many separate instances overshadowed coincidence. Why would Meg keep her son a secret? Why would John stay mum about the connection too? The man had outright lied when he claimed to not know Carol beyond a passing acquaintance. Things started to add up into something more dangerous than Tom cared to think about. He needed to talk to Janie and fill her in on everything he'd learned from his customer.

"I'm sorry, Tom. I didn't mean to shock you about Mrs. Zutterman. It may be another reason why she won't acknowledge her son. Acting in such a manner with a woman in public. I heard the hairdresser had been divorced four times. The last one just recently," she clucked.

He made a show of looking at his watch. "Is that the time? Well, I've enjoyed your hospitality a little too long. I'm sorry, Mrs. Weiss, but I have another meeting to go to. If you wouldn't mind signing the papers, I can get going and will call you to schedule the work once I'm back at the office. How would that be?"

"Oh." The disappointment was clear in her voice.

Tom didn't want to stick around so she could rehash this another time or two. Once was enough for him.

"Of course. Have you got a pen? Oh, I see it." Finally picking it up again, she scribbled her signature, her sight lingering on the bottom amount before finishing her last name.

"Great. I'll send you a copy and call to schedule the work. Thanks again for the delicious coffee, Mrs. Weiss. No, don't get up. Finish yours while I show myself out. Have a good day." Tom hurried out of the house to his truck. He didn't lie about having another customer to go see. A call to Janie could wait until after his next appointment. While Meg would be with her at the office, they wouldn't be alone with Larry there too. John would be working himself, so no danger of his being around her during the day.

A nagging doubt ate at him full of "what ifs." What if John was Meg's son? What if he dated Carol (though according to Mrs. Weiss it seemed more than a casual relationship)? That would mean he was seeing her after he had already asked Janie out. What if John was more dangerous than he let on or even part of the reason Brian went missing? Tom didn't like the connections. He'd arrange to go over to her house after work so they could reason this out.

****

John's white pickup pulled into Janie's driveway at precisely ten o'clock. Her heart skipped a beat, and her pulse quickened as she watched him approach the door. Despite peeking out the window, she waited for him to ring the bell. Things had been moving a little too quickly for her, and she didn't want to seem overanxious for today's outing. Of course, she was excited for both reasons—another chance to be with John and finally getting a look at the Pelter farm. Her emotion came with a healthy dose of guilt. Somehow it seemed wrong to be looking for clues about Brian while going out with her new boyfriend. There, she'd admitted it to herself. She had a boyfriend.

She was lost in thought when the doorbell rang a second time reminding her John waited on the stoop. Flustered, she turned the knob and invited him in.

"I'll just be a second. Let me grab the picnic basket and my sweater from the kitchen."

He followed her without being invited. "I hope those heavenly smells are coming from our lunch." John sniffed the air. "How about I take the picnic basket and you get your sweater?"

Swinging her purse over her shoulder, she swiped up her wrap. With her new keys, she locked up on their way out. Her stomach fluttered with appreciation. John had made this sense of security possible. Finding someone she could lean on soothed her soul. Maybe love could happen twice in a lifetime.

They walked to the passenger door, and he opened it. Flashes of Brian spilled into her head. He'd always done this for her. Doubts about her expedition with John competed for attention, and her vision blurred.

"Anything wrong?" John asked, placing a hand on her shoulder.

Janie looked up. "No…no…not at all." She forced a smile. "Our picnic may get rained on. Those clouds look a bit ominous."

"We can run between the raindrops if a storm happens." He leaned in and kissed her.

Warmth rushed to her cheeks. "I love an optimist," she said, then slipped in through the open door.

John circled the vehicle to the driver's side, swinging the picnic basket. He stopped to secure it inside one of the containers built into the bed of his truck.

As they backed onto the street, Janie thought about the conversation she'd had with her brother three days ago and cringed inwardly. Tom seemed adamant about John being Meg's son. How could it possibly be true? If she could figure out a tactful way to broach the subject with John, she would. But if Tom was wrong, the conversation could get embarrassing, not to mention awkward about her checking him out behind his back. Meg had been a widow for years with no family in town. Her assistant certainly had friends but never mentioned having children. There weren't any pictures on her desk other than the one of Morton, her departed husband.

They rode along in a comfortable silence like an old married couple. No need for constant chatter. After a ten-minute drive, they entered the Long Island Expressway and continued east. It would be thirty minutes before reaching the end of the Expressway, then an additional thirty or forty to where the property lay.

Near the end of their journey they pulled off the pavement onto a dirt road and stopped in front of a set of wrought iron gates with a lock in the middle. On one gate hung a large sign reading "Keep Out—Private Property." The other touted a sign "For Sale—Charger Realty" with the office phone number. They hadn't gotten many bites on this place in the last couple years. Occasionally, someone called asking questions, but it never resulted in a showing.

Staring at the entry, Janie's palms dampened with sweat. The vein in her neck throbbed. She'd waited so long to get here, and now it terrified her at what she might find. As she dug for the keys from the real estate file, John strode to the gates and, without hesitation, pushed them open.

Guess we don't need the keys after all, Janie thought, dropping them back into her purse next to the folded copy of the journal page.

The iron monsters groaned as they swung open. As a precaution, John grabbed two large rocks and wedged one under each side. Back in the truck, he shifted it into gear and slowly bumped along the winding driveway.

Tilting her head, Janie asked, "How did you know the gates wouldn't be locked?" A tinge of suspicion crept into her voice.

"Actually, it never occurred to me to check. I

assumed it would be open as that lock looked ancient and probably didn't work anymore."

"Oh." She leaned back into the cushioned seat, chastising herself for having doubts.

His driving was overly attentive as he navigated the dirt road. Surely, this being a work truck, he wasn't that picky about every hole and rut he went through. *I'm being ridiculous.* She allowed Tom's comments to ruin her day instead of trusting John's good intentions. As if on cue, her cell rang. Tom's number lit the screen. *What is he, psychic now?*

Unsure whether to answer, she found John watching her. "Do you need to get that?"

"Sorry, it's Tom. I better." It was too late for him to discourage her from taking this outing, so she accepted the call. "Hello, Tom."

"Hey, Sis, how're you?" he asked. "Sounds like you're not at work. Are you showing a house?"

"Well, I am in a way." She didn't want to confess she went to the property without him.

"I'm sorry, are you with a client? Call me when you're done."

No sense skirting the issue. She never could lie to her brother. "Tom, I'm just pulling up to an old property we've had listed for a while. Since I've never seen it myself, I thought I'd take a day and come look around." She didn't want to let too much information slip with John listening.

"You're at Brassel Field, aren't you? Janie, you promised you wouldn't go out there alone."

"I'm not," she said sheepishly. Now why on earth would she be embarrassed to let her brother know she ditched work to go on a picnic with her boyfriend? She swallowed. "Actually, John and I decided to make a day of it and brought along a picnic lunch." There was dead silence on the other end of the phone. "Tom, are you still there?"

"Janie, listen carefully. Try not to react or tip him off about what I'm about to tell you."

She didn't like the sound of this and feared he would bring up the nonsense about Meg being John's mother. This needed to stop. "I'm sorry, Tom, I'm losing reception. Look, I'll call you when I get to a better area. Talk to you later." She ended the connection and hit the power button.

"Everything okay? You seem upset?" John squinted his eyes.

"Oh, no, not at all." Janie waved her hand dismissively. "He feels his job as my brother is to give me a hard time about dodging work to go play. Sometimes his joking gets to me, and I need to put a stop to it. I'll call him later." Janie inhaled deeply and sank into her seat trying to calm her frazzled nerves.

John rubbed her hand. "Was that an exasperated breath, or were you cleansing your soul?" he mused.

"What…oh." She flushed with embarrassment from the reaction to her brother's call. "It's silly really. Just breathing in the fresh country air."

Slyly, he commented, "And we live in such a bustling, smog-infested metropolis?"

"Stop teasing. You know what I mean. Yes, we do have woods and trails around our town. This place is more…rustic."

"True. Looks like there isn't a neighbor for at least two acres in each direction. I'm surprised a developer hasn't scooped this place up and built a whole community."

The warmth radiating from his hand lingered on hers. "That's one of the weird stipulations the current owners have attached to the place. They want it sold but don't want to sell to anybody with a commercial use in mind. Could be why it's been on the market for years. With property taxes so high, not many people can afford to keep it strictly as a residential estate."

"The current owners must have the bucks to keep it paid for since they don't seem in a hurry to sell. There's the main house now." John removed his hold and pointed to the left.

The road curved and circled around on itself in front of the house. Another lane led to the barn in back. Mounds of dirt were scattered around the cleared parts of the property. With a mix of overgrown grass and scattered shrubs, not all the grounds could be seen clearly. Janie estimated about an acre of property surrounded the house before the woods closed in.

"John, did you notice tire tracks on the road? They look freshly made as I know it rained out this way a few days ago. Do they continue toward the barn?"

"How could I miss them?" He laughed. "I'm sure it's kids coming back here on Friday nights using this for a spooky Lover's Lane. Either that or they dare one another to come exploring after dark. You have to admit this place is creepy."

"You've got that right. I mean, the house is beautiful, but with the windows all boarded up, it takes on a different persona. Almost as if it were watching us." She gave an exaggerated shiver. "Does the front door look ajar to you? I hope nobody vandalized the place. I know I'm only the realtor, but I still feel responsible. Maybe we should look."

"I'm famished, honey. Dreaming about the delights you might have in the basket, I skipped breakfast. What do you say we eat first and then explore?"

Janie grinned. "Okay. Where should we set up this feast?"

Jumping out of the truck, they scouted for the ideal picnic spot. A lot of the grounds were so overgrown that there weren't many flat spots to choose from.

"That looks like a good location over there." He pointed off to the edge of the forest on the right. "There's a beautiful old oak tree with lots of shade. We can tamp down the grass and set out our blanket."

Janie looked around, then pointed toward the side of the barn. "It looks less jungle-like there with plenty of shade on the one side."

John crinkled his nose. "Well, isn't that a romantic setting," he said sarcastically.

"Oh, I didn't know 'romantic' was part of the criteria." She made air quotes with her fingers. "The oak tree it is."

Opening the side compartment in the truck bed, he retrieved the picnic basket and a blue quilt. Janie linked her arm in his as they meandered over to the edge of the woods. Scraggly weeds and roots pulled at their feet, making it difficult to walk. John set the basket on the ground, and the two of them stomped down the high grass before spreading the quilt. Wisps of overgrown dandelions took to the breeze as they dislodged the weeds with their movements.

Once they were comfortably settled, she unpacked the meal. First, two stemless wine glasses and a bottle of chardonnay from Prancer, another local winery. She handed the corkscrew to John. "Would you do the honors, kind sir?"

"You certainly know how to pack a lunch. I can see you've already retrieved the essential ingredient, but what else do you have in there?"

"Just wait," she said. "I haven't begun to dig out all the wonders of this cache." She pulled out a container of freshly cooked fried chicken, accompanied by homemade potato salad and warm rolls. Next came a container of grapes—three different kinds. Lastly, a homemade apple pie.

"You must have been up at the crack of dawn cooking all this stuff. Or will I find the deli boxes stuffed inside your trash can?"

Janie playfully slapped his arm. "Be polite. I'll have you know I cooked all of it this morning, except for the potato salad. I made that last night."

"I don't suppose there's a pint of vanilla ice cream to go with the apple pie?"

"Sorry. We'll have to rough it."

"I guess I can handle fresh pie un-a la mode."

The cork popped out of the wine bottle with little coaxing, and John poured them each a glass. Handing her one, he picked up his own. "Here's to a wonderful afternoon...and evening?" He waggled his eyebrows.

Janie clinked glasses. "Let's start with the afternoon and see where it leads us." She took a sip from her glass. The liquid tingled down her throat, letting off flavors of fresh citrus and pears. She looked forward to the time when they'd spend the night together. As much as her body stirred with an ache for intimacy, she wasn't sure when she'd be ready to act on those feelings.

John leaned in and gently kissed her. A hint of the chardonnay lingered on his lips. Janie snuggled closer. The wine hadn't even had time to take effect, yet she felt giddy with excitement. Tom's warning got shoved to the farthest corners of her mind.

After a few moments of passion, Janie pushed away. "Can I interest you in some homemade fried chicken?"

He placed a hand on her chin, coaxing her closer. "I'd like seconds on this course."

Pressing a hand to his chest, she stated in a serious tone, "Lunch first, then you can play."

He obediently reached for a plate.

Conversation stayed light, and time slipped by. They ventured into plans together, even trips they might take which included Janie's daughters. A future life blossomed ahead of them. While they plotted and ate, clouds moved in, and a darkening gloom tinged the skies.

After John finished every scrap of a second slice of pie, they packed up the basket. Once more he angled in toward Janie, his fingers sliding along her arm.

It took all her reserve to pull away. She didn't want the moment to end, but the time had come to put her ghosts to rest. "Let's have a look around first. After all, that is the main reason for coming all the way out here."

"But you said after we ate we could play," John said in a mock-childish voice.

Both wore serious faces then burst out laughing.

"Okay," John said. "Let's go take a look around this haunted mansion."

CHAPTER 30

On their way to the residence, John dropped the basket and blanket in the truck bed and grabbed a sturdy Maglite from the cab. "We may need this."

Janie put her hands on her hips. "You're so prepared."

"Didn't I ever tell you I was in the scouts?" he asked in a serious tone.

"After our little tussle by the oak tree, I have a hard time picturing you making it all the way to the final awards ceremony."

"I guess 'Be Prepared' was the only rule I managed to follow."

Janie chuckled and reached for the passenger side door. "Give me a minute to freshen up." She grabbed her purse from inside the cab. When John turned toward the house, she slipped the journal page into her back pocket. For good measure, she fussed with her lip gloss a moment before tossing her bag on the seat. Her skin radiated a happy glow as she checked her reflection in the sideview mirror.

The aging porch creaked and moaned with a voice of its own as they stepped onto it. Being a standard two-story design from the 1920s, the facade had an austere look, devoid of decorations. The original house built by Jacob Pelter had been destroyed by fire. Such a loss since Pre-Civil War dwellings usually got listed as historical landmarks. Used as a garage now, the barn had been built in the 1950s. The one built by William's great-grandfather probably fell down decades ago. Jacob's barn had stood directly behind the house and farther away. Janie guessed the back edge to have been where the forest now began. After poring over schematics of the old property, the location looked right.

The screen door hung ajar. Rusty hinges whined as she pulled it all the way open. Turning the handle on the inner door, she pushed, but it wouldn't budge. She'd forgotten about the key needed for the deadbolt installed sometime in the last decade. Janie ran back to the truck and got it from her purse.

John waited, his lips a thin line.

The bolt slid back easily, but the door remained jammed.

"The wood in the frame must've swelled. Let me try." He stepped in front of her.

Janie backed out of his way.

He leaned into the door and shoved. After a moment's hesitation, it gave way with a loud scrape. John stepped aside and, with a slight bow, motioned for her to go in first.

"What a gentleman."

"I aim to please, ma'am," he said with a slight twang.

Musty air assaulted her nostrils the moment she walked through the entry. Grit crunched under her shoes, and her footsteps stirred up a thick cloud of dust. Janie expected to see William standing in the hallway, backlit by light filtering through boards on the windows. A shudder ran through her as she bit her upper lip.

"Spooky, isn't it," John whispered in her ear.

Janie gave a slight jump. "That's enough of your ghostly notions. This place is scary enough." She veered left into a sitting room. Furniture covered with white sheets gave the appearance of a typical summer home awaiting the owner's next visit. "Enough light seems to be filtering through those boards, so we probably won't need your flash—" A high-pitched scream emitted from her throat as she froze in place. Her flesh tingled with cold.

A figure had arisen from one of the covered chairs in a corner of the room. Thoughts of William returned, but he'd never moved with such fluid motion before. Mostly he appeared before her, hovering above the floor. This time, he walked toward her.

As the figure came out of the shadows, Janie's fear turned to confusion. Scrunching her brows, she asked, "Meg, what on Earth are you doing here? And why were you sitting in the dark?"

Meg continued her approach with an angelic smile on her face. Only then did Janie notice the small gun in her hand. "Did you have a nice lunch, dear? You certainly took your sweet time about it, as if you didn't have a care in the world. I loved the passionate kiss for the appetizer."

"You were spying on us? Meg, what's going on? What are…" The woman's gaze wasn't focused on her.

"Mother." John tensed his jaw. "I told you I would handle this."

Waving the gun, she stepped closer. "Like the way you handled it the last time? I wasn't about to let you go solo after your botching that affair."

"Mother? She really is your mother? I don't understand." Janie's stomach lurched, and bile rose in her throat. Tom was right. Why hadn't she listened? Desperate for closure and happiness, she'd discounted his warnings.

John circled past Janie and stood beside Meg. "Sorry, doll, we're guilty as charged. But where are my manners? Janie, I'd like to present my mother, Meg Zutterman. Mother, I believe you already know Janie Holgram."

"How can that be? Your name is different. I guess if you'd lied about other things..." There were too many implications to grasp. Sweat formed at her temples, and panic ricocheted inside her head.

"Small town, dirty secrets. It's always the same," Meg said. "Obviously, he isn't Morton's son."

"And good ol' Morty loved to point that out every chance he got, didn't he?" interjected John.

Meg patted her son on the arm. "Calm down, dear. Let's not relive that argument again." Looking back toward Janie, she continued, "You see, when I met poor, belated Morton, I was already two months pregnant by an irresponsible dalliance with some passing fool. Morton refused to acknowledge Johnny as his own but agreed to say he was a son from my previous marriage. I had been married before and widowed, so it wasn't hard to pull off. We delayed the wedding until after his birth. Just a little adjustment of the dates. Who would know? Morton made it clear he would never accept Johnny as his own yet would help raise him to be with me. Of course, I agreed. The man was too good of a catch to throw back, given his social stature and, let's face it, well-endowed bank account."

"What does any of this have to do with why you're holding a gun on me?" Janie looked around as if searching for an easy solution to her predicament.

"Patience, my dear. It will all become clear. Why don't you sit down; you look as if you're about to faint. Must be all the wine you drank." She glared at her son.

The woozy haze threatening to overtake her consciousness left her no choice but to follow Meg's suggestion. Sidling over to the nearest chair, she dropped onto the cushioned seat sending puffs of dust swirling in the sunbeams seeping from the boarded windows. All the while her gaze remained glued to the gun in her assistant's hand.

Meg took a seat on the couch opposite while John stood behind his mother.

"There now. Better? Good." Meg went on without waiting for an answer. "Now, where was I? Oh yes, Morton and his well-padded bank account. Unfortunately, the man had been tight-fisted with his money once we got married. Don't get me wrong. We enjoyed quite a bit of it, but not as much as I would have liked. Then, seventeen years ago, when Morton chose to leave this Earth, it turned out he'd put us in debt up to our eyeballs. He'd even cashed in on his life insurance policy leaving me nothing. I had to sell the house and most of our belongings to pay off his debts. All those wasted years for naught.

"Twice during our marriage I asked him to buy this estate when it went on the market. He refused. When I realized the only way to get my hands on the land would be to use the insurance money I assumed I'd be paid at his demise, his time came swiftly."

Janie's jaw dropped. Her mind raced to figure out

an escape plan, but no avenue came to her. She struggled to keep her breathing even and not hyperventilate. "Are you telling me you killed your husband?"

Meg clucked her tongue. "Killed? That's such a nasty term, and, as the police determined, completely unfounded. He lost his life in a boating accident, plain and simple. Too much wine, a loss of footing, and over the side he went. Nothing sinister."

"I still don't understand." Pain blossomed between Janie's eyes. "Why are you interested in this estate?" The words were barely out of her mouth when she stiffened.

They knew about the journal.

They knew what happened to Brian.

They knew why she was here today.

Maybe if she played dumb, they'd believe she didn't know anything.

"Ah, yes, I see your confusion. Let me fill you in on a bit of family history. You see, I am a direct descendent of William Carver." Meg stopped, her gaze never wavering from Janie's face.

Janie's cheeks grew cold and dry. In the dim lighting, her pallor must match the sheets covering the furniture.

"I see his name means something to you. My connection, regrettably, is unacknowledged by that thieving family." She waved the gun.

"You know about the journal," Janie whispered, "and Brian." Tears spilled from her eyes.

"Yes, Brian figures prominently in this story, but not yet. Patience, my dear." Meg wagged a condescending finger in Janie's direction. "I've always known about the journal. That knowledge has been in my family for years. William told his beloved, Becky, he would keep an account of his adventures with his brother in the Civil War. He also needed a place to write down the treasure's location, which his mother would disclose before his leaving the next morning. Becky had seen the beautiful leather-bound book his mother had given to him for his birthday. You see, William was my great-great-grandfather."

Janie leaned into the backrest of the small settee she perched on, waiting for Meg to continue. The headache blooming behind her eyes exploded in agony. Ultimately, she knew the conversation would come around to Brian but didn't know if she wanted the truth anymore.

"William had promised to marry Becky but not until he returned from the war a rich man with his grandfather's treasure. Of course, their parting night of passion resulted in the conception of my great-grandfather—except William's family refused to acknowledge the child as their own kin. Those self-righteous bastards insisted William would never have known a woman without holy matrimony blessed by the church. They turned their backs on my great-great-grandmother.

"After the Battle of Gettysburg, they received word both brothers had perished. Becky never believed it because their bodies were never found. The army couldn't account for their whereabouts, so officials assumed the brothers had either been killed or deserted. Of course, the family believed they'd been killed. Becky told her son someday his daddy would return. She died waiting. Her son went on to marry and produce heirs. He had passed on every word of his mother's story to his children and grandchildren. Until you get to me. I was an only child, and my mother, being William's descendent, passed on Becky's story, hoping someday one of us could reap the benefits of the treasure."

Janie found her voice. "Meg, why didn't one of the other descendants just go dig up the treasure?"

"Supposedly, the location got written down in the journal before he left. When William and Benjamin never returned, their mother, the only living person who knew the exact spot, refused to tell her remaining daughters. She swore she'd never again lose family attempting to retrieve it. Becky, however, knew there was still a chance of digging up the treasure if William's journal could be found. So long as it hadn't fallen into the hands of someone who could figure out where the property sat, it would be safe until they found the book."

Janie watched John's enamored look as his mother told their family history—like he was hearing it for the first time. His eyes glazed as he clung to every word.

Reeling from Meg's confession, Janie attempted to figure how Brian fit into the plan, as well as how to assure her own safety. With Meg's admission to killing Morton, Janie feared for her own well-being and possibly her girls' lives. How stupid she had been falling for John, but how could she have possibly dreamed of his connection with this mess?

Meg paused.

After a few moments of silence, Janie looked up.

"We're not far from the finish line, dear. Have patience. Now, we can fast forward to the day Brian and Larry had their fifteen minutes of fame in the newspaper via a brief article about their finding an old skeleton in the woods. Of course, we know now the remains turned out to be my great-great-grandfather, William Carver. They discovered his identity through the pocket watch, which had been a family heirloom. His bony fingers were wrapped around it. Obviously, he'd been clutching it when he died. The body got removed with everything there and returned to a family plot in Virginia, where the Pelter-Carver descendants still resided. Since there was no mention of the journal, I hoped the young boys, being typical teenagers, had neglected to show that item to the police. All I had to do was bide my time until I could get close to it. Lo and behold, eight years later the two of them opened a real estate office near their hometown. Using my secretarial skills to gain employment at a real estate firm, I learned the business over the following ten years. When Brian's original secretary departed for bigger and better things, it was a simple matter for me to land the job. I guess those phone calls threatening to expose her affair with a married man convinced her to leave town quite hastily." She smirked.

John squeezed his mother's shoulder, and she patted his hand.

"I had decided if I couldn't purchase the property outright and dig until I hit pay dirt, I'd find another way. That opportunity arose when I pointed out to Larry the lot had been for sale by owner for years. Maybe he needed a realtor to broaden the prospects of potential buyers. Of course, Larry acted immediately. I hadn't planned on it taking as many years to achieve my goal, but I knew sooner or later they would produce the journal.

"Secretly, John and I sent anonymous threats about the journal. They were astounded anybody knew about it. Larry backed off and wanted nothing more to do with the property. Brian persisted. One day he slipped up and left the diary in his desk. I read it cover to cover, and it infuriated me when I saw the last page was missing. The page with the exact location of all that wealth." She shook with anger. "I made a copy and left the original, so he wouldn't connect me to the threats."

Taking a moment to compose herself, the angelic smile returned to Meg's face.

They all jumped as a clap of thunder punctuated the brewing tension. The rain had started. With the storm moving closer, the steady tapping on the rooftop beat harder like a drum. A bolt of lightning lit the room for a fraction of a second.

Meg's eyes shone as she pushed on with her story. "Now, Janie, tell me where the final page is."

"I only recently got the journal from Brian's lawyer after the court proceedings, with the final page missing. I don't have it."

"Liar," shrieked Meg, bolting up, causing Janie to almost slip off her seat. "You have it. I know you have it! Why else would you be here?"

Ire rose up through Janie's body. Good. Anger gave her strength and determination—she would need both to get out of there alive. "To find out what happened to my husband. It seems I've finally found someone with the answers." She glared at Meg.

"Your husband was just as much of a fool as you. He claimed to not have the final page either, but I knew he lied. Why else would he spend time searching out information on the original structures? He wanted to find where to dig. That's why."

"Meg, I swear to you, he never left me that information."

Janie hadn't noticed John slip out of the room. He returned dripping wet, holding her purse. "It's not in here, Mother. She must have it on her."

"Then search her," she screeched.

Janie shot up, backing away from him. "Don't you lay a hand on me. Don't ever touch me again, you bastard. How could you do this?"

"Sorry, doll. I must admit, I enjoyed my part. You're a hot lady. Too bad you wanted to move so damn slow. Your friend, Carol, on the other hand, was quite the wild ride." His tongue swiped across his lips. "Too bad she grew a conscience. Her fatal error. You and I could have gone for some wild rides too, if you'd only given in to me." John smirked. "Now hands up and let me search, or I'll rip your clothes off first."

Janie's jaw dropped. "You murdered Carol? You bastard!"

Shrugging, he said, "She left me no choice. As you are now, so smarten up and cooperate."

When she didn't budge, he took a step forward.

"Don't touch me." Her glare pierced through him as she reached into her back pocket. "Here's your precious page." She threw the folded copy onto the floor.

John dove for it, ripping the paper open.

"Well, is it the last page? Don't make me wait. Is it?" Meg pleaded in a manic tone.

"Yes, Mother. Finally, after all this time, we have the remaining piece. If it's the genuine article." He glared at Janie. "How do we know for sure it's from William's journal? This is a copy."

"Give it here." Meg grabbed the paper with her free hand. Studying it intently, a smile spread across her face. "William's handwriting, I'd know it anywhere—it's genuine."

"I gave you what you wanted. Now give me what I want. What happened to my husband?" Janie narrowed her eyes. They'd beaten her, but she still deserved answers.

Both Meg and John remained silent. With a shrug, John replied, "I can't see the harm it would do now. Go ahead, Mother. Tell her what happened to her dear, sweet Brian."

Meg calmly said, "You might as well know before you die."

This didn't surprise Janie. With all the confessions this madwoman shared, there could be no other conclusion.

Meg spoke as if defending their actions. "Johnny never meant to kill him. We both threatened Brian in phone calls over his last month. He'd already been acting jumpy about something, so it wasn't hard to push him into submission. Of course, we told him we'd kill you, Larry's wife, and your girls if he didn't turn over the final page. That fool Larry backed off immediately. The wimp was useless, so we focused on your husband.

"We were quite clever. Sometimes I even taped my threats and had John call him while I was at the office. I don't think he ever suspected me." Meg grinned.

"So, he's dead?" Janie asked flatly. While not a surprise, to hear Meg admit it drove a nail through her heart.

"Oh, yes. John had arranged to meet him out here. Imagine his surprise when he discovered I was in on it too." She gloated. "Much the same way I surprised you. Anyway, he claimed to not have brought the page with the last clues, but he knew the directions. He insisted we work together and split whatever we found. Some nerve. Why should I split my birthright?

"We walked toward the location of the original barn. Brian thought he could make a break for his car and get away. Johnny and your husband struggled, and at some point Brian fell and hit the back of his head on a rock. There was no helping him. He bled so badly it didn't take long before he was gone."

"Murderers," screamed Janie. "You killed him for some stupid fortune that may not even exist."

"No, no, dear. It was an accidental death. Why would we kill him when he had the last piece to our puzzle? I'm sure the authorities would agree it wasn't intentional."

Janie balled her hands into fists, the nails biting into her palms. "The police found his car at Orient Point. Was that an accident too?"

"We weren't about to risk police involvement here. Better safe than sorry. At the time the owners were renovating the property. The county was after them to fill some dangerous open wells before the place could be sold. No workers were scheduled that day, so we decided it would be perfect to meet. We hid Brian's body in one of the wells, and Johnny bulldozed over it. It didn't get noticed. The workers took care of the rest when they returned. I truly am sorry it ended that way, Janie. If he had only cooperated, none of this would have happened. It really was his own fault."

Defeated, Janie asked, "Can you at least show me where my husband is buried?" After all these years, she thought a weight would be lifted from her shoulders once she knew the truth. It didn't happen. She slumped back into the chair as an overwhelming sense of dejection and loneliness swept through her like a hurricane.

CHAPTER 31

Meg stood before Janie, gun in hand, with her son by her side. "Come on, dear, enough brooding. It's time to do some digging."

With wide-eyed astonishment, Janie asked, "You want me to dig? You just told me you killed my husband. Why should I help you now?"

"Ah, ah, ah. We didn't kill Brian. It was an accident, but I suppose you'll believe what you want. Remember, you still have two children, whom, I am sure, you want to remain unharmed. Now get moving! The treasure is all that matters." Punctuating her last remark, Meg aimed the gun at Janie, pulled the hammer back, and a round clicked into place.

As Jenny and Natalie consumed her thoughts, Janie stood, set her jaw, and strode toward the front entry. With her body in motion, she kicked into survival mode, ready for any opportunity of escape. Maybe she could make a break for it once outside. This could be her only chance. Bracing herself before reaching the door, she felt a rough hand tug on her arm.

"I'll be going first, in case you're thinking of making a dash for the woods," John told her, pushing ahead.

She ripped her arm from his grasp. "I told you not to touch me," she seethed.

As he opened the door and stepped outside, a

wooden board crashed over his head. Janie didn't hesitate. She dove over John's limp body and ran down the driveway.

"No," screamed Meg.

A gunshot rang out, and Janie stole a glance over her shoulder. She skidded to a halt. The man holding the plank slammed backward into the front of the house and fell lifeless onto the porch. "Tom," she yelled. Forgetting about her own safety, she ran to her brother's side. "Tom, no. Tom." She rolled her brother over and saw blood seeping from his torso. "Help him. Please, help him," she pleaded.

His head lolled to the side, eyes closed.

"Get up." Meg nudged the gun into Janie's ribs.

Behind his mother, John stood and rubbed the back of his head. He bent over and pulled Janie up by the arm.

"No. Please. We have to help him."

"Nobody can help him now," Meg snapped. "He's just another fool trying to steal what is rightfully mine."

"You mean ours don't you, Mother?" John's voice dripped with sarcasm.

Meg hesitated a moment. "Of course. You know you're always included in my plans, Johnny."

Tom's approach had been masked by the storm, the creaking floorboards of the porch unheard with the crashing of rain and thunder. *Why didn't I listen to Tom? He obviously followed me to the property fearing the worst. Now he is dead from trying to help me. When will this end?*

John retrieved a shovel from the bed of his truck.

"I have another in the trunk of my car," Meg said. "With the two of you digging, we'll get out of here faster."

By the time they reached the barn through the pelting rain, Janie's clothes clung to her body like a stocking. The socks squished in her sneakers with every step.

John slid open the doors of the structure where Meg's car sat parked inside. He opened the trunk and grabbed the second shovel. Back out in the storm, they continued to the edge of the clearing. Having studied the layout of the original farm, John easily located where the northeast corner of the barn had stood. Pacing off the steps as indicated by the last page of the journal, he led them into the woods.

Giddy as a schoolboy, excitement in his voice, he said, "This is it, Mother. The spot where our fortune lies hidden. No longer will the Carvers' 'precious treasure' remain buried on Yankee soil." Turning to Janie, he held out a shovel.

"Go to hell." Her hands remained at her side.

Meg motioned with the gun. "Get started. Remember your poor, defenseless children."

As the storm raged, so did Janie's emotions. Rain flooded through the thick cover of trees. Drops rolled down her face and body. Snatching the shovel, she stabbed into the root-infested soil.

John bounced on his feet as if it were a blessed event. He leaned on his shovel, watching the woman work.

Meg's lips remained in a straight line, displaying no emotion.

Weakly working at the ground cover, Janie pushed foliage aside to get at the dirt beneath.

With an impatient sigh, John dove in beside her.

His pace accelerated with every shovelful.

Despite the man's strength, it took immense effort to get through the roots twining through the soil from the low bushes and plants. After a foot, the dark fertile ground the area was known for made it easier to dig.

Janie robotically stabbed the ground as she was told. Turmoil flashed through her mind—her children, Tom lying lifeless on the porch, Brian's body being hurled into a cold, unmarked grave. Tears mixed with dirt, and rain slid down her cheeks.

When they'd reached five feet down, her shovel hit something solid. Attempting to dig around it, she revealed something smooth and grayish-white. Janie let out a bloodcurdling scream, causing Meg to fire a round. The bullet veered off into the woods.

Janie jumped out of the hole and stared at the thing bulging from the ground.

John used his shovel to push back the dirt, revealing a skull. "Mother, are you sure there wasn't a family plot back here? I wonder if we'll find more bodies."

"Don't be ridiculous. Maybe they buried a servant with the treasure to keep his mouth shut," she spouted, giving Janie a menacing grin. "Nonetheless, be careful not to damage anything valuable. We're close."

He dug out more of the body while the women watched.

When he got as far as the left arm, Janie noticed something odd but familiar. There were only three bony appendages to the hand. A passage in William's journal came to her. She giggled. It grew into a hearty laugh—not one of humor, but mirthless hysteria.

"What are you cackling about? How can you find

any of this funny?" demanded Meg, waving the gun wildly as she gestured with her arms.

Janie roared, leaning on the shovel for support. "The hand...the...hand...look... at...the...hand." She could barely breathe, let alone talk.

Neither Meg nor her son understood the significance, and their gazes remained flat.

Holding the gun steadily in Janie's direction, Meg said, "It's a damn skeleton. Who cares what the hand looks like? Keep digging!"

Janie remained by the rim, not moving. Her voice still laced with laughter, she said, "Her most precious treasure remains buried on Yankee soil."

"What is she babbling about, Johnny? Make her stop." Meg's face reddened.

"Come on, babe, everyone loves a good joke. What gives?" He grinned, as if they were still on friendly terms.

Janie cried, "You idiots. You don't get it. In his journal William wrote to his mother that her 'most precious treasure' remains buried on Yankee soil."

"You already said that. So what? We know he left all their wealth behind when he realized he would die before reaching Virginia." Meg tensed her hand around the weapon.

"More than jewelry and coins remained behind. In the beginning of the journal William referred to his younger brother as his mother's 'most precious treasure.' When Benjamin died from his wounds, his brother buried him on the family's land." Janie put a hand to her forehead. *How could Meg be so dense?*

Color drained from John's face. He stared down at the remains of the corpse with his mouth gaping wide.

Janie got her laughter under control and gestured toward the body. "Look at the hand—it's missing the thumb and pointer finger. Benjamin's fingers were shot off at the battle of Gettysburg. The last page doesn't give the location for the family cache. It tells where William buried the body of his little brother."

"You fool! You have no idea what you're talking about." Meg's tone escalated.

In a flat voice, John said, "Mother, she's right."

Hysteria edged Meg's response. "No, she's not. How could that be? Not after all these years of searching. She's lying to keep the treasure for herself."

John climbed from the hole and dropped his shovel in disgust. "Look at the hand. How can you deny the facts?"

Meg's eyes turned hazy and distant. "No. It's not true. Keep digging. I know it's here."

Janie backed away as far as she dared without raising suspicion.

Suddenly, a young man in Confederate uniform appeared in front of Meg.

"William," Janie whispered.

The specter no longer looked pained, but angry. He hovered over the remains of his brother's body, fists at his side. His mouth opened in a silent scream of rage.

Meg shrieked with terror and fired five rounds into the apparition.

John, who stood directly behind the young soldier, fell to his knees heaving in pain.

A wail echoed through the forest. It came from Meg as her son collapsed on the ground.

Turning the gun on Janie, she yelled, "This is your fault."

Janie held up her hands in defense as she backed farther away.

Meg pulled the trigger repeatedly. Instead of earsplitting booms, the hammer clicked on a spent chamber.

Stunned for only a moment, Janie rushed Meg, who still pointed the useless weapon. Swinging her shovel, Janie let loose a heavy blow to the side of the woman's head. Preparing to strike again, she stopped as her captor lay unconscious.

Janie dropped the shovel and sank to the ground. She rolled onto her back allowing the rain to wash over her face. The storm had eased, but a steady stream continued to fall. Her journey had reached its end. Having all the answers didn't issue the great sense of relief she'd hoped for, yet there would be closure.

What must have gone through Brian's mind during his last moments on earth? Surely, he thought of her and the children.

Janie bolted up and raced for the farmhouse. Mud splashed from under her feet, sucking at her shoes. Her mind focused on one thing—Tom. God, please let him be alive, she prayed, tearing around the side of the house.

Her brother lay in a heap on the porch with a pool of blood staining the boards beneath him.

She slowed her steps, fearing the worst. The wood creaked as she approached his body.

Tom's eyes flew open.

Relief coursed through her when he moaned.

"Boy, Sis, that lady is one lousy shot," he gasped, pushing himself upright with labored breath.

Janie threw her arms around her brother. "You're

alive! You're alive!"

Wincing, he said, "Not if you keep squeezing me. How about whipping out a cell phone and calling the cavalry—or at least someone who knows how to use a bandage?"

Releasing him, she said, "Right away. I'm so sorry I didn't believe you. Tom, you were right about John and Meg."

"Speaking of which, where are those two? Rolling in their treasure?"

"Not exactly…Meg shot John. He's probably dead. I had a little help from a friendly spirit," Janie quipped.

Tom gave her a sharp glance. "You don't mean…"

"Yes, that's exactly who I mean."

"What about Meg?"

"Out cold, but she'll live. She had a little run-in with a shovel."

"Way to go, little sister." Tom hesitated, before asking, "Did they tell you anything about Brian?"

For a long moment she didn't answer. Easing back on her heels, Janie said in a somber tone, "He's buried on the property. One of the covered-up wells."

Tom reached over and squeezed her knee; the motion caused him to gasp.

Looking up, she said, "We can deal with that later. First, let's get you some medical attention."

CHAPTER 32

The aroma of balsamic vinaigrette-and-basil marinated steaks filled the air as they sizzled on the barbecue. Janie and Tom reclined in loungers on her back porch while Jeremy worked his magic at the grill—under his wife's supervision, of course. The redhead watched with arms crossed and an approving smile on her face.

Laughter echoed across the backyard as the cousins played with large plastic rings making bubbles. The huge floating orbs made the place look magical.

"How much longer do you have before the doctor removes those stitches?" Janie asked.

"They come out next week. A little too soon, if you ask me."

Her head tilted toward her brother with a question on her lips.

Before Tom could respond, the screen door around the side of the house creaked then slammed shut. Light footsteps whispered on the wooden boards as Cassie approached. Handing Tom an ice-cold beer, she asked, "You comfortable, honey?"

"Just peachy. Don't fuss over me." He grabbed her hand and kissed the back. "Thanks for the brew."

She brushed a kiss across Tom's cheek, grabbed the empty bottle on the table beside him, and went back into the house where she and Mom were preparing the rest of the meal.

"I see what you mean, you dog," Janie slapped his shoulder. "You wouldn't be milking this whole injury thing, would you?"

Tom opened his mouth wide in mock surprise. "What do you mean milking? I got shot. You can't fake a wound like this."

"The bullet only grazed your side. You knocked yourself out when your head hit the house. At no time were you close to death."

"Grazed? It went in the front of me and out the back. There was blood. Lots of it! So it didn't hit any vital organs, and yes, it wasn't life threatening. You know that, and I know that. Couldn't we keep that bit of trivia just between us? Huh, Sis?" Tom nudged her with his elbow.

"I suppose. After all, you did try to save my life first." She leaned back into her chair.

Tom spit into the palm of his hand and extended it to his sister. "Spit swear?"

Looking sideways at him, she kept her hands in her lap. "You're disgusting."

"You thought it was cool when we were kids," he said, wiping his hand on his denim shorts. "Guess I'll have to trust you at your word."

They watched the progression of bubbles drift across the yard—at least the ones the cousins' dog didn't attempt to eat.

"So, the family retrieved the treasure years ago?" Tom asked. "You said you'd fill me in on the details later. It's later. Spill."

"You're right; I owe you an explanation. The coordinates William wrote in his journal were so the family would know where Benjamin lay buried. He probably hoped someday his brother's body would be moved to the family plot in Virginia.

"When William told Becky of his mother's plan to give him the treasure's location before he left, he thought it was something he would write down. Not being at the Carver home when William departed the next morning, Becky didn't know the significance of the pocket watch. His mother explained how the coordinates were etched on the inside cover. To anybody else, it looked like a calendar date. The family knew they were paces and directions. Meg never knew because her great-great-grandmother didn't have that information. Becky and her child were never acknowledged as part of the family, so it wasn't revealed to them."

Tom sipped his beer. "How did you find this out?"

"When the current descendants learned of Benjamin's remains being found, they were grateful. They moved his body to the family plot in Virginia, where he now lies beside his brother. Given everything that happened with Brian, they felt it only fair I know the end of the story. I've been sworn to secrecy. If I blab, they'll deny it, but who are you going to tell?"

Tom held up his hand "I won't breathe a word to a living soul. I swear." Moving his hand to his mouth, he prepared to spit.

"That won't be necessary." Janie chuckled. "Once the Carver descendants recovered the pocket watch Brian and Larry had found with William's body all those years ago, they waited until the property was put on the market. Purchasing it through a third party, the family name was never linked to the sale. The rest is simple. They dug up the treasure and auctioned it off at a private sale in Europe. Since they had no further need of the land, they sold it. Meanwhile, Meg waited all these years, plugging away in Larry's and Brian's office, all for nothing as it turns out. If only she'd known, none of this would have happened."

"Now she's up on murder charges"—Tom toasted with his beer—"not to mention kidnapping. Are they reopening her husband's case?"

"I don't know, but they've got enough on her for killing her own son, if she doesn't use an insanity plea. She keeps babbling about a young soldier appearing at the dig site, but I'm not talking. The way it looks to the police, Meg decided she didn't want to share with John and gunned him down. Since her greed included covering up Brian's death, as well as threatening Larry and his family, it's not a far stretch to think she'd murder her own offspring. She might even be implicated in Carol's death too."

"Speaking of the soldier"—Tom glanced at her— "have you seen any more of…"

"No. I believe he's finally at peace. I imagine the help he wanted was for his brother's body to be found. Now that they're together in the family plot, his job is done. He fulfilled his promise to his mother by seeing Benjamin brought home."

"I can't believe Larry never knew who threatened him and Brian," Tom said. "Is that why he never came forward when Brian went missing?"

"Yes. They had told him they'd killed Brian and would hurt the girls and me, as well as his wife, if he talked. He thought he could protect us by keeping quiet. Larry said he'd even snuck into our house a couple times to search for the journal. At least he convinced Meg and John that he and Brian had kept this strictly between them. The threats stopped, but he knew they would always be watching. Larry never knew Brian had left the journal with his lawyer."

"Where is it now? Didn't you say William's family offered to let you keep it?"

Janie stared out at the yard, allowing any lingering stress to drain from her body. "Yes, but it didn't seem right. I sent it back with Benjamin."

"Oh, admit it, you didn't want any more…visitors."

"Well, there's that too."

"I don't know. Maybe this could be a whole new career for you?"

Feigning anger, she said, "Stop it. Now."

"Sis, promise me one thing?"

Narrowing her eyes, she asked, "What?"

"If we ever go treasure hunting together, don't leave me behind with a cryptic message on how to find my body. You would make for one ugly apparition."

"You know, if you weren't already injured, I'd hurt you."

"I love you too, Sis. Do you think you could see if Jeremy will be done with those steaks sometime this century?"

Rising out of her chair, Janie said, "Now that's a mystery I can sink my teeth into."

Tom leaned his head back and groaned.

A word about the author…

Terry Segan resides in Nevada. The beach is her happy place, but any opportunity to travel soothes her gypsy soul. The stories conjured by her imagination while riding backseat on her husband's motorcycle, can be found throughout the pages of her paranormal mysteries. Visit Terry's website at http://terrysegan.com.

www.ingramcontent.com/pod-product-compliance
Lightning Source LLC
Chambersburg PA
CBHW051529260626
47170CB00003B/854